a fey tale

a fey tale

KAREN J CARLISLE

Kraken Publishing

a fey tale
An Aunt Enid Mystery,

Copyright © 2021 Karen J Carlisle

The moral right of this author has been asserted.

All rights reserved in all media. No part of this book may be reproduced, stored or transmitted in any form, or by any means, without written permission (except under the statutory exceptions of the Australian Copyright Act 1968).

This is a work of fiction. All characters and events in this publication, other than those clearly in public domain, are fictitious. Any resemblance to real persons, living or dead is purely coincidental.

Cover design and artwork,: Copyright © 2020 by Karen J Carlisle
Icons and internal artwork: copyright © 2021 by Karen J Carlisle

A catalogue record for this book is available from the National Library of Australia

ISBN: 978-0-9944850-5-2
Series: Carlisle, Karen J. The Aunt Enid Mysteries Book 2

Also available separately as eBook

This book is written in British English.
Printed in Australia.
Typeset in Times Roman 10pt.

Published by Kraken Publishing.
www.krakenpublishing.com

To the memory of Mark Calderwood,
a master artist, always willing to help
with obscure research.
Vale, Unca Giles.

contents

aunt enid
protector extraordinaire

bonus extras

chapter one

music flitted through the air, skipped across the tables and danced around the tea room. Enid Turner tapped her toe on the tiled floor. The trumpet was her favourite, with a melody both melancholic and cheeky. Tonight, it played a jaunty tune. The cello, keyboard and drums joined in. The more, the merrier.

A multitude of glass squares set into the roof - each second square offset to form a triangular prism, captured, and redirected, the light to form slow-moving rectangles on the walls.

China tea cups clinked, accentuating occasional lulls in conversation. Tobacco smoke curled up from the tables and clung to the low ceiling. The aromas of bergamot, vanilla, chocolate, and orange mixed with smell of exotic teas and perfume.

Waitresses lifted tea trays above their heads and wove between packed tables. The Adelaide Cafe Refreshment Room always did a bustling trade; Enid and her friends were fortunate to get a table.

Enid reached into her carpet bag, wrapped her gloved fingers around a small glass bottle, and unscrewed the lid. She rested her teacup on her lap, balanced the bottle on its edge, and poured the contents into her drink, smiling sweetly as she replaced the cup on the saucer in front of her.

The cello struck up a new tune. The trumpet added a melody. The revellers whooped. Bodies shimmied, wriggled and twirled in front of the low stage creating a sea of undulating colours: green, blue, pink, and red. A tall, attractive man was the current centre of attention, several young flappers congregated around him.

A jazz quartet. Dancing. Laughter. Enid smiled.

"I haven't seen such a party since the 'Great Picnic.'" Olive Oldham grinned. She appeared to be in her late twenties. Her brunette curls jiggled as she swayed to the music.

Enid replaced the lid on the bottle and slipped it back into her bag.

"It was supposed to be quarantine, not a party." Sylvia Devin glared at her from the opposite side of the table. Her blonde, pin-curled hair clung to her head like a military helmet.

Olive stopped swaying.

Enid glanced across the table. Sylvia was the oldest of the trio, and didn't look a day over thirty-five. Her brown eyes flashed their disapproval at Olive.

"Always so serious, Sylvia." Enid sipped her drink.

"We have our duty," replied Sylvia.

"But it doesn't mean we can't have fun," whispered Enid. "What about Olive's poker games?"

"Shh." Olive's gaze darted across the tea room.

The trumpet player rose from his seat and blasted out a catchy solo. The crowd cheered.

"Do you plan to get drunk on your birthday?" Sylvia glanced at Enid's augmented tea.

"No, I plan to enjoy myself." Enid tapped her foot to the rhythm, despite Sylvia's protestations.

"With that rabble?"

Enid smiled and eyed the young man at the centre of the commotion.

"Enid, he's half your age." Sylvia continued her disapproving glare.

"Or less." Olive laughed. She may follow Sylvia's orders when it came to her duty as Protector, but she could always be relied on when it came to appreciating a beautiful face. After all, she'd been married, against Sylvia's stern protests, three times.

Enid glanced back at the merrymakers. There was something about the young man; tall, lithe, almost-impossibly handsome, surrounded by blondes, brunettes and redheads. He had his pick. But Sylvia was correct; he was too young. Too perfect. A redhead, with her long cigarette holder, cosied up to him and blew a fine wisp of smoke over him, as if marking her territory. He wrapped his arms around her, dragged her into the gyrating fray, and laughed.

Enid's heart skipped.

"He is a bit of a looker." Olive stared at him.

Sylvia sneaked a peek.

"No, Olive," said Enid. "I have a birthday date."

"A date?" Sylvia raised an eyebrow.

"But I thought we could see a film at the Theatre Royal," said Olive. "The Man From Snowy River is playing at the movie theatre. It's your favourite."

Enid stared past her, shook her head, and smiled. A dapper young man in a well-cut suit, dark hair and a jaunty moustache paused on the wrought iron stairs. He returned her smile, lifted his hand off the wooden banister and waved. Her stomach fluttered.

Sylvia looked over her shoulder.

Olive followed her line of sight. "Oh, wowsers. He's dishy."

Enid felt her cheeks burn.

The young man removed his Homburg and adjusted a brown paper package under his arm. His shoes clunked on the metal as he came closer. Enid's heart raced. He was, as Olive had rightly noted, very dishy.

"You're stepping out with Owen Barrington?" asked Sylvia. "The artist?"

"And what's wrong with that?" asked Enid.

"A moustache?" Sylvia's forehead wrinkled as she peered through the smoke-filled room.

"He's not a slave to current trends," replied Enid.

"His parents died from the Flu," whispered Olive. "They left him a bundle. Oh, Enid, he's a catch."

Both Enid and Olive watched him descend the stairs.

"He's very young." Sylvia harrumphed.

"Leave her alone, Sylvia," said Olive. "She's still young." She twisted the ring finger on her left hand. "Let Enid have some fun while she can."

Sylvia lifted her teacup to her lips. "You're old enough to be his gr--"

"I'm twenty-five," said Enid.

"Twenty...?" Sylvia laughed.

"That's what my current birth certificate says," replied Enid.

"Thanks to the Shoemaker." Sylvia sipped her tea. "Never forget, Enid. You're no longer one of them."

Enid huffed and crossed her arms.

"We can't let civilians know we exist. If they learned the truth..." Sylvia leaned forward. "It wasn't that long ago our... skills branded us witches, and had us murdered."

Enid ignored her, and concentrated on Owen's movements as he glided past the tea shop tables; his grin growing larger with each step. The low light fixtures accentuated his strong jawline and glinted in his deep blue eyes.

"I think it's romantic," said Olive.

"You knew about this?" asked Sylvia.

Olive bit her lip.

"How long?" Sylvia frowned.

"Since Easter," replied Enid.

"We cannot allow ourselves to get attached." The furrows on Sylvia's forehead deepened.

"And why not?" Enid retrieved her carpet bag and dumped it on her lap. "Eighty years is a long time to be alone." She tugged off her gloves and laid them on the table. "You may be able to bear it, but I cannot. We're Protectors, not nuns. We can have fun, Sylvia."

"Don't get distracted." Sylvia eyed the discarded gloves as she picked up her bag. "Never let him discover who you really are."

The music stopped. A melodic laughter wafted across the room. Enid's heart fluttered. She glanced towards the band. The perfect young man snuggled into his companion.

"Good evening, ladies." Owen cleared his throat. "Did I interrupt something?"

"No." Enid's gaze snapped back to her companions.

"Just enjoying the band. They're particularly good tonight," offered Olive.

Owen waved for the waiter's attention. "Coffee, please."

"No, thank you," said Sylvia.

Olive shook her head.

"Two," said Owen.

The waiter nodded.

"Owen, these are my old friends, Olive Oldham and Sylvia Devin. I ran into them while shopping in Adelaide Arcade. They were..." She shifted in her seat. "Keeping me company until you arrived."

"Enid was buying hats." Olive nodded. "At the Hatters."

Owen surveyed the table and frowned. "Did you leave them behind?" he asked.

As an artist, he was observant; there was indeed no hat. Enid kicked Olive under the table. Olive's eyes watered as she rubbed her shin.

"Um... I had my eye on a lovely little cloche," replied Enid, "but I thought it best not to have boxes to carry. I wasn't sure what you have planned for this evening."

"Oh, a mystery date?" Olive grinned. "How romantic."

Owen raised an eyebrow, chasing away the lines on his forehead.

Sylvia's leg jerked under the table. Another kick in the shins for

Olive. Olive jolted upright and stifled a gasp.

"Are you alright, Mrs Oldham?" he asked.

"Just a touch of hayfever." Olive coughed. "Spring plays havoc with my sinuses."

Sylvia's chair scraped as she stood. She tucked her bag under her arm and peeled back her white glove to check her Marcasite wristwatch. "The movie will be starting soon."

Olive joined her. "Have you been to the Theatre Royal, Mr Barrington?" Her cheeks were pink.

"Come along, Olive. We'll be late." Sylvia tugged on her arm.

"It was a pleasure meeting you both, ladies." Owen nodded his head in a slight bow.

"And you too, Mr Barrington." Olive winked at Enid.

Sylvia rolled her eyes.

"We'll talk tomorrow, Enid. Goodbye, Mr Barrington." She dragged Olive away from the table and ushered her to the stairs.

Enid sipped her cold tea and waited for the gin to fortify her nerves.

"Do sit down, Owen. I must apologise. Olive has been over-interested in everyone's love life since her husband died in the war."

"I'm sorry. I didn't realise." He sat down opposite Enid.

She placed her gloved hand on his. It was warm. Reassuring. He turned over his hand and wrapped his fingers around hers.

The waiter returned and placed the coffee on the table. Enid sniffed the aromatic steam rising from the cups. It was not an unpleasant smell. She raised an eyebrow.

"Try it." He smiled. "It's all the rage in America at the moment."

She tentatively sipped the dark liquid.

She took another sip. It reminded of her of him. Strong, unexpected, but surprisingly enjoyable - her nose wrinkled - with a slightly bitter aftertaste.

"It's an acquired taste." Owen laughed gently, and presented her with the parcel. "Happy birthday, my dear, sweet, Enid."

"You didn't have to get me a present." She eyed the parcel, wrapped in brown paper and tied with a red ribbon.

"Open it." His moustache twitched as a smile flickered over his lips.

Enid slid off the ribbon and removed the paper wrapping. Inside was a book. She eased it out of its customised Morocco slipcase, ran her fingers over the red pebbled cloth and gilt spine, and slowly turned it over. The embossed gold title read: *A Study in Scarlet.*

Her heart thumped.

"Holmes is my favourite," she whispered.

"I know."

She opened the book. On the first page was a handwritten dedication: For Enid, love always, Owen.

Love? The word was confidently written, without hesitation. Enid swallowed. He'd never voiced his true feelings before. Oh, he'd always been attentive, endearing, but never actually said the word.

Her hands trembled as she turned the page and read the copyright details: eighteen eighty-eight. Her eyes widened.

"A first edition?"

He nodded. "Only the best for my gal."

He took her hand in his and kissed it, with his warm, soft lips. The moustache tickled. Enid's heart fluttered. The world spun around her. Voices buzzed. The murmur of the crowd faded...

She focused on his beautiful face. How could Sylvia deny her this? She'd give up anything for this. Her heart thumped. She held her breath.

Don't get distracted; Sylvia's voice echoed her in her head. She shoved them aside. She *could* have him and be a Protector. Olive had.

A howl of laughter rang in her ears.

"...I've got something to--" Owen's voice was close.

A chair scraped. Something knocked the table. Enid shook her head. Her teacup rattled. Brown liquid crept across the white tablecloth and seeped into the corner of the brown paper.

She snatched up the book and slid her chair away from the table to avoid the liquid drizzling over the edge.

The crowd surged past their table and towards the exit.

"Time to go, I think." Owen held out his hand. "Shall we?"

The crowd slowed, blocking the stairs. Two blonde flappers dried their tears. There was no sign of the intriguing young man or his companion.

"It's all right," said Owen. "I know another way out."

Enid nodded, slipped the book back into the slipcase and placed it in her carpet bag.

Enid squeezed Owen's hand as he led her up the narrow steps. A cold wind blasted down the lane. The tearoom door slammed closed behind them.

Shadows cloaked the lane. Long, dark, concealing.

Enid glanced up at the sky. The sun had dropped out of sight; the sky was dark blue, tinged with orange. Still, it wasn't late enough to warrant such deep, dark shadows. Something wasn't right. She frowned.

The sound of footsteps retreated south, towards Grenfell Street, and stopped.

The hair prickled on the back of Enid's neck. Shivers ran down her arms. She let go of Owen's hand.

A faint smell of smoke lingered in the air. She sniffed; cigarette smoke. But there was something else. She sampled the air again. And froze.

The smell of rotten eggs snatched at her nostrils. She swallowed, and slipped the glove off her right hand as she scanned the shadows.

Her fingers twitched. Their tips buzzed. She couldn't do magic; not in front of Owen. She stretched her hand. The static faded.

Owen paused. "What's wrong, Enie?"

"Can you smell that?" she whispered.

He wrinkled his nose and glanced at the mound of boxes and open bins near the doorway.

"It's just the rubbish," he replied. "I wish they'd put the lids on the bins." He took her hand. "Let's go."

Something moved in the too-dark shadows. A distant giggle in the dark; in the opposite direction, towards the street. Another shiver ran over her skin. Goosebumps trailed down her arm.

"You're cold," said Owen. "Would you like my jacket?"

"No." She turned Owen away from the shadows, putting herself between him and potential danger. "There's something there."

Owen held her closer. "Perhaps you saw the ghosts?"

"Ghosts?" Enid swallowed. Of all the things that could cross over from the Otherworlds, ghosts were the most unpredictable and hardest to control. Even for Sylvia.

Owen wrapped his arm around her shoulder.

"A little boy and his mother." His breath warmed her neck. "She worked in Adelaide Arcade."

"Don't be silly, Owen." She feigned a laugh. "Ghosts don't exist." She apologised to the Aether. Best not to rile them.

Another giggle drifted from the direction of the street. Enid held her breath. Please, not ghosts.

Owen glanced at her, then towards the sound. A loud sigh followed, then more footsteps, fading away. Two silhouettes huddled, then moved away from the lane.

"A lover's tryst?" Owen laughed and kissed her. "What an excellent idea."

Enid relaxed into his arms.

Metal scraped beside them. She spun towards the sound. A pinpoint of light glowed in the dark, deeper in the lane.

The stench of rotten eggs rolled over her. Owen covered his nose.

A metal lid clattered on the rubbish bins.

"Well, that's spoiled the moment." He kissed her hand and winked at her. "Come on, Enie. I've got a birthday surprise for you."

Owen and Enid strolled along the riverbank arm in arm, the sun at their backs. The sun skimmed the top of the City Bridge. The long shadows of the trees beckoned them towards the river.

Owen straightened his Homburg and smiled at Enid. Chocolate ice-cream dripped onto the fingers of her other hand. She giggled and licked her fingers.

His breaths quickened. He longed to do the same. His shoe caught on the footpath, causing a misstep to regain his balance.

"Are you all right, Owen?" asked Enid.

His reply caught in his throat. He fidgeted with the box in his jacket pocket. He removed his hand from his pocket and glanced along the riverbank. It was a week day; everyone was either still at work or on their way home for dinner. They were alone. He sighed, relieved there were no witnesses to his awkwardness.

Enid leaned her head on his arm and crunched into the crisp waffle of the ice-cream cone.

He sucked in a sharp breath to calm his nerves, and led her further along the path towards the River Torrens.

A cool breeze swept across the water and caught the leaves in the gum trees lining the bank. It fluttered around Enid's calves and teased her skirt.

"Fancy a spin on the lake?" He patted Enid's hand on his arm.

"It's getting late, Owen," she whispered, "We'll never find a boat.

They'll have gone home by now."

"They won't say no on your birthday."

A lean man in a straw boater leaned against a lamppost near the edge of the water. A small wooden rowboat bobbed in the water next to him. He checked his pocket watch.

"Cutting it fine aren't we, Barrington?" The attendant shook his head.

"Come on, Enie." Owen picked up his pace and ushered her down the path towards the boat.

"But, Owen, it must be time for him to finish for the day?"

"It's all organised. Cole is an old rowing buddy of mine." He grinned. "And he owes me a favour."

"Good afternoon, miss." Cole doffed his hat.

"Good afternoon." Enid smiled politely. "We're not too late, are we? We don't want to keep you."

Owen pushed a pound note into the attendant's palm, climbed into the boat, and straddled the seat.

"Forty minutes, Barrington. No more." Cole eyed his pocket watch again.

Owen held out his hand to assist Enid.

"Are you *sure* it's no trouble, Mr Cole?" she asked.

"It's fine, miss." He grinned. "And happy birthday."

"Thank you." Enid took Owen's hand and stepped into the row boat. It wobbled.

Owen wrapped his arm around her waist to steady her, guided her onto the seat, and sat down opposite her. Cole untied the boat, nudged it away from the bank with his foot.

"Enjoy yourselves." He raised an eyebrow in Owen's direction, lit a cigarette and drew in a deep breath.

"I'll need that boat back before sunset, Barrington."

Owen patted his pocket and nodded. Time enough to summon up his courage again.

Water dripped from the paddles as they rose out of the water and plopped back through the surface. The landscaped Plane trees on the south bank eyed him, assessing his every movement as the boat glided silently eastward past a boat shed and approached the Albert Bridge.

The silence amplified the thump of Owen's pulse as it raced in his ears. He held his breath, though he knew Enid couldn't hear it. There was no one else on the lake. Perhaps now he could muster his courage? After all, it was just four words...

A lone magpie warbled, snickering at him from a lone red gum on the north bank. He cleared his throat.

"Yes, Owen?" Enid's eyelids fluttered.

He swallowed, and dug the oars into the water.

The lake was silent. Too silent. Plane trees stood sentry on the south bank, their feet planted on the clipped lawn. Scattered red gums huddled together on the north bank, defying the enforced intrusion of the European invaders, as the boat slipped through the water.

A wood duck foraged on the south bank amongst the long grass.

Enid usually found stillness comforting. She preferred the Hills, away from city life. It was quieter there, with only her bees for company. Less complicated. Fewer voices in her head. She could concentrate, and gather her thoughts.

But today there was something else. Something flitted and teased, just beyond her senses; something she couldn't quite discern. If Sylvia were here, she'd be giving a lecture on the lie of the land, and instinct.

Today, her instincts were muddled. Perhaps she was too distracted? She took a deep breath. Owen's moustache was quivering, and she didn't know why.

She watched him lift and turn the oars; he'd removed his jacket, revealing a hint of rippling muscles under his shirt. Other than driving the Lincoln, the only consolation to venturing into town was Owen Barrington... and those rippling muscles.

Owen Barrington: the name wrapped around her tongue. It tasted like toffee: sweet, delicious. But humans, like toffee, didn't last. Protectors lived many lifetimes. Sylvia had counselled both her and Olive many times: *Best not tangle yourself with the ephemeral.* The words were meant to dissuade her, but they'd had the opposite effect.

Owen smiled as he plunged the oars into the water and guided the rowboat into the centre of the lake, then eastwards to the Albert Bridge and the zoological gardens.

Her heart fluttered. He cut a fine figure. Surely he was worth it?

Water dribbled from the oar as he dipped it into the water again.

The wood duck's long, goose-like neck twitched as it jerked towards the sound. It squawked and darted into the long grass under the tall gum.

Owen laughed. "Fidgety blighters."

"It's probably protecting its babies." Enid replied. "And thinks we're out to steal them, poor thing."

The low sun skimmed across the top of the City Bridge, creating a halo around Owen's Homburg. It hid his expression, but she could hear him smiling.

"This should do it." He pulled the oars out of the water and rested them on the bottom of the boat.

The boat drifted forward, closer to the bridge, turning slightly towards the sunset. He stared at Enid, his deep blue eyes uncertain, as if he'd swallowed a hive of bees.

She closed her eyes, and let her head fall back. The fading sunlight illuminated her eyelids. A cool breeze caressed her cheeks.

The oar creaked against the wooden boat. A magpie warbled its approval.

This was perfection. Fresh air, nature, and Owen all to herself.

"Enid?" Owen's gentle voice drifted quietly on the breeze, like liquid caramel.

"Yes?" Her heart raced. Excitement rippled over her skin.

"The past six months have been wonderful." His voice echoed off the high banks surrounding them.

Oars creaked. The boat wobbled. Water lapped the hull. Shadows played across her closed eyelids.

Was this a proposal? She wanted to hear the words. She wanted to whisper: yes!

"What I'm trying to say is..." He hesitated.

The magpie warbled a last serenade, spread its wings, and took flight.

Enid took a deep breath, to breathe in every memory of the moment. The aromas of fresh-turned soil, cut grass, and warm eucalyptus filled her lungs. A foul, sulphurous smell of rotten eggs assaulted her nostrils. She screwed up her nose. Her eyes flickered open.

"Perhaps we should go back, Owen?" There it was; that word again. She shook her head.

Concentrate! Owen was a civilian. She was sworn to protect them. She glanced back at the setting sun, peeking through the trees. Whatever it was, the darkness would embrace it. She shifted on the seat. As Protector, she should investigate. "It is getting late. I'm sure Mr Cole will want dinner."

The excavated river banks rose on both sides, cut into a hillock and built up to accommodate the Albert Bridge and its decorative mouldings. They cast deep shadows across the water as the boat drifted closer.

Owen lowered one knee onto the bottom of the boat. His hand rummaged inside his jacket on the bench seat.

Something moved in the shadows beneath the bridge. A pebble plopped into the water.

Enid's muscles tensed. "Did you hear that?"

"Probably just another wood duck."

A panicked peal of chittering erupted.

"And feeding time at the Zoological Gardens." He chuckled.

The boat had turned so the sun was at his side now. It twinkled in his brilliant blue eyes and highlighted his fastidiously-groomed moustache.

Something metallic scraped along the rocks.

Enid peered into the shadows under the bridge. The foul smell of rotten eggs wafted across the water, stronger now. The stench caught in her throat. The air smelled of troll.

A bounty hunter, here in Adelaide? *Impossible.* Trolls were the bounty hunters of the Fae world. They usually hunted criminals or political refugees from the Otherworlds. They didn't care about the politics of humans, and she'd never heard of one crossing into this world to hunt a Protector. They didn't care for much, really, other than money. And magic. They coveted it. If this one had crossed through Earth's Shell, then you could bet magic was involved.

Enid rubbed her nose and searched the darkness. Something red flickered under the bridge.

There was another scrape, louder this time.

Every muscle in her body tensed. She had to protect Owen, but she had no Focus; she'd been too distracted. Sylvia would be livid. She slipped off one of her gloves and clutched her bag: tapestry with bone handles. No metal. She cursed under her breath.

Enid rose slowly, searching for a substitute Focus; something metal to channel the magic.

"What's wrong?" The twinkle in Owen's eyes faded.

"I left my umbrella at home." Enid replied in the calmest voice she could muster. Her Focus was at home in the umbrella stand by the door, ready for action... but not today. Today the action was here. And her umbrella was not. Her stomach knotted.

"But it's a beautiful day."

While Owen scanned the sky, Enid scanned the boat. The oars?

Sunlight reflected on the brass bands at both ends of the oars, and flowed along a metallic strip tracing down its length. She prayed it would be enough.

The boat twisted further in the water, presenting its bow to the bank, sliding silently under the bridge.

The sun kissed the horizon now, extending the shadows of the riverbank over the boat and under the bridge, creating a prefect sanctuary for a troll bounty hunter to snatch up its prey.

Owen shifted his balance and took a deep breath, apparently oblivious to the movement.

Enid peered over his shoulder. A pinpoint of red light flickered, turned to face her, and narrowed.

Troll! She wanted to scream the warning, but what could she do with a civilian present?

A low growl rumbled in the darkness. A large grey-skinned head emerged from the shadows. An angry fist followed.

Enid yanked off her remaining glove and snatched up the oar, as soil and stones rained into the rowboat.

Owen's eyes widened. There was no time for him cry out. A large rock slammed into the back of his head. He slumped forward, his head landing in Enid's lap.

A lion roared in the distance.

The troll grinned. Crooked teeth ground as it lunged in Enid's direction.

"*Frange*," she hissed.

Sparks crackled around her hand and coiled along the brass strip on the paddle. With a flick of her wrist, she raised the oar, swung it wide over Owen's head, and slammed it into the troll's exposed left leg.

She shoved Owen to one side and lunged forward.

"*Abi*," she hissed.

The troll howled and recoiled. A gust of sewer breath blasted her face. A wave of nausea washed over her.

The troll's eye flared red, and faded as it retreated further into the shadows.

"*Regrade!*"

Green light arced from her fingers and twisted along the oar. The rowboat lurched away from the bank into the middle of the lake, then slowed.

The lion roared again, as if in approval.

Enid collapsed back onto the seat of the boat and examined Owen; his eyes were closed, his face pale.

"Owen?" her voice trembled.

There was no answer.

She placed her hand under his nostrils. There was a faint warmth. She let out a ragged breath, and ran her free hand over Owen's dark hair. Fresh blood smeared her palm. Her heart sank.

"No!"

She pulled him close and scanned the bank. The troll had gone. Only the sentinel trees stood watch.

"*Sano.*" She clutched his motionless body. The amulet around her neck burned against her skin. Its green glow seeped from under her dress and pulsed along her arm around enveloped Owen's body.

Enid clasped his head against her chest. Her skin buzzed. Light crackled, and wound around them.

"Please," she whispered.

Owen remained motionless. The buzz along her skin faded as the energy fizzled and faded. Still he didn't move.

Her muscles ached. Her lungs screamed. She gasped for air.

"Please let him live." She kissed his neck.

Owen coughed and gasped.

"Well, that was unexpected," he mumbled.

She pushed his head from between her breasts. A cold rush of air tugged at Enid's blouse. Owen blinked, his attention still on her cleavage.

Enid's cheeks burned.

He raised his hand and cradled the back of his head.

"What hit me?" He examined the red-smudged palm. His smile faded. "Enie, what's going on?" He glanced back towards Albert Bridge, now over a hundred yards away.

How could she explain the troll attack? Or her duty to protect the Earth from such creatures and incursions from the Otherworlds? Or magic? She swallowed. What would Sylvia do?

"Enid?" His voice was still weak.

Enid's chin crumpled. She knew what to do, but she didn't have to like it. She kissed his forehead. Her fingers wrapped around the shaft of the oar.

"*Oblivísce.*"

Green static crackled along the wood and sparked in Owen's face.

"Bloody hell!" He flinched hard against the side of the boat. It shuddered. His eyes rolled up, exposing the whites of his eyes. His body convulsed.

Enid's stomach churned. She felt sick. Her *Memory Magic* was dangerously unpredictable at the best of times. What if it went wrong? But she had no choice; Sylvia wouldn't hesitate to remove all his memories, if she had to.

The oar jerked in her hand. The air shuddered around them. A crack splintered down the shaft of the oar, splitting the wood. The metal burned, searing her palm. She dropped the oar and shoved her hand into the water.

"I'm coming!" Mr Cole's rowboat jiggled in the water as he waved his arms.

Owen stared into space.

"Blast and damnation." Enid caught her breath. She was exhausted; there wasn't enough magic left to conceal her work, and her makeshift

Focus on board was spent.

She slipped Owen off the seat, pressed the oar into his hand, and wiped blood on the bottom of the boat to explain a concussion.

"Are you all right?" Mr Cole's rowboat thudded alongside.

Their boat jolted.

"What?" Owen shook his head.

Sylvia's voice shouted in her head: Rule one: *Don't involve civilians. Ever.* Enid swallowed, hoping the *Memory Magic* had worked.

"Did I miss something?" he asked.

"That lightning storm came out of nowhere," replied Mr Cole.

"Lightning?" echoed Owen.

"Dry lightning. A freak of nature." Air whistled through Mr Cole's teeth. "Lucky you both weren't killed."

Enid's heart skipped. Lightning was as good excuse as any. If Mr Cole believed it, having witnessed the incident himself, then others would likely to believe it as well.

"My God, Barrington, you're a lucky man."

"Yes, I am." He winked at Enid and leaned forward. The spark had returned to his eyes. "Did we have a good time?"

"Yes." She smiled sweetly.

Mr Cole rolled his eyes, and pried the scorched oar from Owen's hand. "I'll fetch a doctor."

Owen shook his head. His face greyed. His eyelids fluttered.

"Are you sure, mate?" Mr Cole frowned.

A spot of rain sploshed on his nose.

"You were right about your umbrella." He chuckled.

chapter two

the muslin curtain flapped against the window frame. Water bubbled in the kettle on the stove top. The kettle whistled impatiently. Hot air rolled over Enid's skin.

She opened her eyes. She was in her own kitchen, with its new cream-enamelled Metters & Co. Stove, and fully stocked pantry. Her favourite teacup - fine cream china, with pink roses painted around the rim - sat on the table in front of her. The first gift Owen had given her.

"You've been neglecting your bees again." Sylvia tsked as she emerged from the pantry, a jar of sunny-yellow lemon butter in one hand and a covered earthenware butter dish in the other. She plopped them on the kitchen table. "If you're not careful, they'll leave." She snatched up the kettle, filled a teacup on the bench, and ferried it to Enid. "Then who will they talk to?"

Enid leaned her elbows on the kitchen table and let her head drop into her hands. Hair skimmed her chin. Her head ached. Her shoulders ached. Her arms ached. She stretched her fingers. The tips were still numb.

Steam rose from the teacup. It had an unfamiliar, peppery aroma. She lifted the cup to her nostrils, examined the translucent red liquid, and sniffed the tea again. There was a sweetness to the smell she couldn't place. She frowned. It wasn't the usual Echinacea-brew Sylvia flavoured.

"A berry tisane?" she asked.

"Amongst other things." Sylvia smiled. "And a little something I picked up from a friend in Chinatown." She slathered two scones with lemon butter.

"What is it?" asked Enid.

"Drink it, and rest." Sylvia pushed the scone-laden plate in front of Enid. "You've ignored your training." She crossed her arms. "You allowed yourself to be distracted, let a troll surprise you, *and* forgot your Focus."

She took Enid's hand and examined her fingers. Small blood-coloured blisters marked the tips.

"*Memory Magic*?" Sylvia rolled her eyes. "You know it's not your best discipline." She let Enid's hand fall back onto the table. "If it doesn't take, I will have to fix it. Again. *Permanently*."

Enid sipped the tisane. Its tart, fruity taste rolled over her tongue. No salty... She swallowed. A peppery tang lingered, tantalising her taste buds. She raised an eyebrow.

"That's different." The strong aftertaste reminded her of the coffee Owen had bought her.

"Chinese Magnolia Vine," said Sylvia. "Five flavour fruit."

"I'll be fine." Enid pushed the teacup away. "I just need a strong coffee."

"Coffee?" Sylvia screwed up her nose. "This is better." She pushed the cup back in front of Enid. "It enhances mental endurance. Lord knows you could use more of that. What were you thinking? Tracking a troll, with a civilian in tow. You're supposed to protect civilians, not flirt with them."

"That's not fair." Enid glared at her. "Olive's had three husbands, and--"

"I can't have both of you distracted." Sylvia tapped the rim of the teacup. "Drink up."

"It's a bit sweet for my taste." Enid stared at the tea. Her tongue tingled, and burned. She sucked in cool air and leaned back in the kitchen chair. "It's got a kick to it."

The corner of Sylvia's mouth flickered. "Drink it all."

Enid took a deep breath and drained the cup. She knew better than to argue with Sylvia.

"I can--" A knot of air rose up her oesophagus, burning all the way. She grimaced, and rubbed her chest.

Sylvia turned her back on Enid, and washed the teacup. It clattered on the drying rack.

"Olive should be back soon." She pushed aside the curtain. "Eat your scone, and lie down. I'll let you know when she arrives."

Enid sank her teeth into the scone and licked her lips. Not quite as good as hers, but still tasty.

A motorcar rumbled in the distance. Her heart skipped at the sound of the familiar throaty roar.

A horn blared outside. The gate squeaked. An engine whined, and gears ground.

Enid winced, and lunged toward the window.

"My Lincoln!" She pushed past Sylvia and scanned the driveway.

Her sleek, red 1919 Lincoln Tourer lurched forward and shuddered to a stop mere inches from a squad of garden gnomes. The gravel crunched. The motorcar's door flung open. Olive jumped out and slammed it shut.

The motorcar rolled.

"No!" Enid gasped.

Olive leaned back into the cabin. The vehicle shuddered to a halt.

Enid dashed out of the kitchen and burst through the front door. The screen slapped shut behind her as she caught her skirt on her beloved hydrangeas.

"Relax, Enid. The motorcar's fine." Olive scooped up Enid's arm, ushered her back into the cottage, and sat her down at the kitchen table.

"Tea, Olive?" Sylvia re-filled the kettle.

"Excellent." Olive pulled off her driving gloves and dropped them onto the table.

Enid didn't answer. Her mind was listing the possible destruction Olive could've wrought on her precious Lincoln. She'd assess the damage later.

"Are there any scones left?" Olive eyed Enid's half-eaten scone.

"You can have mine," replied Enid. "I've lost my appetite."

"You'll need to fetch the lemon butter." Sylvia nodded in the direction of the pantry. "And the milk's in the cold safe on the veranda."

Jars rattled in the pantry.

"Any sign of the bounty hunter?" Sylvia replaced the kettle on the stove top.

"No," came the muffled reply. Olive returned, loaded with scones, and a jar of lemon butter.

"Are you sure it was a troll?" asked Sylvia.

Enid nodded. "I think it may have been in the alley, behind Adelaide Arcade, when Owen and I left." she replied. "I could smell it."

"Was it *Glamoured*?" Olive emerged from the pantry. "I've never seen a *Glamoured* troll."

"You've never seen a troll." Sylvia placed three clean teacups on the table.

"Whatever possessed you to track a troll?" asked Olive.

"I wasn't tracking it," huffed Enid.

"Well, it was tracking you," said Sylvia.

Olive's hand paused in front of her mouth. A yellow dollop fell onto her plate.

"But, a bounty hunter? After a Protector?" She stared at Sylvia, waiting for an explanation.

"No, they wouldn't dare." Sylvia frowned.

"And in the daylight?" Olive swallowed a mouthful of scone. "Don't they turn to stone in the sunlight?"

"That's an old wives' tale," Sylvia scoffed.

"They're usually true," replied Olive. "Like the bees."

"Not this one." Sylvia spooned some honey from a jar and let it drip into her cup. "It's a fairy-tale, designed to make us feel safe."

The kettle whistled. The cap on the spout jiggled, as if to lighten the mood. Sylvia lifted the kettle, and hesitated.

"Are you sure it was a troll?" She stared through the window and scanned the front yard.

"Positive. With one red eye. And it stank like rotten eggs. Worse than Olive after eating her infamous onion pie." Enid grinned.

Olive licked her fingers. "Pardon?"

"And there was *Elemental Magic*," Enid continued. "Water."

"I thought trolls could only use *Glamour Magic*?" asked Olive.

"There have been reports..." Sylvia moved to the bench and filled the tea pot. "Some have minor magics. I suppose they could manipulate the water by moving the rocks on the water bed?" She carried the pot back to the table and slid into her chair. "But, a troll here? In Adelaide? After a Protector?" She shook her head.

"It was there," chirped Olive. "I recovered a whole sack of troll dung. It's acidic. Perfect for the hydrangeas." She chuckled. "Using their own excrement against them."

"Not in my Lincoln?" Enid jumped to her feet. Her head swam. She grabbed the edge of the table.

"Relax, I dropped it off at Sylvia's on the way here," replied Olive.

Sylvia glared at her.

"You'll clean the seats before you go," grumbled Enid.

"Drink your tea," whispered Sylvia.

"Always with the tea," mumbled Enid. She gulped down the new concoction. It tasted of apple, with a mellow, honey-like sweetness. Floral and woodsy. She sniffed her cup. Chamomile, Valerian, and... A sour-sweet note clawed her tongue. But there was no zing; this wasn't the pick-me-up. Her eyelids quivered. She pushed her chair away from the table.

"Sylvia?" Enid's eyelids fluttered.

Sylvia snatched up the cup from her hand, and turned to Olive.

"Stay here, Olive. Make sure she rests for at least twenty-four hours. I'm going to consult the Books. Surely there's another reason why an Otherworld bounty hunter would be here?"

Olive nodded.

"Come on, Enid. Off to bed." She slipped Enid's arm over her shoulder and ushered her out of the kitchen. "It's for the best. Sylvia knows what she's doing. She's been a Protector longer than both of us together."

"No, I have to find that troll." Enid's vision blurred.

"Perhaps The Shoemaker may be able to help?" Olive's voice seemed muffled.

"No." Sylvia glared at Olive. "I forbid it."

Olive grumbled. Enid shuffled towards the hallway.

"Sylvia, what have you done?" Enid's words slurred. "You, bit..." Her head drooped onto her chest. *Bollocks.*

"Don't worry. You're an Eternal," replied Sylvia. "You'll sleep it off."

The morning sun glared off the bedroom mirror. Enid's favourite garden gnome, Red, stood guard at the window sill. Enid squinted, feeling her way along the bed toward her wardrobe. She dressed slowly, her arms aching with each movement, and shuffled down the stairs.

Olive was in the Sitting Room, her feet curled up on the settee, playing Patience and nibbling on baked goods from the pantry.

Enid tapped her foot.

"You're up?" Olive's feet thudded onto the thick rug.

"How long was I asleep?" Enid ran her hand through her hair.

"A day and a half." Olive popped another mouthful of Devil's Food cake in her mouth.

"What?" Enid strode into the hallway. "Where's Sylvia?"

Olive trailed after her, still nibbling on her cake.

"Sylvia said you are not to go anywhere until you've had breakfast."

"What about the troll?" asked Enid.

"Sylvia has been looking for it."

There was a knock on the door. Red was already waiting by the threshold; garden gnomes seemed to have a sixth sense about these things.

"Are you expecting anyone?" Olive frowned.

Enid rubbed her temples and shook her head.

The grandmother clock in the hall struck eight.

"And so early?" said Olive.

Enid slipped her umbrella from the stand near the front door; this time she wasn't distracted.

"I'll get it, Enid." Olive shook her head and slipped in front of her. "You're still not strong enough." She opened the door.

Thomas Bellchambers stood on the veranda, examining Enid's hydrangeas. He was a gentle soul, in his fifties. Keen eyed and, some would say, unkempt. But he cared for his wildlife more than his appearance. Though, to give him his due - or possibly due to his wife's influence - his beard and moustache were always well-groomed.

"Good morning, Enid." Thomas removed his frayed cap and wiped his boots on the woven door mat. "And this must be Mrs Oldham?"

"Good morning, Thomas." Enid bundled her visitor into the sitting room, opened the curtains, and glanced over the shambles Olive had left in the Sitting Room. "I'm afraid I wasn't expecting visitors this morning."

"I do apologise for the unannounced visit, but I have a proposal for you." His clear blue eyes smiled mischievously. "One I think you'll enjoy."

"Really, Mr Bellchambers." Olive raised an eyebrow. "Do tell."

"Put the kettle on, Olive."

Olive pouted and marched into the kitchen.

"How is your family, Thomas?" asked Enid.

"The children keep Eliza busy." He placed his hat on the chair beside him.

"And the Sanctuary?" Enid stacked the discarded cake plates and placed them on the bookshelf.

"I hope to have more support for the sanctuary soon," he replied.

"Your track could use some repairs. It took a week to settle the Lincoln after my last visit."

"Indeed, that is the reason I am here."

Enid straightened the magazines, and placed them next to her copy of *A Study in Scarlet* on the table next to the settee.

Thomas picked up the *Australian Beekeeper Magazine* and flipped through the pages. "How are your bees?"

"They've been all abuzz for days." She tidied away Olive's deck of cards, and sat opposite him. "They won't tell me what has them so excited."

"Ours have been fussing as well," Thomas frowned. "I can't get near the hives."

"That's odd." The tea tray rattled as Olive returned.

"You have a way with them, Enid," he said. "I thought perhaps you could work your wonders, and calm them down."

"The Howler hasn't been back, creating a stench, has he? He does have a sweet tooth." Enid screwed up her nose. The Houghton Howler was a strange beast, scientifically known as a Thylacine. To the Protectors, it was yet another refugee from the Otherworlds. She'd last tracked it to Humbug Scrub. "It takes days for the reek to leave the hives."

Thomas shook his head. "I'd have noticed."

"Was that your proposition, Mr Bellchambers?" Olive poured Thomas a cup of tea.

"It's one I think you'll enjoy, immensely." He clapped his hands. The mischievous gleam returned to his eyes. "I have an important visitor coming to Humbug Scrub, all the way from England." He glanced at the book on the table, and grinned.

Enid leaned forward.

"Eliza suggested we have a picnic to celebrate." He paused, possibly for dramatic effect. His moustache twitched. "She's making her native currant pie."

"I like currant pie," whispered Olive.

"I was hoping you would bake some of your divine scones and lemon butter for the occasion, Enid."

"Is that all?" Olive plopped on the settee, next to Enid.

Enid elbowed her.

"There will be eleven in the party, plus you, of course. Twelve if Mrs Oldham would like to join us." Thomas sipped his tea.

"Who's the special visitor?" asked Olive.

"Ah, now that would be telling." He chuckled.

"I bet I could guess." Olive stretched her un-gloved hand towards her handbag.

Enid shook her head. Olive huffed and placed her hands on her lap.

"Put her out of her misery, Thomas." Enid raised her teacup to her lips to hide her smile at her friend's frustration.

"Very well." His smile broadened. "Mrs Oldham, would you like to accompany Miss Turner to a picnic at Humbug Scrub cottage, Wednesday next, in honour of the famous author," he leaned across the table. "Sir Arthur Conan Doyle."

Olive gasped.

"He's coming here, to Humbug Scrub?" Enid's cup clattered onto its saucer.

Thomas nodded.

"And you're inviting me?" she continued.

"Us?" squealed Olive.

Thomas nodded again.

"Do you think he would sign your book, Enid?" asked Olive.

"There's one more thing," said Thomas. "Nothing too onerous, I assure you. Reverend Farrow's daughter has been invited. She wishes to join the Field Naturalist Society. Her father thought it wise she experience the bush a little before making her decision." He cleared his throat. "Unfortunately, her father can no longer attend, so Miss Farrow requires a chaperone."

"I'd be happy to help." Enid's heart raced. A small price to pay to meet her favourite author.

"Then it's settled."

"I'll take the Lincoln," said Enid. "I can drive Miss Farrow, if she wishes."

"I think she'd like that," replied Thomas. "You're closer to her age."

Olive coughed.

"Shall we say ten? That will give me time to show Dr Doyle the wildlife sanctuary before luncheon."

"And time to chat to the bees," said Enid.

"I'll have to tell Sylvia," whispered Olive.

"She doesn't need to know," replied Enid.

"But--?"

"Owen's not going, so I won't be distracted," replied Enid. "And it is only a picnic."

"She won't be pleased." Olive bit her lip.

"You do want to meet Sir Arthur, don't you?"

Olive nodded.

"Then Sylvia doesn't need to know." said Enid. "Promise you won't tell her."

chapter three

nid had packed the motorcar by the time Reverend Farrow dropped off his daughter, Agnes, at nine in the morning. He'd twitched nervously each time the young woman had mentioned Sir Arthur's name. He explained he had previous engagements, thanked Enid for chaperoning his daughter, and left Agnes with instructions to only speak about the weather, the roads or the flora and fauna, then retreated back to the city.

Olive arrived at the last minute, clutching a Sherlock Holmes book in one hand, and her leather handbag in the other. She had kept her promise not to inform Sylvia of their outing, though Enid thought that it more likely due to Olive's wanting to meet Sir Arthur, than out of any loyalty to her. Olive was, after all, Sylvia's protegé.

Agnes Farrow's green eyes flashed excitedly, as she climbed into Enid's new Lincoln Six Tourer. Agnes' flame red bob tapered at her nape and skimmed her cheeks. It complemented her emerald, drop-waisted shift dress with its high hemline and her impractical three-inch heels; unexpected choices for a minister's daughter. Her eyes darted over the dashboard, as she traced the door with her lace gloves. She opened her beaded purse, extracted a pair of round sunglasses and slipped them on.

Sunlight warmed Enid's leather driving gloves. Trees lined the road;

their shadows raced over the Lincoln's red bonnet. A pale wooden fence, strung with two metal wires, lined the road through Golden Grove, along the Barossa Road.

The drive had been awkward, fraught with long silences, punctuated with deep sighs and bouts of excited chatter, on Agnes' behalf.

Enid dodged potholes and road gullies carved by the winter rain, as they followed the trail through bushland; a second growth of wild bush and brilliant yellow wattle had sprung up since the bushfires. Occasionally they caught a glimpse of the two cars - of Sir Arthur and invited dignitaries - ahead.

With each bump in the road, the shoulder bag with her first edition copy of *A Study in Scarlet*, poked into her rib.

Olive squeaked in the back seat. She squeezed her eyes shut and gripped the door handle with a gloved hand, the other resting on one of the tins of Enid's freshly-baked scones. A basket sat beside her on her lap, containing a round cake tin, a container of sandwiches, and three jars of lemon butter.

"What's this knob for?" Agnes jiggled in the front passenger seat and poked the dashboard. "And this one? Oh, I'd love to learn to drive."

"Why don't you?" asked Enid.

Agnes sighed. "Father says it's unseemly for a young lady to drive."

Unseemly? Enid straightened up in her seat and held back a frown. It was a new decade. The world had survived the Great War, and the Spanish Flu; surely the Reverend could accept a woman driving a motor vehicle?

Enid yanked the steering wheel to one side to dodge a pothole. Her umbrella, wedged in the seat beside her shifted, and threatened to tumble onto the floor.

"How old are you, Agnes?" she asked.

"Twenty-one," replied Agnes.

"Surely you're old enough to make your own decisions?"

Agnes bowed her head.

"I wanted to attend Sir Arthur's lecture," she said. "But Father wouldn't buy tickets." She turned to face Enid. "Do you think he'll talk to us?"

Olive grunted in the back seat.

"I thought you were visiting Humbug Scrub, on your father's behalf," replied Enid, "to learn more about the wildlife sanctuary, dear."

"Um, yes..." Agnes sat back in the seat and straightened her skirt.

"Why didn't he come himself?" asked Enid.

"He thought it would imply he supported Sir Arthur's theories," replied Agnes. "He says it's best not to meddle with things one doesn't understand."

"Sensible man." said Olive.

"Perhaps keeping to the subject of the sanctuary is a wise choice." Enid frowned. She smiled when Agnes announced they'd caught up with the two-car motorcade.

"That's them." Agnes and pointed to a dark motorcar in front of them.

Enid slowed their motorcar.

"I hope you packed extra scones," said Olive.

Enid smiled. Olive was always predictable when it came to things gastronomic. Her favourite was chocolate cake.

"There's a Devil's Food Cake in the tin. I baked it just for you, Olive," she said. "Still friends?"

"Perhaps," replied Olive.

Enid returned her attention to the road ahead. A thick stand of trees marked the turn for the private track to the Bellchambers' wildlife sanctuary.

"Oh, can't you drive faster?" asked Agnes.

"Those fences were put there for a reason," grumbled Olive.

"Where's the fun in that?" Agnes pouted. "I want to feel the wind on my face! If my hair doesn't fly, then we're not going fast enough."

"What's the fun in life, if we don't take a risk now and then?" Enid smiled. Olive was a poker player; she loved excitement, yet loathed motorcars. "Don't you think so, Olive?" She gripped the steering wheel.

"No, Enid." Olive cringed. "Must you go so fast?"

The first two cars turned right onto the track.

"Right, right!" Agnes clasped her hands on the dashboard and squealed.

Enid turned the wheel. The sun glared over the windscreen as she followed the motorcade.

Olive went pale, and wrapped both hands around the back of Enid's seat. The scone tin on her lap clattered against the door handle. Glass jars rattled in the basket.

"Please?" she groaned.

Enid kept her attention on the way ahead. Something had moved in the trees. A glint of red. She sucked in a breath and peered into the shadows.

"What's wrong?" asked Olive.

"I thought I saw a tr--" She swallowed the words. There was a civilian in the vehicle.

The steering wheel jerked to the side. The car slid.

Agnes squealed. Enid felt Olive grab the back of her seat.

Gravel crunched under the wheels. Stones clattered on the metal chassis and bounced off the radiator grill. A cloud of dust rose from the road, obscuring her vision of the trees ahead.

"Slow down, Enid," pleaded Olive.

Road dust crept into the cabin and enveloped them. Enid held her breath.

Olive coughed loudly.

Agnes laughed. "What a hoot!"

Agnes grabbed the wiper handle and pulled. Grit scraped the glass.

Enid winced and slammed her foot on the brake. The cloud of dust wafted behind them.

The umbrella thudded onto the floor, rolled, and thumped against her ankle.

"Your umbrella!" Specks of dust settled on the dark lenses of Agnes' sunglasses. She leaned down to retrieve the umbrella. Her red hair fell forward and tickled her nose. "You won't need this." She laughed. "It won't rain today. I can tell, you know. Father calls me the *Human Barometer*." She screwed up her nose. "It's not a very pretty nickname, is it?"

Enid reached for the umbrella and shoved it on her lap.

"Why are we stopping?" asked Agnes. "We'll never catch up now."

"The stones were chipping the chassis paint," replied Enid, as she caught Olive's attention in the rear vision mirror. She inclined her head in the direction of the trees, and resumed searching the shadows for the source of the red glint of light.

Olive peered into the trees, and shrugged. "I don't see anything."

"There they are!" Agnes pointed further along the track.

The lead car flashed red in the sun as it turned along the track.

Enid's shoulders relaxed. The red glint had just been a reflection off the car. She scolded herself for an overactive imagination. A troll, indeed. How could it know she would be on the road to Humbug Scrub this morning? She checked the umbrella on her lap, and took a deep breath. Besides, she had not forgotten her Focus this time.

"Will we be there soon, do you think?" asked Agnes. "I can't wait to meet him."

Olive leaned forward, her breath brushed Enid's right ear. "Whatever possessed you to bring her along?"

Enid whispered her reply: "We're supposed to be chaperones, remember. That was the deal, in exchange for an invite to the picnic."

Olive shook her head, picked up the scone tin, and fell back into her seat. "She'll probably eat all the cake."

The Lincoln braked at the end of the dirt track. Leaves rustled in the eucalyptus trees, their fragrance chasing away the smell of hot motor oil and warm gravel dust. Wind danced over a paddock of knot grass, like a long skirt over a plush carpet. Its purple flowers swayed.

Enid opened her door. The cool breeze swirled around her calves, teasing her skirt. Two cars - one black and one red - were parked only a few yards ahead near the property fence, already emptied of their passengers. She peered at the red car. The paint was expensive, and shone like a mirror. The red glint must have been a reflection.

Agnes swung open the passenger side door, slipped on a sheer sun hat and jumped onto the gravel.

Olive snatched up her handbag, and cleared her throat. Agnes jumped to attention, and opened the back door for her.

"Let me take one of those for you, Mrs Oldham."

"Call me Olive. Mrs Oldham sounds so... Well, *old*." Olive offered her the scone tin and hooked the food basket over her arm.

Enid unpacked the picnic rug from the back seat and joined Olive on the other side of the vehicle. A trio of bees flitted in her direction. Their wings tickled her cheek.

"Good morning." Enid laughed. "Are the birds behaving now?" She waited.

The bees circled her head.

"Good. I'm glad they saw sense." The corner of her lip curled. "No other unexpected visitors?"

They buzzed to the negative.

Agnes picked her way through the gravel, in her high heels, towards the parked cars. She straightened her skirt, licked her lips and circled to the opposite side of the two parked cars. Her shoulders slumped.

"They've gone ahead," she said.

"Don't worry, Agnes," said Olive. "They won't start the picnic without us. Mr Bellchambers is quite partial to Enid's scones and lemon butter."

Enid secured her umbrella on her arm and blushed.

Agnes smiled and walked towards the property fence. She lifted the latch bar in two gloved fingers, as if it would bite her.

Enid eyed the girl in the side mirror and laughed under her breath. City girls.

Agnes dropped the bar back into its keep. The rusty gate screeched as she swung it open. She examined her gloves, screwed up her nose, and dusted them off.

"Come on, Olive." Enid adjusted her shoulder bag and led her through the gate, nodding at Agnes as they passed. "Don't forget to shut the gate, Agnes."

Agnes rattled the gate, then wandered up the track after them.

The bees flew in the direction of the homestead, and circled back, buzzing to get Enid's attention. She nodded.

"They're setting up beyond those trees." She waggled her umbrella in the direction of the paddock up the hill. "Follow me."

The trio trudged up the hill, following the chicken wire fence, towards a clearing on the other side of the homestead. White, rectangular wooden beehives stood in the tall grass on one side of the walking track.

A lone bee flew in their direction, hovered near the fence, and returned to the closest hive. Enid smiled. Soon there'd be a buzzing welcome party to update her on all the latest news.

The women followed the smell of wood smoke from Mrs Bellchambers' baking. Enid's stomach grumbled. It was like... What was that scientist Sylvia met during her travels through Europe? Pavlov, wasn't it? And his dogs.

Her stomach grumbled again, this time louder.

"Was that you?" whispered Olive.

Enid nodded. "I didn't have breakfast this morning." She rubbed her stomach and trudged faster up the hill.

Agnes hobbled after them, past the lake and up to the other side of the homestead.

The clearing was scattered with yellow dandelions and buttercups, and surrounded by ancient grey gums swaying in the gully breeze. Magpies warbled in the branches. A crow squawked in complaint, and flew in the direction of the lake.

Rugs had been laid out over the knot grass, in front of the old log cabin - a relic of the old mine.

The picnic party was a largish one. A couple sat on one of the rugs, sipped cups of tea, and chatted to a well-dressed, clean-shaven man in a light suit and hat. He puffed on his pipe and nodded politely in reply to their conversation. Two boys laughed and squealed as they darted between the trees, and ran down towards the lake.

Thomas Bellchambers stood in the shade, chatting with two gentlemen, and looking decidedly uncomfortable in a three-piece suit. Enid smiled. She knew Mr Waite by sight: the symmetrical face and full, immaculately trimmed beard, and spectacles perched on his aquiline nose.

The second man was taller, of solid build, with a thick greying moustache, and inquisitive eyes. He glanced in their direction. His short, dark tie popped out from under his waistcoat as he tipped his fedora, then returned his attention to Thomas.

The grass rustled; a fourth man moved out of the shadows of the trees. He pressed a camera against his body and studied the viewfinder.

A screech pierced the air. The taller, inquisitive man pointed upward to an eagle in flight, and grinned. The other men looked skyward. The taller man pulled a notebook from his coat pocket, jotted down notes and nodded.

Thomas spoke inaudibly, smiled and led the men towards the picnickers.

"Ah, Enid, you made it," he said. "Wonderful. You remember Mr Waite, Director of the Institute Museum?"

"Yes, of course." She shook his hand. "Lovely to see you again, Mr Waite."

"And you, Miss Turner." Thomas turned to Enid's travel companions. "Have you met Mrs Olive Oldham?" he asked Mr Waite.

They greeted each other.

"And this must be Miss Farrow? Agnes, I presume?" Mr Waite's gentle eyes smiled. "I haven't seen you since you were a child. My how you've grown." He shook her hand enthusiastically. "Your father tells me you wish to join the Field Naturalist Society?"

Agnes nodded.

Enid bit her lip. She suspected Agnes was more interested in meeting Sir Arthur, than the local fauna or flora.

"This is Mr Whitington, from *The Register*," continued Thomas. "He's writing an article on Sir Arthur's visit to our sanctuary."

Mr Whitington glanced up from his camera, nodded, and returned to examining the viewfinder.

Thomas stepped aside.

"And, ladies, this is Sir Arthur Conan Doyle, author of--"

"Sherlock Holmes." Agnes clasped both hands around his.

Enid clutched her shoulder bag, calculating the best moment to ask him to sign her first edition.

"A pleasure, Miss Farrow."

A red glow flooded Agnes' cheeks.

"Did you attend any of my lectures?" he asked.

"Sherlock Holmes is my favourite," she cooed.

Sir Arthur's lips smiled, but his pale blue eyes remained lifeless.

Enid's hand twitched. She'd seen that ingenuous smile before. Sylvia had mastery of it, particularly when humouring Enid about one of her plans. The mention of Holmes seemed to bother him. Perhaps the rumours were true; perhaps he *had* killed off Holmes on purpose? Her hand fell from her bag.

"That's enough, dear." She placed a hand on Agnes' arm. "I'm sure Sir Arthur would like to eat lunch."

Agnes' cheeks flamed. She disengaged her grasp and clasped her hands behind her back.

"I hear you follow cricket, Sir Arthur," said Olive.

"Yes." His moustache twitched. "I hope to catch a game when in Melbourne next month."

"Excellent." She grinned and led him towards the other guests.

Enid followed. Olive never took risks without knowing the odds. She'd done her homework, obviously interested in more than just his... books.

A crow growled loudly in the trees. A chorus followed. He had returned, and brought his companions; their wings fluttered as they took flight, cawing and circling.

Enid counted them. ...five ...six. She glanced at her fellow Protector. Olive was already eying the bird. Furrows creased her forehead.

Stones crunched down the hill.

"Good morning, everyone." Eliza Bellchambers dodged clumps of tall grass. She wore a simple dark blouse, a matching ankle length skirt, sensible boots and an infectious smile. In her arms was a tray with a pie dish and covered plates.

Enid had known Thomas for many years, sharing apiary tips; she'd only met his wife on a few occasions, always with their brood of offspring in tow. Today the children were nowhere to be seen.

"I've brought scones and lemon butter," said Enid. "And this is for you both. A gift for inviting me." Enid handed Thomas one of the scone tins. "And there's a jar of lemon butter in the basket as well."

"Thank you. I'll have to hide that from the children." Thomas grinned.

"Your lemon butter is legendary in our household." Eliza laughed and set the dishes on the rug. "I baked a native currant pie, especially for Sir Arthur."

Sir Arthur licked his lips.

"I've sent the other drivers up to the house for lunch," continued Eliza. "Your driver can join them, if he wishes, Miss Turner."

"Miss Turner drove us." Agnes grinned. "Oh, it would be so exciting to drive, but Father says a young lady should allow the gentleman to drive a motorcar."

"Really? Well done, Miss Turner." Sir Arthur leaned close to Enid's ear. "You know how it feels?" he whispered. "The freedom, the wind in your moustache?"

Enid's cheeks burned. She'd never dreamed to meet the author of the Great Detective, let alone share a secret with him.

Agnes stifled a giggle.

"I do apologise. You know what I mean." He laughed. "Was that your red Lincoln following us along the drive?"

Enid nodded.

"Most excellent. I'd love to take her for a spin sometime."

"Only if I can join you," whispered Olive in her other ear.

"It would be my honour, Sir Arthur," said Enid.

His moustache twitched as he smiled. Jolly creases formed in the corner of his eyes.

"Please, call me Arthur," he said.

"Thank you, Sir--" Enid nodded. Her heart skipped; first name basis with the great Sir Conan Doyle. "Arthur."

The two young boys ran up the hill, plopped onto one of the picnic rugs, and grabbed a plate.

"Your sons?" asked Enid.

"Yes," replied Sir Arthur. "The country air is the perfect tonic after being confined on a ship for months."

"Miss Turner." Eliza smiled. "...Enid? Has Thomas introduced you to Dr Anderson and the Kyffins yet?"

Thomas opened his mouth to reply, and hesitated.

"I thought not." Eliza rolled her eyes. "He does tend to be forgetful when given the chance to show off the sanctuary." She sliced a piece of currant pie and offered it to Sir Arthur. "I'm surprised he hasn't shown you the Mallee fowl eggs yet." She winked at her husband. "But lunch first, or the pie will go cold."

Sir Arthur clapped his hands together.

The party sat down to lunch on the slope below the old log cabin. The two boys ate politely, then shadowed the journalist, Mr Whitington, as he continued to record the day's outing. Dr Anderson and the Kyffins sat together, continuing their conversation. Sir Arthur sat with Mr Waite and Thomas, on the rug next to Enid and her companions - much to Agnes' delight. She shuffled to the edge of the picnic rug, as close to Sir Arthur as possible. Eliza joined them.

Enid overindulged in Eliza's sublime baked goods while Olive kept an eye on the circling crows, tracking where each landed. She hovered next to Enid and scanned the picnicking group and counted quietly.

"Thirteen, Enid." She frowned. "That's not a good sign."

"Relax," whispered Enid. "It's a glorious spring day, and we're on a picnic. The worst that could happen is we get invaded by ants."

"And the crows? Six, Enid. You know what that means," she hissed under her breath. "Death."

"Or gold." Enid patted Olive's hand. "It depends on which superstition you prefer."

"Don't let Sylvia hear you say that." Olive scanned the trees. "You're a Protector, Enid. You shouldn't make light of such things."

"Cake?" Enid removed the cake tin from the basket, opened it and cut a large piece of chocolate cake. "You don't have to be on guard twenty-four hours a day." She slipped the slice of cake on a plate and handed it to Olive. "Enjoy the picnic. Just for a few hours at least."

"Tell me, Thomas, how are your lovely ibises?" she asked.

"You have ibises?" asked Sir Arthur.

"Yes," Thomas replied, "I trained two. Birds have much more sense than many creatures, I find." His shoulders slumped.

Enid nibbled on her sandwich. The bread seemed to stick in her throat. This didn't bode well.

"They were both picked off by some local..." He paused, as if looking for an appropriate word for mixed company. "*Sportsmen*," he said finally, though his true meaning was felt in his tone.

Sir Arthur frowned. He placed his pie back on the plate.

"Unfortunately, it happens, despite our precautions," said Thomas. "The concept of a sanctuary for the local wildlife hasn't been accepted by some of the locals."

"Well," Sir Arthur dusted crumbs off his trousers. "I shall see about that."

Mr Whitington returned from a short walk up the hill. He wound on the camera film, circled the picnic group and paused to check his viewfinder again.

The boys trailed behind, whipping at the long grass with sticks as they passed under the tree where the crows had last been seen. Olive eyed the tree tops, her chocolate cake touching her lips, and held her breath. There was silence.

She let out a long breath, relaxed her shoulders and popped the cake into her mouth.

"Tell me about your lake, Mr Bellchambers?" asked Mr Whitington.

"Yes, I thought we'd start there, before venturing up the hill." Thomas rose from the ground. "We've lost too many Mallee fowl eggs. The moisture here isn't good for hatching, so I've constructed my own mound."

"Excellent." Sir Arthur picked up his own camera, slung it around his neck and slipped on his fedora. "You are living so close to nature, Mr Bellchambers, do you ever see fairies?"

Agnes' eyes widened.

Thomas froze mid-step. His gaze darted over the group. He shook his head.

"No," he replied.

"But the little folk are always with us on every country walk."

This time it was scone and lemon butter that caught in Enid's throat. She glanced at Olive. Her friend's smile had dropped; her fingers were wrapped tightly around her handbag.

"Our lives would be improved if they were recognised," continued Sir Arthur.

"You'd have more luck finding them back in England." Thomas slipped on his hat, sweeping back his hair as he did so.

"Doesn't your friend, Mr Houdini, say otherwise, Sir Arthur?" Whitington' voice was clear and strong. His eyelids narrowed as he waited for his reply.

"I'll convince him one day." Sir Arthur patted his camera and smiled.

Olive opened her handbag. Static electricity in the air. Enid swallowed. Olive played the odds, but surely, even she wouldn't risk anything in front of so many people.

"More cake?" Enid picked up Olive's empty plate.

Thomas cleared his throat. "We'd best be on our way, if we're going to see everything before dinner time."

Sir Arthur jotted down more notes and joined Thomas. Dr Anderson and Mr Waite followed.

"May I come too?" asked Agnes. "If it's alright with Miss Turner?"

"In those shoes?" asked Olive.

Enid glanced at Agnes' patent leather Mary-Janes, with their three-inch heel and shiny silver buckles.

"Are you sure, Agnes?"

Agnes bit her lip. Her eyes seemed to plead for permission.

Enid's eyelids fluttered. The sun was warm, the food soporific. She stifled a yawn, took a deep breath and selected a tuna paste sandwich. She'd been baking scones into the wee hours. Perhaps the walk would exhaust the girl's enthusiasm.

"Very well." Enid yawned; she could snatch a nap while they were on the Grand Tour. "You go. I'll wait here."

Agnes grinned and skipped after them.

"Thirteen people at lunch." Olive's hand caught Enid's gloved wrist. "Six crows. Mark my words, Enid: these are not good signs," she whispered. "Don't close your eyes, Enid."

Enid peered into the gum trees behind them. There was no noise. No movement. The bees meandered amongst the dandelions and purple flowers of the knot grass.

"The crows have gone, Olive," she whispered back. "And the bees are quiet. They'd warn me if we were in danger."

"I hope you're right." Olive relaxed her grip.

"You just need to trust them."

Bees flew across the picnic area, and buzzed near Enid's head.

"You won't let me down, will you?" said Enid.

They circled her head and flew off up the hill.

She stifled another yawn as she passed Olive the remaining slice of chocolate cake. Olive sighed, placed her handbag on the rug next to her and took the plate.

Enid stretched, and lay back on the picnic rug.

"Trust me," she mumbled.

The fresh smell of eucalyptus enveloped her, coaxed from the leaves by the afternoon sun. Bees fluttered around her head, buzzing a soft lullaby. She lay back on the warm wool rug and closed her eyes.

chapter four

bees buzzed excitedly around Enid's head. Their shadows flickered over her closed eyelids.

"Hush," she whispered. "Leave me sleep. It was a long drive, and I'm not used to bakers' hours."

The shadows flickered faster. Wings brushed her cheeks.

A thunder crack shook the air, and thumped her eardrums. Her head pounded. The sharp smell of ozone clawed her nostrils.

Enid's eyelids snapped open. Her hand landed off the edge of the picnic rug. Powder drifted onto her fingers. She lurched onto her elbows, and banged her forehead into an unsuspecting bee.

"May I, Miss Turner?" Mr Kyffin tugged at the corner of her rug. "There's a storm coming. We're decamping to the cottage."

Enid nodded, picked up her picnic basket, and stood to one side. A mushroom was crushed where the rug had lain. She examined her fingers; they were covered in mushroom spores. She wiped them on her skirt, and scanned the ground as Mr Kyffin picked up the rugs.

There was another mushroom. And another. A shiver ran down her spine. They'd been picnicking inside a Fairy Ring. No wonder she'd fallen asleep.

She surveyed the paddock for Olive, to warn her. Olive was nowhere to be seen.

Tree branches swayed in a brisk gully wind. Dark, green-tinged clouds crept over the hills. Enid frowned; it was too warm for hail.

A bee landed on her nose and twitched furiously.

"I know," whispered Enid. "It's all very odd."

Another crack of thunder rolled across the darkening sky. And another. A rush of ozone followed each peal.

China chinked behind her. Crumbs tumbled over the edge of plates as Eliza juggled an armful of plate and containers. Mrs Kyffin collected up the remaining crockery. Her husband pulled up the final rug and flung it over his shoulder.

"Oh, look a fairy ring." Mrs Kyffin bent down to pick a mushroom.

"Don't touch it!" Olive appeared from behind the stand of gums the crows had occupied earlier in the morning, and slipped her handbag off her arm.

Mrs Kyffin froze.

"Why ever not?" She straightened up slowly, a look of puzzlement on her face.

Enid glanced back at the sky. Thunder rumbled. The clouds were dark as soot. Her stomach squirmed. Where there was thunder, there was lightning. If Olive attempted to channel Aether now, the extra energy could be dangerous. *Nature Magic* was always predictable. She placed a hand gently on Olive's arm, and turned to face Mrs Kyffin.

"They could be poisonous," she said in a calm voice.

Mrs Kyffin snatched back her hand, and straightened up. The crockery in her arms rattled.

"We must've been sitting inside it all along," said Eliza. "How delightful."

"Sir Arthur will be pleased," said Mrs Kyffin. "Perhaps there are fairies around us, and we just can't see them?"

Her husband kicked the last rug, on the ground, with his foot. Mushroom spores floated into the air.

"The hills are full of them," he said. "Some chap wrote a book about them." He returned his attention to collecting the rugs.

"Fairies?" asked his wife.

"No." He scowled. "Mushrooms."

His wife waved him away. "I'd love to see a fairy," she cooed.

"Be careful what you wish for," whispered Enid.

Olive took Enid aside and indicated the now-broken ring of mushrooms on the ground. "They surround the entire clearing."

A hunting horn trumpeted in the distance. They turned towards the noise. Everything seemed normal - other than the darkening sky, the thunder and the newly-found Fairy Ring. Enid eyed the rest of the party. They'd returned to hurriedly packing up the picnic, apparently oblivious to the sound.

Olive examined the mushrooms. Frost-tipped grass crunched under her feet. Chill air fingered Enid's neck and crept down her spine.

The tree branches shuddered around them.

"Did you see the sky?" Enid's breath frosted as it left her mouth.

Olive's eyelids narrowed. She blew out a slow breath. A cloud of steam issued from her mouth. Her face paled.

Nature Magic. Enid's stomach knotted.

"I wish Sylvia was here," whispered Olive. "She'd know what to do." She snapped open her handbag.

Enid swallowed. Olive's poker face was renowned; she'd never seen her this worried.

Drops of rain plopped on Enid's cheek. She flinched.

"Oh, dear!" Eliza flicked droplets from her hair. "Tell Thomas to meet us at the house, please Miss Turner? I'll pop the kettle on and we can finish your delicious scones." She ushered Mr and Mrs Kyffin along the track to the house.

The clouds rumbled as if in reply.

Footfalls thudded down the hill behind her. The journalist, Mr Whitington, clutched his hat close to his chest, shielding his camera.

He slid to a halt next to Enid and Olive, shook the rain off his hat, and stomped up the path towards the cottage.

Thomas and Dr Anderson arrived next, their clothes dripping. A large drop of water splashed onto the doctor's spectacles.

"Storm's coming." Thomas caught his breath. "Did I hear Eliza mention tea?"

Enid nodded. "They've gone back to the cottage."

Sir Arthur's camera jiggled around his neck as he strode down the hill behind them.

"Where are the boys?" asked Enid, trying not to let her concern show in her voice.

"We sent them back to the cottage for a snack." Sir Arthur grinned.

Another gully wind rushed through the scrub, tugging at Enid's skirts. Sir Arthur's fedora skittered into the long grass. He spun on his heel and snatched after it.

A blue-winged dragonfly swooped past him. He stopped mid-stride, pressed his camera against his torso, and hesitated. The dragonfly hovered, then circled his head and darted off towards the closest stand of trees. He grinned, and marched off after it.

"Mr Whitington and I will escort the ladies back to the house," said Dr Anderson. "The chill is coming in. They'll catch their deaths."

"Mr Whitington has already left," said Olive.

Agnes squealed as she limped down the hill and stopped at Thomas' side. Strands of wet hair clung to her jawline.

"Where's Sir Arthur gone?" she asked. "We can't leave without him."

"Off hunting local insect life." Enid motioned to the trees. She caught Olive's attention, and frowned.

"I'll fetch him." Olive trudged off towards the trees.

The men nodded and made their way up the hill, along the walking track. It seemed narrower now, overgrown with weeds and grass. The trees seemed closer, too. Bushes sprang from ground where they'd sat less than an hour before. The smell of eucalyptus clawed at Enid's throat, but this time there was something else... Something familiar. Something from her childhood. Memory was a strong magic.

She took a tentative sniff, not really wanting to know the answer. There; the smell of secluded English forest, of moist oak, and freshly disturbed earth.

"A Thin Place?" she whispered to Olive.

Olive spun on her heel, a metal fountain pen in her un-gloved hand.

Enid peered up the hill where most of the party trekked. Smoke rose from the old pioneer log cabin. The smell of pine and tea tree now filled the air. Branches swayed in a silent wind. There was no sound. No birds. And...

Enid's heart froze.

The bees were gone.

A second horn trumpeted, ricocheting off the ancient tree trunks, disguising its exact point of origin.

Thomas jerked his head in the direction of the noise. Olive stepped in front of him, as Agnes turned to face the trees. Dr Anderson paused further up the track, just visible through the newly-erupted, ancient oak trees.

Enid took a deep breath and stood her ground.

Strips of bark peeled off their trunks in fractured movements, as if tugged by an indecisive invisible force. Leaves convulsed, plunged, then froze mid-air. Rain fell on Enid's shoulders, dripped into her gloves, and tumbled to ground around her. It tumbled from the leaves of the tall grey eucalyptus trees, in fits and starts, halting a few feet above the ground.

Olive raised her 'pen arm', in lurching movements. Time was slipping, jolting like a film at movie house, caught in a malfunctioning projector.

Another shudder; the rain droplets and bark peelings plummeted to the ground.

Sleeping butterflies stirred in Enid's stomach.

Something crashed through the undergrowth. Her muscles tensed.

"There's something out there?" yelled Dr Anderson.

A large, brown rabbit, with a gnarled horn jutting from its head, skittered through the bushes. Its blazing eyes turned to face Enid as it raced past, and bounded into the trees on the other side.

Enid flinched. The Otherworld magic must be strong to bleed into this reality before its protective shell had been breached.

Agnes gasped and grabbed Thomas' arm.

"It's just a rabbit, dear." Enid patted Agnes on the shoulder.

"Flaming nuisances." growled Thomas.

"I thought I saw--" Agnes frowned, shook her head, and regained composure.

Enid eyed the young woman.

"A trick of the light?" Olive feigned a smile.

"Perhaps the mushrooms spores were hallucinogenic?" Enid dusted the remnants of the spores from her skirt, to lend credence to her subterfuge.

Another horn sounded. The ground vibrated under Enid's feet.

The trees - oak, elm, and fir, gum and tea tree - were now close enough to touch, to examine where the bark had peeled. Two worlds were overlapping.

There was a deafening crack and a blinding flash. A strong, sharp stench of Ozone swept over them. The hair on the back of Enid's neck stood on end.

Light flickered in the distance, and grew steadily. A deluge of iridescent colours surged out of the wood - brilliant greens, blues, pinks, reds, and golds tumbling and sparkling in the still-growing glow behind them.

Agnes gasped. "Dragonflies!" She held out her hand to them.

The horn sounded for a fourth time.

"Enid," whispered Olive, "the rain's stopped."

"Finally!"

"No," Olive spoke slowly, "the rain has *stopped*." She pointed to the drops of water suspended in the air around them.

Enid glanced at Thomas and Agnes. Thomas stared into the trees, his eyes unblinking.

"Thomas?" asked Enid.

"I should've told Sylvia." Olive cursed under her breath. "We can't let civilians see this."

"Time's stopped. They're frozen," said Enid. "They can't hear you."

"As Protectors, we must be immune," continued Olive.

"But that's not..." Enid examined Thomas. He wasn't breathing. Agnes stood on the other side of her, hand outstretched. Her eyes wide, her mouth open, her cry frozen. "No one on this world has magic this strong." She peered up the hill. Dr Anderson stood motionless as well.

The dragonflies circled back towards the group and buzzed above their heads. The colours shifted as she watched.

Enid's heart raced. Dragonflies didn't usually glow. And these moved with purpose. She grabbed for her umbrella - her Focus. Her heart froze. She struggled to breathe. It was gone.

A dragonfly, with luminescent green wings whizzed up to her. Its wings buzzed. A giggle echoed in her head. It hovered in front of her nose, and turned. Its face was thin and pale, with delicate features. Haunting black eyes stared at her. It blinked, raised its slender finger and shook it as if berating her.

The world spun. The light imploded with a crack. And everything went black.

The wood was dark, with a distinct lack of glowing dragonflies. Enid blinked, waiting for her eyes to adjust. A large, dark moon squatted in a starless sky. It skimmed above the canopy of distinctly un-Australian-looking trees, providing no light.

Thrashing noises tracked through the undergrowth, behind her. The fresh aroma of disturbed tea-tree swirled through the air. Far off to the left, something thudded the ground. The thrashing sound moved closer.

The butterflies in Enid's stomach fluttered. She scanned the unfamiliar shadows. No moonlight penetrated the dense wood. It was as if she'd crawled into her oven, and shut the door tight.

She swept her hand through the air, searching for a reference point - hoping Olive was by her side.

There was a slow gasp nearby. Her heart pounded. She shuffled a step closer to the noise, and reached tentatively in its direction.

"*Illumino.*" Olive's voice rang through the still air.

Enid's palpitations calmed; she wasn't alone.

The air sizzled. Blue light flared, at chest height, next to her. It glinted in Olive's green eyes. A blue filament of light extruded from the glow, circled down Olive's arm to her un-gloved hand, and traced the engraved inscription along her fountain pen. Light pooled in a ball at the tip of the nib, illuminating several yards in diameter.

Agnes stood to Enid's right, staring wide-eyed in Olive's direction. Thomas stood on the other side of her, facing in the opposite direction. The track was no longer visible, and nor was Dr Anderson.

Lightning crackled through the clouds, arcing towards the trees. A shining sphere glimmered and expanded in the distance. With a crackling flash of light, it shifted, and floated slowly forward. Small glittering lights flitted ahead of it, darting through the tree trunks as if drawing the light with them.

"The protective shell is breaking." Olive's voice was louder than expected.

Enid jumped.

A second flight of Fae rushed into the clearing. They flitted around the group, twirled in the air, and formed a guard, just inside the damaged mushroom ring.

The advancing light sphere flickered brighter. Air pressed against Enid's chest, pushing her away from the trees. She struggled to stand her ground.

The light pressed forward. Olive winced. The skin on her cheek flattened, pressed by the invisible barrier.

Enid grimaced, and stepped back to relieve the pressure. There was a faint pop under her heel.

An earthy smell wafted up from the ground. Fine dust-like particles tickled her nostrils. She spluttered, and glanced down at the mushrooms crushed under her feet. Her heart skipped. She'd crossed inside the mushroom ring.

The light sphere intensified, advanced further, and paused at the edge of the ring. A rumble of thunder rolled over them. The light shimmered and twitched. The bottom edge touched the ground. Silvery green sparks crackled around its circumference. The sphere distorted, grew larger, and flattened to form a flat, vertical disc of light a few feet taller than Enid herself.

The smell of sulphur clawed the back of her throat.

"Something's creating a portal, trying to break through," she said. But, there were so many Otherworlds beyond the protective shell. It could be any of them. She glanced back down at the mushroom ring. "Fae?" she asked. There were many types of 'fairy'; the Fae was but one of their ilk, and one of the more unpredictable.

"Most likely." Olive swallowed. "I wish Sylvia was here."

Sylvia had met a Fae once, as a child. In Scotland. And, according to Olive, she still had nightmares. Her voice echoed in Enid's head: *Never trust the Fae*. Every muscle in Enid's body readied for defence. Not just any Fae could open a portal from the Otherworlds.

Enid's fingers twitched. She'd need a Focus to have any chance against Fae, and her umbrella was missing. *One day, when you need it most, you'll forget your Focus*; Sylvia's voice haunted her. Today was that day. She clenched her fist and cursed under her breath. She'd be in for a stern lecture from Sylvia.

...if they survived.

"*Claudere porta.*" Lightning crackled from the tip of Olive's pen and fanned over the disc. It sizzled and smoked where it touched the light. Her hand trembled. The pen glowed. She grimaced.

A loud pop. The energy fizzled.

The portal brightened. Jagged lines appeared on the surface and splintered inward from the edges. Air hissed through the fractures. The sharp smell of ozone followed.

Olive stepped in front of Enid and pointed her fountain pen at the portal.

Fractures sped across the surface, reached the opposite side, and stopped. The surface quivered. Vibrating shards of light leaked through them. The portal snapped open. Its surface rippled in a myriad of swirling colours.

Enid and Olive stood ready; they had civilians to protect.

Shapes twisted, formed. Dozens of dragonfly-Fae buzzed around a central luminous figure on the other side of the doorway. A glowing, silvery ribbon snaked through the portal, widened and coalesced into a pale, lithe limb of perfect proportions, glistening silver in the faint moonlight. Its body filled the portal and glided over the threshold, accompanied by a guard of dragonfly-Fae.

The creature, clothed in pale flowing garments, stood seven feet tall. Fireflies hovered at the hem of the gown, preventing the fabric from being soiled on the ground. Glittering, star-like flecks dusted its flowing black hair, crowned with a headdress of gold, silver and emeralds and adorned with branches of horn and wood. Violet eyes blazed from a fine-featured face.

By the creature's side was an Otherworldly-hound, tall and elegant, tethered to its master by a silver chain.

The Fae within the mushroom circle paused mid-flight, and bowed. This was the Fae Queen herself. It explained the *Temporal Magic*; all the legends about falling asleep, and lost time in the Fae world were her doing. Enid swallowed a curse; she should have suspected it.

She glanced at Thomas and Agnes. Few mortals who encountered the Fae Queen escaped without consequences.

"Show no emotion," whispered Olive.

"Are you sure?" Enid caught her breath. Gone was Olive's cheeky bravado; she was calm, cautious.

"I trust Sylvia." Olive's face remained blank. "It's a sign of weakness to Fae. On no account, agree to *anything*." The fountain pen in her hand wavered.

A twig snapped behind them.

Enid held her breath, determined not to cry out.

A shadow moved between the trees, and advanced towards them.

Olive crouched and raised her fountain pen, as if wielding a sword.

Sir Arthur burst from the bushes, just beyond the mushroom circle. He removed a hand from his pocket, dusted off his trousers, and lifted his camera up in triumph.

"Let's see Houdini rationalise that one." He chuckled.

The dragonflies wheeled in the air. Their intensity brightened as they swirled around him. He grinned, stood his ground, and wound on the camera film. The shutter clicked.

"Magnificent!" He lined up his camera, clicked the shutter, and spun around to follow the fluttering rainbow. He wound on the film and crept closer, slowing with each step. One foot fell onto a clump of mushrooms. Spores spat into the air. He stumbled in jerky movements, glanced down, and froze mid-step.

A heartbeat.

Time slipped.

He hurtled forward into the circle. He blinked, regained his balance, and dropped his camera. It dangled from the strap around his neck.

Enid willed him to remain silent.

"Is that..." His ragged breath wheezed in her ear. "The Fairy Queen?"

"Keep your mortal quiet." The Fae Queen glared at him.

Suspended rain droplets shuddered in the air around them.

"Shh." Enid dragged him closer. "These are the Fae, and they're nothing like your fairy stories."

The Fae Queen waved her hand in their direction. Her violet eyes flared gold. The last of the blue light at the tip of Olive's fountain pen fizzled.

The newly arrived Fae Guard surrounded Enid and her companions, creating a ring of light. Their queen stepped forward.

"Who speaks for the mortals?" The air quivered.

"I do." Olive lowered her fountain pen, and straightened her shoulders.

"Are you Protector of this world?" she asked.

"I am this world's Protector," replied Olive.

"As am I," said Enid. "We are many."

"I need only one." The Fae Queen scanned the group. Enid felt her presence sifting through her mind. The Queen turned to face Enid. "You are bound to this world. Will you represent it?"

Enid nodded. The butterflies in her stomach beat the walls of their cage.

The Fae Queen leaned closer, the violet colour around her cat-like pupils drained from her eyes. "The Fae Heir has been taken."

"We've seen no child," whispered Sir Arthur.

"Silence!" Her pupils flared.

Enid elbowed him.

"I trust not the lying tongue of this man of Earth," hissed the Queen. "We've dealt with his kind before. Where is my child?" Her eyes burned black. "Are you in league with our enemies?" Her skin shone like darkened steel.

The butterflies in Enid's stomach were now even more eager to escape. Had they landed in the middle of a war between the Otherworlds? She swallowed.

Olive squeezed her arm. She shook her head.

"Then return the Heir by midnight on the last day of the full moon, or this world is forfeit."

"But we don't--" Sir Arthur's voice caught in his throat. He spluttered and gasped for air.

The Fae Queen glared at him. Both turned to face Enid.

"If the Heir is returned safely, your part of the contract will be complete. I give you my word."

"And if we don't accept?" asked Olive.

The Queen leaned towards Olive, her face darkened, her eyes still completely black.

Hair bristled on the back of Enid's neck.

"If you return the Heir I will let your world live."

Sir Arthur cleared his throat, and thrust his hands on his hips. "We accept!"

"You idiot," growled Olive.

"It was full moon two days ago." He grinned. "That gives us a month."

"Time moves differently in the Otherworlds." Enid nodded in the direction of their motionless companions.

"When is your next full moon?" asked Olive.

"Three of your suns," replied the Queen.

"You fool." This time Olive elbowed Sir Arthur in the stomach.

It was too late now. The deal was struck.

"Can we trust her?" groaned Sir Arthur.

"Shut up," said Olive.

"Insolence!"

The Fae Queen turned, glided back towards the portal, and stepped over the broken line of mushrooms. She raised her hand. Her court buzzed after her.

"You have three of your suns." Her voice drifted back towards them - a whisper on the wind, a memory of a fading dream. Her silhouette melded into the swirling light.

The portal snapped shut. The darkness retreated. The sun blazed in place of the Otherworld moon. Gum tree trunks knocked gently in the retreating wind; the thick wood had faded back into the Otherworld.

"Will they keep their word?" asked Sir Arthur.

"The Fae keep their word," replied Olive. "If your goals match theirs, then all well and good. But they always win."

"Then, we have a quest." He clapped his hands. "How exciting!"

"It's more like an ultimatum," said Enid.

"And we can't afford a civilian getting in the way," said Olive.

Enid's heart sank into her stomach. She lowered her voice: "No, Olive, not *Memory Magic*."

She'd used it on Owen, and it had cost her dearly. Only time would tell how much of his memory had been lost. Would he remember his interrupted proposal? Or was the moment lost forever. *Memory Magic* was unpredictable. Even Sylvia hadn't mastered control of it. And there were *always* consequences.

"There's no other way," said Olive. "We can't let anyone know we've made a deal with the Fae." Olive lowered her head, avoiding Enid's gaze.

What she really meant was if Sylvia found out, she'd have their hides.

Enid's shoulders slumped. "What if it goes wrong?" Sir Arthur was a brilliant man, and she didn't want to lose Mr Holmes.

Olive raised the fountain pen. It was expensive, with exquisite etchings, and engraved: *To my darling wife, love always, Frank. 1915.* Personal items provided a strong Focus to channel magic. Perhaps that would help?

"But you need me." Sir Arthur's eyes widened. "I know about the Wee Folk. I can see them." He clasped his camera in his hand. "I can help you."

"If you get in the way, or cross them... We can't save you." Olive glanced at Enid. "Best he doesn't know it's coming."

"Who are you people?" He raised his hands and stepped back.

Olive's amulet glowed blue under her blouse. Deep blue sparks crackled around the tip of the pen.

"*Dormi*," A puff of blue smoke ringed Sir Arthur's head.

"Wha--?" He breathed in the vapour. His eyelids drooped.

"Don't take too much, please," whispered Enid.

"He'll think he fell asleep after the walk. He'll remember the picnic, but he'll have a heck of a hangover in the morning.

"*Oblivisce.*"

The air shuddered. A spark appeared in the air, about an inch from the pen's nib. A beam of blue light formed a point of light on Sir Arthur's forehead, and seeped into the skin. He sucked in a sharp breath. His hand spasmed around the camera.

"That's how it's done," said Olive.

"And the others?" asked Enid.

"They won't remember anything." Olive examined Thomas and Agnes, still frozen in the moment before the Fae arrived. "The Fae Queen made sure of that." She examined the camera around Sir Arthur's neck. "Now it's our turn. No one can see his photos."

She clicked the latch on the back of the camera, removed the canister, and extracted the film.

"That was bright." Thomas moaned behind them, and lowered his head into his hands.

Agnes wobbled. Her eyes watered. She blinked, lowered her arm and rubbed her shoulder.

Voices shouted further up the hill. Footsteps thudded down the, now clear, walking track. Eliza's skirt fluttered behind her. Her face was pale.

Thomas rushed up the track, and cradled her in his arms.

"You need to come. There's been a--" She struggled to catch her breath. "Murder!"

chapter five

magpies warbled in the trees, as the group raced up the fenced track toward the Bellchambers stone cottage. Thomas led, followed by Agnes.

A drift of bees fussed around Enid's head.

"No, I don't know who it is," she replied. "Yes, I'll let you know when I find out."

They buzzed in front of her face.

"What do you mean, 'they're here'?" She halted mid-step. A drop of water dripped from her wet hair and dribbled down the back of her neck.

Sir Arthur jogged up the path behind Enid and Olive, apparently unaware of his recent ordeal. Perhaps luck has been on Olive's side. Again. She had a knack for beating the odds.

He slowed as he caught up.

"The bees won't hurt you, Miss Turner. They're considered messengers between us and the spirit realm, you know. Perhaps they're trying to warn us of something?" He smiled and continued up the path after the others.

The back flap of his camera slapped against his chest. The exposed loose film tumbled out, caught in the back flap, and crinkled. Enid winced. He'd be devastated when he discovered his precious film was ruined.

"Don't worry," said Olive. "He won't remember what photos he took." She smiled and followed the others up the track.

A muffled shriek echoed down the track. Enid's heart jumped. Had the murderer claimed a second victim? She waved her 'messengers' away, and dashed up the path after Sir Arthur.

A large brick chimney clung to the corrugated roof at one end of the Bellchambers' stone cottage. The building itself was small, not large enough to fit the entire clan. The children usually slept in nearby outbuildings.

A single hydrangea bush grew in front of the veranda. It had been an innocent-looking gift. Eliza was a keen gardener, and her favourite colour was blue. It was a safe way to ensure the ground was tended; acidic soil not only blued the flowers, it would protect a known Thin Place - and them - from just such Otherworld incursions. Each culture had their legends, based on the Thin Places - standing stones, graveyards, sacred places - points where Otherworlds touched this one.

Enid examined the flowers as she neared the cottage. The petals were blue, the tips tinged pink. She frowned. Eliza had been neglecting her garden. No wonder the Fae had broken through.

A faint smell of sulphur hung in the air. Enid wrinkled her nose; it didn't bode well.

Someone was crying inside the cottage. Enid's heart lurched into her throat.

Please, not one of the children...

She glanced back at the hydrangea flowers. There was only a faint tinge of pink on the petals. Surely there was still enough protection for the living areas?

Ravens scratched on the metal roof. Six ravens. They greeted her with a throaty growl. One called to her: a short series of 'caws'. It wanted her to follow. It spread its wings, and swooped over their heads towards the side of the house.

She followed.

Olive ran to meet her.

"It's no one we know. The children are safe." She lowered her voice, and indicated the roof as they walked to the back of the cottage. "Did you see them?"

"Yes," replied Enid.

"Six," said Olive. "Six crows."

"Ravens," corrected Enid. Olive was a city girl, more interested in playing cards, and unpredictable magic, than the local wildlife.

"Still a bad omen," whispered Olive.

They rounded the corner of the cottage. Mr Waite stood guard near the back door. Water dribbled off the brim of his hat as he nodded in their direction.

Thomas and Mr Waite stood near a body. Dr Anderson crouched beside them. Agnes moved away from the group, rubbed her arm, and peered at them over the top of her dark sunglasses.

The Doyle boys bustled out the back door. Mr Waite spread out his arms, blocking their view of the corpse. As a zoologist, he was likely the most experienced at wrangling two inquisitive boys. They jostled to push past him.

"Shall I take the boys inside?" he asked.

"Please do," replied Sir Arthur. "Their mother won't be pleased if they come home talking about dead bodies."

The screen door slapped against the door frame. The boys complained as they were ushered inside. Mr Whitington emerged from the cottage and strode past them.

"Mrs Bellchambers has telephoned the police." He surveyed the scene, scribbled notes in a little notebook, and took some photographs.

"That's all we need," grumbled Olive. "It'll be all over the news. If Sylvia finds out..." Olive's hand trembled.

"She'll understand." Enid clasped Olive's hands in hers.

"No." Olive pushed Enid's hands away. "We don't say anything. We return the Heir, and all will be right with the world."

Agnes clutched her purse and stared at the corpse.

"The poor girl," whispered Olive. "She's had a sheltered upbringing. I don't think she's seen a dead body before."

"Her mother died from Spanish flu," replied Enid.

"Who is it?" Agnes sniffed and flicked wet hair from her chin.

"Our driver," replied Mr Waite.

"Go inside, Agnes." Enid rested her hand on Agnes' arm to usher her inside. Agnes flinched.

"I need to help." The girl's gaze tracked Olive as she joined the men.

"You can," said Enid. "Mrs Bellchambers will need help with the children."

Agnes shook her head. "They're tucked up in their beds." She avoided Enid's gaze, but there was fear there.

Enid frowned. "It's safer inside."

"You're not my father," she said. "I'll stay."

"As you wish, dear." Enid joined the huddle near the body.

The twisted body of a man lay at the base of the broken fence, only a few yards from the back door. The fence looked as if trampled, as if by a large horse.

While Mr Whitington fiddled with his camera, Enid stepped into the vacated space. A ripped, dark-coloured jacket was caught on the broken fence post. A man in dark trousers, white shirt and braces lay on his side, one arm over the fence, as though he'd been trying to escape. His flattened chauffeur's hat lay on the other side of the fence.

Rolled up sleeves exposed his forearms. Bruises had already formed on one arm. Long gashes trailed along the other. Blood pooled around the head and chest, and drenched his mop of hair.

"Did you notice his neck?" whispered Olive.

Faint linear bruises on the side of his neck tracked up to a set of darker oval marks surrounding a crushed Adam's apple. Enid eyed the marks: twice the size of a human hand, and dusted with a fine grey powder. She opened her mouth to reply, and hesitated, aware Agnes was close by. She nodded.

Olive moved closer and whispered in her ear: "I think our bounty-hunter troll has tracked you down."

Enid scanned the hillside for any sign of her nemesis. The late afternoon sun cast long shadows amongst the trees. It would be sunset in an hour or so. She struggled to keep her breaths even. Trolls moved faster in the dark.

"Definitely dead, I'm afraid." Dr Anderson rose slowly and shook his head. "He was strangled, and his head bludgeoned by a blunt object."

"Whoever murdered him, wanted to be certain of the job," said Sir Arthur.

"You've worked with the police, Sir Arthur." Thomas stood next to him. "What do we do now?"

"No one touch the body," he replied. "We must preserve the crime scene for the Constabulary." He checked the sky. "How long until the constabulary arrive?" His moustache twitched. "We'll be losing the light soon. They're likely to miss vital evidence in the dark."

He picked up his camera. The loose film crunched as he wrapped his fingers around the camera.

"What on--?" He sneered, tipped the film canister into his hand, and cursed under his breath. "My photos are ruined!" Creases marked his forehead. "My fairies," he whispered. "How...?"

He remembered the fairies? Enid frowned.

"Oh, Sir Arthur..." Olive patted his arm. "They were dragonflies."

"Dragonflies?" He pulled his arm away. "What are you saying, woman? I know what I saw. We all saw them." He turned to face Agnes. "You saw them, didn't you?"

Agnes shrank back into the shadow of the veranda, and said nothing.

Her gaze remained fixed on Enid and Olive.

"We can't have him blabbing about fairies, Enid." Olive tugged Enid's sleeve.

"Hush," whispered Enid. "We've got an audience."

"You must have seen them, Dr Anderson?" asked Sir Arthur.

"I'm sorry, Sir Arthur. I saw the storm coming, and a flash of lightning. That was all." Dr Anderson covered the driver's face with his jacket.

"Mr Bellchambers?" The crease in Sir Arthur's forehead deepened.

Thomas shook his head. "The last thing I remember was the flash of light."

"That lightning strike was too close," said Dr Anderson.

"Lightning?" Thomas turned to Dr Anderson. "No wonder my head is ringing."

Sir Arthur's face reddened. "I know what I saw."

"We're lucky to have survived," said Olive.

Enid recognised the twinkle in Olive's eye; she would latch onto the comment and concoct a story. She excelled at that.

Enid remained silent. She didn't feel comfortable gas-lighting Sir Arthur, even if it was for his own safety.

A camera flash flared. Mr Whitington stepped over the body to take another photo.

"Good idea, Whitington." Sir Arthur snatched his camera. "I'm sure the Constabulary will appreciate the use of your camera to document the scene."

"Perhaps we should all go inside for a cup of tea while we wait for the Police to arrive." Thomas opened the back door.

"Excellent." Dr Anderson nodded. "I highly recommend a strong, sweet tea."

Agnes didn't move. Her gaze darted from the body, to Enid and Olive, to Sir Arthur, and back to the body.

"Miss Farrow?" Thomas held out his arm and offered her his elbow.

Agnes blinked. A polite smile flickered over her lips.

"You don't have anything stronger, do you?" She took his arm and allowed herself to be ushered towards the house.

"I don't think your father would approve," he answered.

Her polite smile faded.

"Perhaps a little fortification is in order, Dr Anderson?" asked Thomas.

Dr Anderson nodded. "I dare say we could bend the rules, this once. It isn't everyday you're caught on a hillside in a lightning storm."

"Even your father can't argue with doctor's orders," said Thomas.

Mr Whitington checked his watch. "I need to contact the paper. If I'm quick, I may be able to make the evening edition."

He strode inside. The screen door slapped shut behind him. Dr Anderson followed them into the cottage. Sir Arthur hovered near the broken fence, and stared back down the hill.

Sir Arthur took a deep breath, wound on the film in the borrowed camera, and examined the dead driver. He turned his back to them and slipped his hand in his coat pocket. Enid eyed him out of the corner of her eye. A few seconds later, the camera flashed again.

"Sir Arthur's logic is infallible," Enid said to Olive. "He could have helped us."

"*Mr Holmes'* logic is infallible," corrected Olive.

"We can't just leave him like this," said Enid.

"We can't have him asking questions, either."

"I meant--"

"I know what you meant," said Olive. "But you know the rules as well as I. No mortals allowed. He mustn't tell anyone. If the Bounty Hunter discovers the Fae Heir is here, he will forget all about you. The Heir to a Fae kingdom is much greater prize."

Enid's heart sank into her stomach. She understood Olive's meaning.

"We had no choice," replied Olive. "If Sylvia found out, he'd be up for much worse."

Enid frowned. Olive was correct. If Sylvia found out Sir Arthur had ensnared the Protectors in a Fae contract, she would be furious.

"Best not mention his involvement," she said.

Olive nodded. "Best not."

Sir Arthur trembled. Enid rushed to steady him. His pupils contracted to pinpoints of black. His eyes rolled upwards, showing the whites of his eyes.

"Can you hear me, Sir Arthur?" she asked.

His pupils wobbled, snapped open, then stabilised. His shoulders drooped. Enid and Olive each grabbed an arm. His knees buckled.

Enid lifted his head to face the fading sunlight. His pupils contracted, reacting normally to the light. She smiled.

"Olive, are you sure he'll be all right?"

Olive nodded. "A delayed reaction, that's all. I think he'll be all right," she said. "Get him inside. And no more talk of fairies. We don't want the others to remember anything."

They helped him towards the back door.

"It's getting dark," said Enid. "What if the bounty hunter returns?"

"I'll have a quick scout out to see if it's still lurking around," replied Olive.

"But, it's too dangerous."

"You can't do it," said Olive. "What would you do if you found it? You've lost your Focus." She extracted her arm from around Sir Arthur's. "You'd just better hope the troll didn't filch it." She grinned. "Then, it wouldn't be *me* in trouble."

Enid glared at her.

Olive retrieved her fountain pen from her handbag and removed the lid to reveal the sturdy, sword-like nib. A blue glow shimmered around its tip.

Enid laughed quietly.

"What?" asked Olive.

"The pen--"

"Don't say it," said Olive.

Sir Arthur moaned and leaned against the door frame.

"Best you take him inside before the police get here." Olive stepped away from the cottage, moved into the tree line, and was gone.

Enid slipped her arm under Sir Arthur's and transferred his weight onto her shoulder.

"Come on, Sir Arthur. Let's get you a cup of tea."

The entire picnic party had gathered in the main room of the Bellchambers' cottage.

Enid ushered Sir Arthur to a chair next to the fireplace at the other end of the room, and plumped up his cushion. The unnatural chill, that had heralded the Fae Queen, still clung to her bones. She flicked her damp hair from her eyes and sat down at the well-used, rustic dining table.

A crisp, white curtain framed the window. A vase of fresh hydrangea blooms sat on the table, another on the small table between the wooden chairs near the fireplace in the main room. Old prints of the English countryside hung on the stone walls.

Dr Anderson and Mr Waite removed their soaked jackets. Small pools of water formed around their feet. Thomas stoked the fireplace at the end of the room until flames crackled in the hearth. Dr Anderson and Mr Waite huddled next to the fire.

Mr Whitington removed his coat and hung it on the back of a chair close to the fire. He cocked his head in their direction, and scribbled in his notebook. Mr Kyffin consoled his wife, and offered his handkerchief.

Agnes hovered near the doorway, her hair drenched. Water dripped from her silk dress onto the wood floor, and seeped into the faded rug.

The door opened.

All eyes locked on it. Mrs Kyffin squeaked.

Olive entered the room, and shrugged. "I forgot my handbag."

She joined Enid at the dining table.

Mrs Kyffin buried her head in her husband's shoulder.

"Mrs Kyffin found the body," Enid whispered to Olive, as she sat down opposite.

"Poor thing," replied Olive.

A low hum of conversation filled the room as Thomas lit the gas lamps.

"Really?" Mrs Kyffin's voice rang through the room. She wiped her nose and sniffed. "Fairies?"

Mr Waite nodded.

Mr Whitington stopped writing and raised his head.

"Well, there are the floating lights," replied Thomas, "in the far paddock."

Sir Arthur sat hunched near the fire, his head still cradled in his hands.

Enid's stomach knotted. She'd hoped Olive's *Memory Magic* would quash all talk of fairy encounters. It'd been a necessary risk, and they still didn't know how much of Sir Arthur's memory, or Sherlock Holmes, had been erased. Had it all been for nothing?

"What's all this talk of fairies, Sir Arthur?" Mr Whitington poised his pen, ready to take more notes.

Sir Arthur's forehead wrinkled.

"Pardon?" he mumbled.

"You said you had photos," said Mr Waite.

Sir Arthur stared at the two cameras in his lap - his own, and the one commandeered from the reporter to document the scene of the murder.

"Did I?" He lifted up his own camera. The film cascaded into his lap.

"I'm afraid the film's ruined." He picked up Mr Whitington's camera and examined it; the vacant look in his eyes faded. He looked concerned.

"I'm afraid Sir Arthur isn't feeling well," said Enid.

Mr Whitington lowered his pen and leaned towards Sir Arthur.

"If you have no more use for my camera..." he said.

"Yes, yes." Sir Arthur shook his head and handed it to him.

Mr Whitington hugged the camera and smiled.

Eliza hurried in from the adjoining room, a stack of towels and blankets in her arms. She handed them out to her guests. Agnes nodded her thanks, and remained near the front door as she patted her hair dry.

"I believe this is yours, Miss Turner?" Mr Kyffin approached the dining table, and handed Enid her umbrella. "I must've packed it up with the picnic rugs." Mr Kyffin glanced at her damp hair. "My apologies." He returned to his wife's side.

Enid grinned. "Thank you." Her fingers wrapped around the handle. A faint buzz tingled her skin.

Eliza returned shortly with a tea tray and poured everyone a cup of steaming tea.

"Crispies, anyone?" She placed a plate of golden-coloured flat biscuits with oats on the table.

"It's a new recipe, from a Melbourne magazine," she whispered to Enid. "The secret is the golden syrup. Tell me what you think."

Enid sniffed their rich aroma; her mouth watered. She nodded and took a bite. Syrupy, yet not too sweet. "Delicious. May I?"

Eliza nodded and offered her a second one.

Sir Arthur raised his head.

"Where are the boys?" There was urgency in his voice.

"Don't worry, Sir Arthur," replied Thomas. "They're safe, with the children, in one of the outer buildings."

"Thomas?" Eliza caught up the corner of her apron and wrung it in her hands. "What if the murderer is still on the property?"

Enid clutched her umbrella.

"But, it's..." Olive glanced at Enid and cleared her throat. "*He's* gone. One of the motor cars is missing. I'd say he stole it."

Eliza let out a slow breath and straightened her apron. "Thank goodness."

A knock on the door made everyone jump.

China rattled on the tea tray. Eliza's face turned white.

"The children--" Her gaze darted towards Thomas.

Everyone held their breath.

Enid's heart raced. Surely the murderer wasn't foolhardy enough to return to the scene of the crime, and expose himself to all these witnesses? That only happened in detective novels.

She gripped her umbrella. Olive unlatched her handbag and pulled out her pen.

Thomas picked up the fire poker and opened the door slowly.

A tall clean-shaven man, in a brown suit, stood at the threshold. Behind him were three Police officers, resplendent in their navy uniform and black boots.

"Good evening. I'm Detective Leonard." He removed his bowler. "Mrs Bellchambers telephoned about a murder?"

Eliza nodded.

"I'm Mr Bellchambers," replied Thomas. "Let me show you where--"

"No need, Mr Bellchambers," said Detective Leonard. "My men will secure the area."

"Around the back," said Thomas.

The detective motioned to the two officers at the back. They peeled off and strode towards the back of the house.

"May we come in?" asked Detective Leonard.

"Of course." Thomas stood aside.

Detective Leonard entered, followed by the remaining Police officer.

"I hope to get you all home in time for supper." He hung his hat on a coat hook behind the door.

There was a collective sigh. Mr Whitington checked his watch and frowned.

"Who discovered the deceased?" asked the detective.

The officer at his side pulled a notebook from his pocket, and readied himself to take notes.

Mrs Kyffin sniffled and raised her hand.

"And you are?"

"Mrs Maisie Kyffin," replied Mr Kyffin. "I'm her husband, Evan."

The Officer made notes.

"My wife is very upset," continued Mr Kyffin.

"I have to establish the facts, Mr Kyffin," said Detective Leonard. "I need to know everyone's whereabouts during the afternoon."

They nodded.

"You can all vouch for each other's whereabouts this afternoon?" he asked.

"Yes," replied Thomas. "I took Sir Arthur, Mr Waite and Mr Whitington for a walk to show them the sanctuary," said Thomas.

"Mr and Mrs Kyffin returned with me when it started to rain," said Eliza.

"And you are..."

"Eliza Bellchambers. I live here." She straightened her apron.

"Then we all returned when it started to storm," said Dr Anderson.

"Storm?" asked the detective.

"Lightning storm," said Enid, re-enforcing the assumption by the group to explain the time slippage.

"Strange. We had no storm in town." He turned to the officer behind him. "There wasn't a storm predicted for today, was there Jenkins?"

"Not that I'm aware of, sir."

Perhaps they wouldn't accept the pretence to explain the Fae magic. Enid placed her umbrella in her lap.

"We're a long way from town," said Olive.

"We often get storms here, Detective Leonard," said Thomas. "The moisture plays havoc with the Mallee eggs."

The detective shrugged. "Very well. I'll need to take the rest of your names."

Mr Whitington raised his hand, and twiddled his pencil.

"Mr Whitington, Adelaide Register. I was assigned to write about Sir Arthur's visit to the sanctuary."

"Sir Arthur Conan Doyle?" asked the officer.

"Doyle? As in Sherlock Holmes?" Detective Leonard side-eyed the officer.

Sir Arthur nodded slowly. He clutched his head and groaned.

"The very same Mr Conan Doyle who has a migraine," he whispered.

"Sir Arthur was the closest to the lightning strike," said Dr Anderson.

"And you are?" asked the detective.

"Dr Anderson."

The officer continued taking notes.

"I was with the group all afternoon, until the storm," continued Dr Anderson. "We were returning to the house, when Mrs Bellchambers informed us of the murder."

Mrs Kyffin buried her head back in her husband's shoulder. He patted her on the back.

"Mrs Kyffin has had a great shock," said Dr Anderson. "I recommend keeping her interview short."

The detective nodded. "I'll interview Mrs Kyffin first. Then those who returned to the house first. You can accompany your wife, Mr Kyffin."

"I think that's an excellent idea," replied Mr Kyffin.

"Is there anywhere private?" asked Detective Leonard.

"In the kitchen," said Thomas.

"That just leaves--" The detective eyed Agnes, who hadn't moved from her spot near the doorway. "Miss...?"

"Agnes Farrow," she replied. "But I came with Miss Turner, and Mrs Oldham. I didn't know I was coming until yesterday. My father arranged it."

"I see," he replied. "Miss Turner and Mrs Oldham?"

"I'm Olive Oldham." Olive raised her hand. "And this is my friend, Enid Turner."

Mr Whitington shifted in his seat and checked his watch again.

"Looks like we'll be here a while," he said. "May I use the telephone? I need to lodge my story before closing."

"After I get your statement." The detective's gaze tracked down to the camera cradled in the reporter's hands. "You were taking photos all day, is that correct?"

Mr Whitington nodded.

"It may have recorded something you didn't notice."

"But my story?"

"We'll return it when we're done," replied Detective Leonard. "You may report Sir Arthur's visit only."

Mr Whitington handed him the camera.

"And you are not to mention any details about the murder," continued the detective.

Mr Whitington slouched in his chair. His gaze flicked to the telephone.

Sir Arthur downed his cup of tea and he rested his head against the wall.

"Are you all right, Sir Arthur?" asked Detective Leonard.

Sir Arthur mumbled a reply and closed his eyes.

"Very well," said Leonard. "After you, Mrs Kyffin." He motioned towards the kitchen.

Her husband trailed after her.

They returned not long after. Mrs Kyffin's eyes were red-rimmed. Her chin quivered. They sat quietly in the far corner. The room went silent.

Mr Kyffin lit up a cigarette. Smoke curled into the air and drifted towards the fireplace chimney. Agnes stepped away from the doorway. Her gaze locked onto the cigarette in his hand.

Detective Leonard remained in the doorway. "Mrs Bellchambers, would you please come in?"

Eliza wiped her hands on her apron, followed the detective into the kitchen, and returned five minutes later. She straightened her apron, picked up the plate of Crispie biscuits, and circulated around the room.

Enid took one and nibbled on the tasty morsel. Agnes shook her head. Eliza moved slowly towards the fireplace. Mr Kyffin puffed on his cigarette and declined.

It was Mr Waite's turn. He grabbed a Crispie, and followed Detective Leonard into the other room.

Agnes shuffled a few steps closer to the fireplace, sniffed the smoke-filled air, and licked her lips. She whispered to Mr Kyffin. He nodded and offered her a cigarette. Her eyes lit up as she inserted it into a long, metal cigarette holder, lit the end, and drew a deep breath. Her muscles visibly relaxed as she drifted back towards the front door.

"What would her father say?" Olive raised an eyebrow.

"I'm more interested in what Detective Leonard is saying." Enid rose from her chair and inched closer to the kitchen doorway as Mr Waite entered the room.

Olive shadowed her. "What are they saying?"

"Shh!" Enid crunched on her biscuit and leaned on the door frame.

Detective Leonard sat opposite Mr Waite. A gas lantern illuminated a half-eaten mushroom pie on the kitchen table, between them.

"He was our driver," said Mr Waite. "He was a big man. Well over six feet tall."

Enid's lowered her Crispie biscuit.

"He had to slouch in the front seat," continued Mr Waite. "Hit his head each time there was a bump on the track."

"The bruises did indicate very large hands, sir," said the officer. "Larger than any of the men here."

Enid leaned into the room. "Did he wear an eyepatch?" she asked.

"Please, Miss Turner." Detective Leonard leaned back in his chair. "Let me ask the questions."

Enid took another bite of her biscuit and pretended to stare out the window, still listening to every word.

"Did you know him, Mr Waite?"

"No. He was hired for the day."

A point of light flared in the darkness, outside the window. The Crispie dug into Enid's lip. She peered at the reflections on the glass, trying to ascertain any detail that would reveal who, or what, it was loitering in the dark.

The orange light glowed again, longer and brighter this time. The light revealed a young woman with a red bob.

Agnes?

Mr Waite's chair scraped on the stone tiles at the conclusion of the interview.

The orange light faded.

"Did the driver have an eye patch?" Enid asked Mr Waite as he left the kitchen.

"Miss Turner!" Detective Leonard rose from his chair, and buttoned up his suit jacket.

"Did he?" She stepped in front of Mr Waite.

"No," he replied.

Detective Leonard ushered her out of the room and shut the door.

Enid stepped back, and whispered to Olive: "The driver was a troll."

"Are you sure," asked Olive.

"A man well over six feet, with large hands?" replied Enid. "It can't be a coincidence. A little *Glamour Magic*, and it could look like anything." Enid remembered the foul smell, and its one red eye. She raised her eyebrow.

"But, we followed *it*. How could it know we'd be here?"

Enid rubbed her chin. "There are many Thin Places through the Hills. Some only known by the Elders. Any one of them could provide a portal to cross over from the Otherworlds." She shoved the last of her biscuit in her mouth. It had to be their bounty hunter. "Perhaps he wasn't here for me? Perhaps he was after the Fae?"

Detective Leonard returned to the main room.

"Did anyone see where the driver went?" he asked.

They all shook their head.

"He was gone by the time we arrived," said Eliza.

"The chauffeur company sent him," said Mr Kyffin.

The front door clicked open. Two officers scraped their boots on the doormat and entered the cottage.

Agnes slipped into the room behind them, moved away from the door, and settled on a chair near the fire.

"He's gone, sir," said the first officer. "We can't find any sign of him on the property."

"The children?" Eliza's voice was shaky.

"All accounted for," said the officer.

"But what if he comes back?" she asked.

"We'll leave an officer on their door overnight." Detective Leonard nodded at the officers.

The second officer clicked his heels in acknowledgment and exited the cottage, presumably to guard the children.

Eliza lowered herself onto the chair beside Thomas. He clasped her hands and whispered in her ear.

Sir Arthur moaned and rubbed his head.

"It's been a long day," said Olive.

"We won't take much longer," replied Detective Leonard. "It appears none of you were alone after the driver went up to the house, except you, Mrs Bellchambers."

"Me?" gasped Eliza. Her apron fell out of her hands. "I didn't--"

Thomas' chair scraped and hit the wall. He stood in front of his wife.

"Relax, Mrs Bellchambers," said the detective. "Your wife can't possibly be the assailant."

"Her hands are too small," said Enid, without thinking.

Everyone stared at her.

"Miss Turner?" asked Detective Leonard.

"It's obvious," said Sir Arthur quietly. "The bruises were made by a larger hand. Even bigger than mine."

Enid smiled. Olive's *Memory Magic* hadn't dulled his powers of observation. There was hope for Mr Holmes yet.

Detective Leonard entered the room.

"Who can tell me more about strange lights?" he asked.

"I saw fireflies," said Mr Waite.

"There was mention of fairies, sir." The second officer joined the detective.

"Fairies, Jenkins?" The detective scoffed. "We don't investigate children's stories."

"The gentleman mentioned Sir Arthur has photographs."

"I think I'd remember if I saw any Wee Folk," mumbled Sir Arthur. His face was pale. He looked as if he would throw up.

Olive kicked Enid's shin under the table. *It worked*, she mouthed.

"Sir Arthur isn't well." Enid thrummed her fingers on the table and glared at Olive.

"Perhaps the lightning strike was closer than we thought?" Dr Anderson checked Sir Arthur's pulse.

Enid remembered the pie dish on the table. If she spread enough doubt, perhaps everyone would forget about fairies?

"The mushrooms?" she asked.

"Mushrooms?" Detective Leonard raised an eyebrow. "The pie dish in the kitchen?" He ducked back into the kitchen and returned with the pie plate. "Mushrooms, wasn't it, Mrs Bellchambers? Didn't someone at your Museum write a book on them, Mr Waite?" He didn't wait for a reply. "I've heard there's hallucinogenic mushrooms in these hills."

"There's a purple one... makes you see moon men," said Officer Jenkins

"And fairies?" Mr Whitington made a note in his notebook.

"Perhaps you picked them, for the pie, by mistake?" asked Detective Leonard.

"I know which mushrooms to pick." Eliza crossed her arms and huffed.

Thomas shook his head. "Those mushrooms only grow in Autumn, Detective Leonard."

"We didn't have mushroom pie for lunch." Sir Arthur's faint voice was gruff.

"I baked that pie for the drivers," said Eliza.

"Could explain the missing driver, sir," said Officer Jenkins.

Detective Leonard nodded.

"You won't mind if I take this to have analysed?" he asked Eliza.

Excellent. Their attention had been deflected from investigating the talk of fairies.

"There were mushrooms in the paddock where we picnicked," said Enid.

The detective turned to face her. His eyes narrowed, as if assessing her.

"Sir Arthur stepped in them," added Olive.

"He could have breathed in the spores." Dr Anderson checked Sir Arthur's eyes. "It would account for his headache," he said. "And nausea?"

Sir Arthur nodded once. His hand trembled.

"He really doesn't look well," said Dr Anderson. "Perhaps we should get him home."

"Officer Jenkins will take care of it," said Detective Leonard.

Officer Jenkins helped Sir Arthur to his feet.

"Thank you for your hospitality, Mrs Bellchambers." Sir Arthur bowed and shuffled to the door with the officer.

"Excuse me, Detective?" Mr Whitington stood by the telephone, tapping his foot. "May I ring the paper now?"

The detective nodded.

Mr Whitington grinned and grabbed the handset.

Olive's hand slipped into her handbag. She whispered under her breath. Energy crackled along the cord. The smell of burnt hair wafted into the air. Mr Whitington growled and dropped the handset.

Enid bit her lip to stifle a laugh. The corner of Olive's lip curled. She snapped her handbag shut.

"Residual static from the lightning strike?" suggested Olive.

"May I leave?" Mr Whitington shoved his notebooks and pencil into his satchel.

"Certainly. Jenkins, bring the car."

"No thanks, I'll drive the rental back myself."

"We can't let him print anything about the Fae," Enid whispered to Olive.

Olive nodded.

"Could I cadge a lift with you, Mr Whitington," she asked. "Enid lives locally, and I'm going back to the city."

"If you must." He strode out the door.

Enid grabbed Olive's hand, as she stood to leave.

"Are you sure? One case of amnesia is explainable," she whispered. "Two cases could invite questions."

Olive's hand tapped her handbag and waved her away.

"I know what I'm doing." She tucked her handbag under her arm and marched out after Mr Whitington.

Enid stared out the window, at the moon; only a sliver of shadow marred it. There wasn't much time to find the troll, but there was someone who might be able to help. The question was: would he?

She picked up her umbrella and made her farewell. She had to talk with the Shoemaker.

chapter six

The Lincoln motorcar roared through North Adelaide. Enid's hair tickled her skin. She held her breath as it approached the bridge, where Owen had been attacked by the troll, relaxing only when she saw the gates of the Zoological Gardens.

Olive sat in the passenger seat, her face contorted as if in pain.

A family of ducks waddled across the road in front of them.

"The ducks!" Olive dug her fingers into the dashboard. "Slow down, Enid!"

Another vehicle putted past them in the opposite direction, slowing to avoid the ducks. Enid stomped the brake. Olive flinched.

Enid grinned; it was Olive who had insisted they visited the Shoemaker, against Sylvia's orders.

The morning sun flashed across the windscreen as the Lincoln turned into the street along the River Torrens. The sounds of the waking city grew as they neared North Terrace; the clop of horse hooves, the clang of a tram bell fading into the distance, and the murmur of commuters as they rushed to work.

Enid checked her wristwatch. *Nine a.m.* Her lunch date with Owen was at one; there was plenty of time to visit the Shoemaker. She'd met him briefly, decades ago: a crotchety old creature, bent over his workbench, and the soft, hypnotising tap of his cobblers' hammer.

He'd taken care of her for a time. Sylvia originally introduced them - not by choice - when Enid was accepted as a Protector. After her mother's amulet had left its mark. The amulet had remained with her since, along with its magic, inherited from her mother. Both a blessing and a curse.

It warmed her skin as if in reply. Enid placed her hand over it.

"Keep both hands on the wheel!" Olive squeaked. "And watch out for the--" She flinched and raised an arm defensively.

A horn blared in front of them. A whistle shrieked.

The policeman on the corner footpath glared at her, blew his whistle again, and pointed to the sign on the light pole in the middle of the intersection. Bold, black letters read: *Keep Left*.

Enid nodded in reply and tugged the steering wheel. The Lincoln veered back to the left side of the street.

"Pay attention, Enid." Olive moaned, slid back into her seat and covered her eyes.

"It's perfectly safe." Enid patted Olive's gloved hand. "We've arrived."

She parked in front of the row of shops on the south side. A stone-brick building, painted white, with arched windows on the first floor, loomed above them.

"You can look now." Enid chuckled. "I thought you liked a thrill?"

"I'll stick to poker, thank you."

A bell tinkled as the door of the adjacent store opened. Piano music drifted into the street, and silenced as the door clapped shut. A customer tucked a clarinet case under his arm, tipped his hat in their direction, and continued on his way.

Olive grabbed the motorcar door handle, and opened the passenger side door.

"Let's do this before Sylvia finds out." She straightened her cloche, swung her feet onto the footpath, and strode into the shop.

Enid grabbed her umbrella from the back seat and followed her.

Rows of shoes lined the shop walls. The scent of fresh leather was intoxicating. A young man, in a plain grey suit with cuffed trousers, greeted them.

"Can I help you, ladies?"

"We've come to see the Shoemaker," replied Enid.

"We don't make custom shoes, Miss." He tugged at his white gloves and raised an eyebrow. "Is there anything else I can help you with? Perhaps something for your husband?" He waited. His foot tapped.

Enid surveyed the rows of polished black, chestnut, tan, and white shoes - a varied collection of Oxfords, Brogues, low-sided Oxfords and wingtips. Tucked away in the far corner was a line of polished, but plain, work boots.

Olive cleared her throat. "Brogues, dark brown, size..." She glanced over the wall. "Thirteen."

The young man nodded, ran his hand along the row of laced shoes closest to them. He paused, tapped his finger on the toe of a shoe, and frowned.

"I'll have to check the storeroom," he replied. "Wait here."

He spun on his heel, and marched through the doorway at the rear of the store, labelled in red letters: *Employees Only*.

"He doesn't know the Shoemaker?" whispered Enid.

Olive removed a glove as they moved to the back of the store. Enid followed, and peeked into the corridor beyond. There were two doors, one on either side. The one on the left was slightly ajar. Muffled voices leaked through the opening: the young man and a woman.

Olive crept further down the corridor, halted at the end, and motioned for Enid to follow. She waved her hand in an arc in front of the blank wall.

The air buzzed. A faint, door-sized shape shimmered in the surface.

"Touch it," whispered Olive.

Enid slipped off her gloves, and pressed one palm against the blank wall. Her fingers tingled.

"Open it," said Olive.

Enid wrapped the fingers of her other hand around the handle of her umbrella and whispered: "*Revelo.*"

There was no response.

Olive shook her head. "It's Otherworld magic. Just *feel* it."

Enid pushed her hand against the cold bricks, and willed it to open.

There was a click.

The bricks squirmed as the wall gave way under her hand, and extruded from the wall and enveloped them.

The mumbling voices faded. The corridor darkened and snapped shut behind them. The world went silent.

Enid sucked in a sharp breath. "Where are we?"

Olive nudged her forward a step.

A pale green ball of light flickered to life in a wall sconce beside her. A dark tunnel, carved out of rock, curved ahead of them.

"Are we in an Otherworld?" she whispered.

"Not entirely," replied Olive. "This is a Sanctuary. Like a wardrobe. A place where magic can hide. Only those with the right key can unlock it."

"I had a key?" asked Enid.

"You were a child last time you were here," replied Olive as she eased her further forward. "Do you remember?"

"Just after..." Enid touched the amulet around her neck. It was cold. Her eyes widened. "It's--"

"Our magic doesn't work in here." Olive ushered Enid further along the tunnel.

Another ball of light illuminated on the wall. It brightened as they approached, and faded as they passed, then another.

"This is a place of *Old Magic*, much older than ours. It belongs to the creatures of the Otherworlds."

Enid gripped the handle of her umbrella. Sylvia blamed the Otherworlds for the post-war pandemic. An Other refugee had crossed into Europe, during the War, hoping to hide amongst human refugees in the confusion. It didn't take long for it to spread home via the returning soldiers.

"I thought we were visiting The Shoemaker?" asked Enid.

"Yes."

"But Sylvia won't--" Enid chewed her lip.

"That's why we won't tell her," said Olive.

Enid twisted the umbrella in her hand. It seemed Olive had many secrets.

They paused at a set of wooden stairs, descending into a pool of darkness.

"I don't remember this." Enid hesitated.

"This time we're sneaking in the back door."

"Why?" Enid remembered his smile, his fluffy whiskers and kind violet eyes. "He is friendly. Isn't he?"

Olive paused, and readjusted the bag on her arm.

"It's been a long time," she said.

The air cooled as Enid and Olive descended the wooden stairs; each footstep's echo swallowed up by the darkness. The staircase ended at a level tunnel.

The earthy aroma of wet soil teased Enid's nostrils. She reached out her hand. The wall was damp and cold.

"Isn't the water table close to the surface here?" She slowed, listening for the sound of dripping water.

"The Sanctuary is outside our world," replied Olive. "We need to keep moving."

The tunnel opened into an empty hallway. Enid stepped into the corridor.

Another wall sconce flared. Green light reflected back off the smooth, glass-like obsidian walls and floor, and illuminated the corridor. A row of empty light sconces continued along the walls ahead of them.

Another step forward.

The walls hummed. Dark arched outlines formed on both walls. The wall shimmered inside the archways, creating a hall of tall mirrors, each with a different hue. A faint smell of ozone filled the air, growing stronger as they approached the archways. Each archway buzzed and fluoresced, in turn, as they continued.

One remained silent. Dark grey, devoid of colour. A stench of sulphur mixed with the ozone. Clouded streaks marred the obsidian around the edges of the archway and across the floor.

Enid hesitated. "Are you sure this leads to the Shoemaker?"

Olive hovered behind her.

"We're almost there." She pointed towards a white glimmer in the darkness at the end of the hallway, and froze.

"Olive?"

Olive cocked her head. Her eyebrow twitched. Her gaze remained fixed on the dark archway. A faded grey mist swirled under the glossy surface.

Olive clutched her handbag. Her eyes widened. Her lips quivered.

"Olive?" Enid's stomach squirmed.

"Can't you hear it?" Olive smiled. Her left hand twitched, and moved in the direction of the portal.

"I don't hear anything." Enid peered into the archway. The swirling motion stopped.

Olive shook her head.

"What's wrong, Olive?"

"This way." Olive drifted towards the white door, one eye still on the grey portal.

The door was old, but it looked innocuous enough. Cracked white paint curled at the edges of the door panels. A bronze rectangular plaque appeared on the door. Lines swirled and curled on its surface. Letters formed and solidified into words, written in a flourished hand. The language was unfamiliar.

Enid raised her umbrella and whispered: "*Revelo.*"

Nothing. No buzz. No shimmer. The words remained the same: indecipherable.

Enid's heart sank.

"I told you," Olive whispered in her ear, "our magic won't work here." Her gaze flicked back to the grey archway. "By necessity."

Enid inspected the doorway. A thin, recessed line of shiny, steel-grey stone was set in the obsidian floor, just in front of the door.

"What is that?" Enid indicated the line.

"Protection," replied Olive. "Cold iron." She scanned the plaque on the door. "Knock four times," she instructed.

"You can read it?"

"An old friend taught me." Olive stared at the door. "At least I hope we're still friends," she whispered.

Enid raised an eyebrow. There was a story there; one Olive seemed reluctant to share.

The light spheres behind them began to fade, as did the writing on the plaque. Enid frowned; there was no time to indulge her curiosity.

She took a deep breath and knocked on the door four times.

The door clicked and shimmered. A muffled voice emanated from the other side.

"State your name and point of ingress." A woman's voice, with a European accent.

"Don't mention me." Olive pressed her bare finger to her lips.

"Why ever not?" Enid frowned.

"Don't just stand there." The voice was faint. "This is a safe place."

A gentle wind urged them forward towards the wooden door. It gleamed brightly as the approached.

Olive's hand pressed into her back. "After you." There was a hint of uncertainty in Olive's voice.

Enid swallowed, closed her eyes, and walked closer.

The door hummed faster. Energy prickled over her skin. A faint ticking sound surrounded her, growing louder. Enid's muscles tensed, preparing for an inevitable thud.

"State your name and ingress." The woman's voice was closer, and quite distinct.

Enid opened her eyes.

A cacophony of clocks hung on the walls, each with its own voice adding to a steady, unified chorus. A fire flickered in the far corner of the room. Three carved wooden chairs sat under a curtained window on the left wall. The curtain shivered invitingly.

Enid's fingers twitched. She felt Olive's hand on her arm.

"Best not look." Olive's breath brushed her ear.

Enid's heart raced. Olive was a gambler; nothing thwarted her bravado, yet she wouldn't risk it...?

"Welcome." A woman sat behind a carved-oak desk next to the fire.

The flames sputtered and danced in the hearth. Light caressed the woman's features, illuminating pinpoints of fire in her blue eyes. A light brown tendril of hair fell from her loose bun, and tumbled over her cheek. Wire-rimmed spectacles clung to her forehead. She opened a ledger, scribbled notes, then dropped her spectacles onto her nose, and squinted, as if assessing Enid.

"Human?"

Enid nodded.

"No one informed me we were expecting a human." She sniffed, and flipped through the pages of the ledger. Lines formed in her forehead. She scribbled more notes. "Usually they're running away from you lot."

She leaned back in her chair and twiddled a silver talisman around her neck, with her ink-stained fingers.

Enid peered at the talisman - a blue stone inset in a white eye-shaped stone.

The woman's gaze lingered on Enid's sleeve cuff and traced the visible edges of the silvery scar on Enid's forearm. Her eyes blazed like neon lights.

"You're a Protector?" It was more of an accusation, than a question.

Enid tugged down her sleeve.

"Tell your friend to step forward so I can get a good look at *both* of you."

Olive sighed and stepped forward.

"You?" The woman eyed Olive, leaned forward and grabbed the edge of the desk, her fingers reaching under the lip of the desk as if reaching for something.

"He's told you about me?" Olive edged Enid behind her. Her voice was calm. "I can explain."

The woman's gaze shifted towards the doorway.

"How did you cross the threshold?" She rose from her chair.

The fire flared.

Enid flinched.

"What's going on, Olive?" Her voice trembled unexpectedly.

"This is Miss Enid Turner," said Olive.

The wall crackled and buckled beside them. A line of light rose from the floor and traced out an archway. The inscribed area shimmered and faded, creating an open doorway. A short figure with a cane stood in the opening, silhouetted by green light.

"Enie?" The familiar voice resonated through the room. "It's been too long, Little One." The figure moved into the room, limping as he approached.

He hugged her. A blanket of pipe and wood smoke embraced her. She inhaled slowly, drinking in the memories, and allowed her shoulders to relax. Whiskers tickled her nose.

The woman cleared her throat.

"Ah, yes, this is my..." He hesitated.

The woman's eyelids narrowed.

"My assistant, Miss Caimanos," he continued. "I'd be lost without her.' He stepped back and examined Enid. "Let me look at you."

He chuckled. Crinkles formed at the edge of his violet eyes. Firelight glinted off the gold and silver beads in his beard. It was greyer than she remembered.

"You've cut your hair." His gaze slipped past her. His arm stiffened, and dropped to his side.

"Miss Fraser?" He smiled. "You haven't aged a day."

Olive blushed. Miss Caimanos tapped her fountain pen onto the ledger page.

"Orrug." Olive twisted the plain gold band on her left hand. "It's *Mrs* Oldham, now."

"You're married?" The gleam faded from his eyes.

"Widow," she whispered. "The war."

A grim smile flickered over Miss Caimanos' lips. "There's always a war."

Olive fingered the silver chain at her neck. Her Protector's amulet peeked out from under her blouse; its sapphire glinted in the firelight. The Shoemaker's gaze settled on the amulet.

Miss Caimanos turned a page of the ledger.

Olive clasped her handbag.

Enid raised an eyebrow. There was obviously history between them.

"You've redecorated." Olive indicated the adjacent room. "The threshold decoration is new."

"A new millennium always stirs things up," replied the Shoemaker.

Miss Caimanos huffed and placed her hand defensively on the ledger. Another long silence.

Enid fidgeted. They didn't have time for jealous rivalry. They had less than three days to complete the Fae Queen's quest or the world was forfeit.

The Shoemaker shuffled back towards the fireplace and leaned on his walking cane of carved wood. Its delicate silver inlay of leaves gleamed in the fire light. He patted the head of the cane.

He caught Enid's eye and smiled.

"Consequences of living dangerously. To be expected in my line of work. I'm sure you understand."

"Do you often get interlopers?" asked Enid.

"Too many Fae," said Miss Caimanos curtly.

Finally, some information.

"That's why we're here." Enid sat on the middle chair under the window. The curtain twitched again. She pressed her hands onto her lap, trying to resist the urge to peek behind it. "We are in need of your assistance. Aren't we, Olive?"

Olive bit her lip and nodded.

"It depends on what you want, *Mrs* Oldham." Miss Caimanos slapped the ledger shut. "We had a deal, remember?" She eyed Olive. "The Protectors wouldn't meddle in our affairs, if we didn't meddle in yours."

The Shoemaker joined his assistant behind the desk.

"Is this true?" Enid turned to Olive. "Is that why Sylvia forbade us to come here?"

Olive and Miss Caimanos glared at each other.

Enid jumped out of the chair.

"For the love of--" Enid sucked air in through clenched teeth. They were acting like children; Olive was old enough to know better. "We haven't got time for this. Tell me about the Fae."

"You've had a Fae encounter?" asked Miss Caimanos.

"The Fae Queen, herself." Olive sat down next to Enid.

The Shoemaker's cane thumped against the desk. He leaned in close and whispered in Miss Caimanos's ear.

Olive clutched her bag to her chest and lowered her head.

Enid's heart sank. Olive seemed to always end up with a losing hand, when it came to men. How would she play this one?

Enid eyed the trio. What were they not saying? She leaned on the opposite side of the desk. It was her turn to take a risk.

"I don't care what's happened between you," she said. "We need your help. If we don't return the Fae Heir, this world is forfeit."

Miss Caimanos gasped. "Forfeit?"

"A Fae pact?" The colour drained from the Shoemaker's face, as if he'd drank one of Sylvia's infamous herbal concoctions. "I am sorry," he whispered.

Olive looked the Shoemaker in the eye. "Please, we need to find out why someone is trying to kill a Protector."

"After a Protector?" The Shoemaker shook his head.

Miss Caimanos re-opened the ledger and flipped back a few pages.

"Please," said Enid, "have you had any new arrivals from the Otherworlds?"

"No." Miss Caimanos grabbed his arm and shook her head. "We mustn't. No one crosses the Fae."

He patted her hand. "It could be considered a service to them."

Miss Caimanos frowned.

"Kel..." The Shoemaker put his arm around her shoulder. "We can trust them. I've known Enid since she was *ein Mädchen*. She won't betray us."

Miss Caimanos glanced at Olive.

"And we can trust Olive..." He cleared his throat. "Mrs Oldham." He turned to face her. "Can't we?" There was doubt in those eyes. What had Sylvia done to make them worry?

Olive's fingers relaxed. She rested her handbag on her lap.

"I give you my word," she replied. "If you will take it."

They sat there for a few moments, staring, with - what seemed like - an eternity of words unspoken.

The Shoemaker stood back and retrieved his cane.

"Very well," said Miss Caimanos. "A bounty hunter arrived via a portal in the hallway, about a week ago."

"And you didn't inform us?" Olive's hand rested on the clasp of her bag.

"The papers were in order." Miss Caimanos ran her finger down the page. "He was tracking an unnamed Otherworld criminal."

"Unnamed?" asked Enid.

"It was..." She tapped her finger on the page. "What is it the flyboys say?" She raised her finger. "*Top secret*. And your Miss Devin has made it very clear she wanted nothing to do with off-world affairs."

"But," hissed Olive, "it tried to kill Enid on her birthday!"

"Enie?" The Shoemaker's face reddened.

"I'm fine," replied Enid. She waved aside his concern; there were more important items to address; she needed to know if this was the troll who'd attacked Owen. "Did it have one eye?" she asked.

The Shoemaker and Miss Caimanos both looked confused.

"Your Miss Devin insists we don't interfere with Otherworld politics," replied Miss Caimanos.

"Answer her question," said Olive.

The Shoemaker slipped a monocle in front of one eye and examined the ledger page.

"No, it did not have one eye," he replied.

Enid's shoulders tensed. Then how did her troll enter this world?

"You still aid refugees?" Olive placed a gentle hand on Enid's arm.

The Shoemaker nodded.

Enid smiled. The old gnome still had a sympathetic heart. He caught her gaze. His moustache twitched. He stroked his beard to hide a faint smile.

"Do they all arrive through the Sanctuary portals?" asked Olive.

"In matters of life and death, yes," he said calmly. "And not officially."

"This is why--" Olive slapped her hands onto her lap and harrumphed.

Enid patted Olive's hand. It was her turn to calm Olive.

The Shoemaker raised an eyebrow. "She doesn't know you're here?"

"Sylvia doesn't know about the Fae," Olive replied.

"And the Bounty Hunter?" asked Miss Caimanos.

Olive shook her head.

"I thought Protectors shared all their secrets?" A smile flickered over Miss Caimanos' lips as she leaned back in her chair.

"It's personal," said Olive.

"There's no time to bicker." Enid huffed and cradled her head in her hands. Her mind raced. Miss Caimanos had mentioned only one troll. "I don't care if you help Otherworld refugees, or your grudge with the Protectors," she said. "The police have a troll bounty hunter in their morgue, and there's a reporter nosing about for a story." She lifted her head and glowered at the Shoemaker and his assistant. "And there's a second bounty hunter out there."

The Shoemaker snapped to attention.

"Two trolls?" Miss Caimanos swallowed.

"How was the portal in the hall destroyed?" asked Enid. "Did the second one force its way in though the Sanctuary?"

The metal beads in the Shoemaker's beard clinked as he shook his head. "Nothing escapes the Sanctuary."

"It didn't enter via the Sanctuary." Miss Caimanos' voice was calm. "That portal was destroyed in 1900." She looked Olive in the eye. "Ask your friend, Miss Devin about that one."

"Sylvia?" Enid frowned.

Olive's face was blank. She didn't know?

"Ah, more secrets." Miss Caimanos toyed with her pen. "It appears Protectors have them too."

Olive's eyes narrowed. "Then, how do you explain the second troll?"

Miss Caimanos glanced over the ledger. Her eyes widened.

"The Fairy Door?" she whispered.

"It's a possibility." The Shoemaker frowned.

"What's a possibility?" asked Olive.

"One of the Fairy Doors near the Botanic Gardens was destroyed two days after the bounty hunter arrived," he replied. "It could have been another arrival."

"Fairy door?" Blood pounded in her ears.

"It's what the locals call them," replied the Shoemaker.

"I've never heard of them," said Olive.

The Shoemaker hesitated.

"Is this the bit where you tell me I have only three questions?" asked Enid.

"That's wishes," replied Miss Caimanos.

"And, no. We're not Djinn." said the Shoemaker. "Fairy Doors are portals, bridges between this and the Otherworlds. Possibly Fae in origin. No one knows."

"They appeared late last century," said Miss Caimanos.

"Those little doors on the foundation stones of buildings?" asked Olive. "The ones that look like they were made by an Arts and Crafts sculptor with a dollhouse fetish?"

"They are *Old Magic*." The Shoemaker's moustache twitched. "Very old magic. Shielded from even the Protectors."

"How many are there?" asked Olive.

Enid bit her lip. That was their second question.

"There were seven of them. They provide escape routes from the Otherworlds. It's why the Sanctuary was created here, to ensure nothing untoward came through."

"We save persecuted creatures." Miss Caimanos leaned forward, her face flushed.

"I thought--" Olive rose to her feet. Her bag slumped to the floor. "Why didn't you tell me?" She paced the room. "How did we not know?" she mumbled. "Sylvia will be livid." She paused by the desk. "The refugees? They don't all remain here, do they?"

"No." The Shoemaker's beard jewellery jingled again, making him sound like jolly Saint Nick.

"Most get new identities and move on to other worlds," replied Miss Caimanos.

"A few stay," added the Shoemaker.

One of the clocks chimed behind her.

Olive glanced at it, and frowned. "Haven't you got a lunch date, Enid?"

"Yes," replied Enid. "But we've been here less than an hour."

"Have you forgotten time moves at a different pace here?" said the Shoemaker. "An hour here could be three, or more, in your world."

"This is the time topside, in Adelaide." Miss Caimanos tapped the clock nearest her.

"Half past twelve?" Enid checked her wristwatch. The second hand wobbled over the five. She held it to her ear. Nothing. She tapped the crystal face.

"You don't want to be late." Olive was already by the doorway, her bag clutched under one arm.

chapter seven

nid followed Olive through a door leading to a lane off Gawler Place. Bin lids clattered at the end of the blind lane. The pungent smell of rotting fish and eggs rolled over them.

Enid's eyes watered. She held her breath and dodged a workman unloading a trolley of crates. He set two boxes by the back door of the corner shop, and knocked. The door opened. A man in a white coat collected the boxes, and nodded at Enid and Olive.

The stink of two-day old refuse followed them. Enid ventured a quick breath. And a touch of sulphur? She glanced along the lane.

"Troll?" she whispered.

Olive's nostrils flared as she sampled the air. She shook her head.

"It's just the Chemist." She indicated the back door behind them.

She ushered Enid through the lane, towards the main street.

A stooped figure in a shamble of clothes leaned against the brick wall at the corner, his head encapsulated by a ball of acrid smoke. A dented metal cup sat on the footpath in front of him. Enid grabbed Olive's arm and froze.

"Relax, Enid." Olive rummaged through her bag and fished out a few threepence.

The silver coins clattered into the veteran's cup.

Rundle Street was busier than expected, even for a Monday lunch-time crowd. A cacophony of aromas surrounded them: the rich odour of horse dung, cigarettes and petrol fumes, mixed with roast chicken and roast potatoes, freshly baked bread, and beef and gravy pies.

Enid's stomach grumbled as she settled behind the Lincoln's steering wheel. She checked her wristwatch. The second hand ticked reassuringly.

"It's almost one o'clock," she said. "I don't want to be late. Crank her up will you, Olive."

Olive cranked the engine.

Enid pumped the accelerator. The engine turned over. The chassis floor rumbled under her feet. She closed her eyes and let her muscles relax. The Grand Central Hotel was only a block away. There was still time.

Olive tapped on the windscreen.

Enid's snapped open.

Olive leaned on the door and poked her head into the motorcar.

"Can I cadge a lift to the hotel?" she asked. "Someone should check on Sir Arthur, after yesterday's shenanigans.

Enid nodded. "Jump in."

Olive climbed into the passenger seat and straightened her skirts.

Enid thrust the gear shift lever into neutral, opened the throttle, and hit the starter. The engine purred.

"Those tales of humans disappearing into the Fae world for a hundred years?" she asked.

"Are likely true," replied Olive. "A few days, or weeks, could be years in this world."

Enid sucked in a quick breath.

"Relax, you'll get there in plenty of time," said Olive. "Besides." She grinned, "I'd wager Mr Barrington will wait."

Enid's cheeks burned.

The early afternoon sun streamed in the north and west windows of the Winter Garden Room. The hotel's famous exotic ferns screened the area from the other patrons, creating a private oasis in this part of the room.

Owen Barrington sipped his tea and counted the diamonds in the pattern of the carpet. He tapped the pot on the silver tray. Almost empty. He checked his watch again.

A quarter past one.

He fingered the ring box in his pocket, cursed under his breath, and lit a cigarette. His hands shook; he mustn't lose his nerve this time. He gulped down the last of his tea. Why had hadn't he asked while they were boating on the lake? It'd been perfect.

A pain stabbed in his head. He winced and rubbed his temple. Perhaps a little Dutch courage? He raised the other hand to get the waiter's attention.

Another stab of pain. Owen grit his teeth. The pain subsided.

A waiter appeared from behind one of the large potted exotic ferns, and nodded.

"Yes, Mr Barrington?"

"Scotch, please."

The waiter nodded, ducked back behind the fern, and strode off through the arched doorway of the lattice room partition. Owen stared after him, and imagined his Enid walking through the same doorway. The green leaves of the roses on the stained glass set into its surround were almost the same colour as her eyes.

His heart raced. He'd rehearsed it many times. He'd ask her. She'd consent. He'd present her with the ring. The diamonds would dazzle spectacularly in the sunlight. He'd chosen the table next to the window for that reason - so the ring would have a chance to match her brilliance.

A glass clunked softly on the table in front of him.

"Do you want to order lunch now, Mr Barrington?"

Owen swirled the amber liquid in the glass.

"I'll wait until Miss Turner arrives," he replied.

"Very well, sir." The waiter adjusted the white towel on his arm. "The band will be going on break soon."

"Perhaps they can break a little later?" He opened his wallet and removed several crisp notes, folded them and pressed them into the waiter's hand. "Twenty minutes?"

"I'm sure they wouldn't mind, for you, Mr Barrington," he replied.

Owen swigged his scotch and eyed the entrance.

"She'll be here," he whispered.

The waiter smiled, retreated past the wall of fernery, and approached the band. The violinist nodded in Owen's direction, and continued playing. The waiter slipped the notes into the pocket of the soloist, before returning to his station by the archway.

A pale silhouette flickered over the rippled glass panels of the partition. It paused next to the waiter. He nodded and pointed towards the oasis sanctuary.

Owen lowered his glass.

"Sorry I'm late." Enid tugged off her gloves and draped them over her bag as she sat down opposite him. She hung her umbrella on the edge of the table.

"It's not the motorcar?" He turned the glass in his hand. It would be a shame if it was. It was a fine piece of craftsmanship, worth keeping after the wedding. And a private chauffeur would ensure she'd never have to worry about running late.

"No, the Lincoln's fine. My watch stopped." She smiled. "And parking was horrendous."

Owen's heart raced. That smile. It was worth the wait. He clasped her hand and ran his thumb over her soft skin. She was here now. He'd always wait for her.

"Then all is forgiven," he said.

"Another pot of tea, Mr Barrington?" The waiter hovered beside the table.

"I've taken the liberty of ordering lunch." Owen nodded to the waiter.

A smile flickered over the waiter's lips as he set Owen's teacup on the tea tray. He nodded in the direction of the string quartet.

Enid sat back in her chair.

The tray clinked against Owen's glass as the waiter removed it. Owen's hand twitched under Enid's.

"Is something wrong?" she asked.

He caressed her wrist. "I--"

Music embraced them; a playful tune.

Enid's eyes widened. "My favourite."

"For you, my love," he whispered.

She blushed. Her eyelids fluttered. His heart pounded.

Owen's eyelid twitched. Why hadn't he asked her on her birthday? A boat ride on the lake, all alone, with a glorious sunset of mauves and oranges - with just a hint of pink; no canvas could do it justice.

Pain clawed his temple.

He winced. This wasn't how he planned it. He slipped his hand from hers, straightened in his chair, and glanced at the glass of whisky on the table; he needed a stiff drink.

Instead, he slipped his hand into his pocket.

The waiter returned with gold-rimmed Royal Doulton plates; gold-garland roses traced their circumference, echoing the stained glass flanking the entry archway. The combined aromas of perfectly-cooked filet mignon, chateau potatoes, and asparagus calmed his nerves.

"There's Devil's Food cake for dessert, with French ice cream," he said.

Enid licked her lips; a slow, and deliberate, movement. "My favourite." Her lips glistened as she smiled.

"I know," he whispered. The moment was perfect; beautiful music.

Delicious food. Perhaps this *could* make amends for the birthday debacle? It was now, or never.

He took a deep breath.

"Enid, I want to ask you..." His fingers wrapped around the velvet ring box.

Sunlight caught in her hair, creating a glowing halo. He caught his breath. A Botticelli angel. Soon to be *his* angel. Nothing would interrupt him this time.

"Owen, you look pale. Are you unwell?" Enid leaned closer. The sunlight flared over her shoulder.

Flashes of the sun glaring off the water bombarded his memory. Angry shadows followed. Pain stabbed his eye, and seared along the optic nerve. A dull crack echoed in the back of his brain. His hand shot out of his pocket.

"Owen?" She sounded concerned. "It is the concussion?" she asked. "The doctor said you should rest."

Shit. His temple throbbed. He rubbed his head. He groaned. Not again.

The band went silent.

Damn it! His bloody head was damned inconvenient. A wave of nausea washed over him.

"Here, drink this." Enid pressed the whisky glass into his hand.

He gulped it down. Smooth. Rich. Such a waste to guzzle it all in one go.

Enid waved over the waiter. "Another whisky for Mr Barrington."

"Shall I fetch the doctor?" The waiter was at his side.

"No," said Owen. "I'm fine." He dug his fingernails into his palms.

The moment had passed.

"Coffee?" He asked Enid.

Her nose wrinkled.

Owen smiled. There was still a chance to redeem the situation.

"Two coffees. Not too strong," he instructed the waiter.

He felt her hand stroke his arm.

"Relax, Owen. It will pass." She lifted his hand and entwined her fingers in his. "Did you work on your painting today?"

Visions of chartreuse, cobalt green, *terre verte* and Naples yellow washed over his thoughts. His pulse slowed. His vision began to clear.

"If I perfect a sponged wet wash, I could emulate Sergeant's technique and finally do the light in the gums along the Torrens justice."

"I thought so." She rubbed his index finger. "Viridian, if I'm not mistaken."

He examined his fingertips. Traces of water colour lingered under his nail. He smiled; clever girl. She was trying to distract him. She knew him too well.

"Well spotted. Perhaps I'll make a painter out of you yet?"

She laughed and kissed his finger. "My talents lie elsewhere."

Owen laughed and kissed her hand.

Her sleeve caressed her wrist. A faint, silver scar peeked out from under the cuff. He traced his finger along it. His heart ached, imagining the pain it must have caused. One day she'd trust him enough to tell him how she got it.

The waiter returned with two fine china cups, matching the dinner setting. Steam curled up from the black liquid in them.

Enid untangled her fingers and placed her hands on her lap.

"Anything else, Mr Barrington?"

"Perhaps a Bex?" He glanced at the clock on the wall. Another ten minutes until the orchestra returned from their break. He raised an eyebrow.

The waiter leaned in close and whispered in Owen's ear. "A lady was asking about Miss Turner."

Owen pushed aside a frond and peered at the doorway. A woman with brunette hair lingered under the archway, scanning the room. It was

Enid's friend, Mrs Oldham.

Owen cupped one hand over his pocket, and passed another note under the table to the waiter. He just needed a little more time alone with Enid.

"We're not to be disturbed," he said.

The waiter nodded.

"Very well, sir." The waiter nodded and slipped past the ferns.

The wet, earthy smell of the ferns reminded Owen of the Botanic Gardens, and their long picnics on the grass. Talking. Sharing. They had no secrets. His heart sank; she hadn't spoken about her outing at Humbug Scrub.

"How was your picnic with the great writer?" he asked.

Enid lifted her coffee cup to her lips and took a sip. She grimaced, and eyed him over the rim.

"It's an acquired taste," he said.

Her grimace faded. She looked him in the eye and licked her lips again. She was avoiding a reply.

He let a smile catch his lips. He knew her tactics; he wasn't going to let her avoid the discussion that easily. "I bet your lemon butter scones were popular."

Enid nodded and took another sip.

"I suppose your young charge was excited to meet a celebrity?"

Another sip.

"Did he sign your book?"

Enid swallowed the last of her coffee and stared into her cup.

"No," she said.

"Celebrities rarely live up to expectations when you meet them." He clicked his tongue.

"He was charming," Enid cooed.

Owen raised an eyebrow. Doubts nagged his thoughts. He wanted to know her secrets. He wanted to be part of her life. All of it. Yet, she still shut him out of her escapades with her friends.

The ring box in his pocket grew heavy.

He feigned a sigh. "I suppose we mortal men don't stand a chance."

She smiled sweetly, and swallowed a mouthful of coffee. "Owen, it was just a picnic."

"I should take you on another picnic," he said.

A frown flickered over her forehead. "I've gone off picnics." She stabbed one of the chateau potatoes on her plate.

Owen's hand fell from his pocket. He couldn't ask her now. He glanced at the empty bandstand. The musicians should be returning from their break soon. Enid loved music. And dancing.

He smiled.

"You haven't forgotten the ball tomorrow night, at the Dance Palace?" he asked.

Her eyes lit up.

"Fancy dress, don't forget. I'm Romeo, and you are my Juliet."

"You do have gorgeous legs." She leaned in close and giggled. "I'd love to see you in tights."

There. That was it: the Enid he loved. The woman he was going to marry.

"And I, yours." He clasped her hands.

Her cheeks flushed. "Unfortunately, those costumes were spoken for."

"Very unfortunate." Owen's sighed.

"Not to worry, I found replacements." She lowered her voice. "An infamous couple."

"Infamous?"

"Very." She grinned.

"Most excellent." Owen chuckled.

A cello twanged on the dais, followed by few violin notes.

Finally! Owen slipped the ring from his pocket. He gulped the dregs of his coffee. This time his courage wouldn't fail him. He laid his hand on the table, making sure the box was hidden, and rehearsed the words in his head: *Will you--?*

A tapping sound broke the silence.

Owen glanced at the orchestra. They were still setting up.

Tap. Tap.

Owen stared into Enid's eyes, willing the music to resume. He had to keep her focused on the moment. He didn't want to break the spell.

"Enid, I love you."

Tap. Tap. Tap.

He glanced at the window behind her. Olive Oldham's hand pressed against the window pane, mouthing something inaudible, and pointing to Enid.

No. Owen clasped Enid's hands tighter. *Play the damn music.*

Mrs Oldham's nails tapped the glass again.

Enid blinked and turned towards the noise.

"Olive?" Her hands slipped from the table. "What's the matter?"

Owen slumped back into his seat. Why hadn't he asked her on the lake? Pain thumped behind his eyes.

Not again.

A sweet melody filled the Winter Garden Room. Owen sighed.

Too late.

Mrs Oldham pointed towards the foyer, and marched towards the front door of the hotel.

Enid nodded. Her chair dragged on the carpet as she rose.

"I'm sorry, Owen. I love you." She hovered for a moment. "I just..." She kissed him on the head. The ferns shivered, as she slipped past them and strode out of the room. A front jabbed his neck. He winced.

He clutched the ring box in his hand and peered through the ferns after her. Mrs Oldham was waiting. Their conversation was animated. Enid glanced back, in his direction.

Mrs Oldham spoke again. Enid bit her lip. She spun on her heel and wove her way back around the tables, towards him.

Owen shrank away from the over-sized fern, and slid back into his chair.

Enid avoided his gaze as she slipped on her gloves.

"I'm sorry, Owen." She picked up her bag. "I have to go."

"But, Enid." The corners of the ring box dug into his palm. "I need to--"

"Sorry. I wish I could stay." She patted his shoulder. "This is important. I'll make it up to you, I promise." She unhooked her umbrella from the table, and left.

Owen clenched his jaw. He cursed under his breath. Why hadn't he asked her?

Pain gripped his skull.

The waiter cleared his throat.

"Your Bex, Mr Barrington." He lowered a silver tray. A small, rectangular, white paper packet lay on the tray next to two glasses, one full of water, the other with a dram of whisky. "Shall I have Miss Turner's car moved into the back lane, Mr Barrington?" he asked. "Are congratulations in order?" He eyed Owen's hand on the table. His smile slipped.

The corner of the velvet ring box peeked out between Owen's finger and thumb. He pushed it back under his palm.

"I am sorry, Mr Barrington. The ladies have gone upstairs. I thought--"

"So did I." Owen massaged the bridge of his nose.

The waiter glanced into the foyer. "I must remind you, sir, the management frowns on female guests in the gentleman residents' private rooms."

"That won't be a problem." Owen opened the medicine packet. His hand hovered over the whisky glass. "Upstairs, you say?"

The waiter nodded.

Why were they going upstairs? The question rattled in his brain. He thrummed his fingers on the table. He didn't like surprises. He had to know what was going on.

Owen tapped the analgesic powder into the whisky, swirled the liquid and downed it in one gulp. The empty glass clunked on the tray.

He eyed his lunch. A half-eaten asparagus lay in congealed meat juices. Two chateau potatoes stared blankly at him. His stomach churned. He pushed aside the plate.

"I'll take my dinner in my room, tonight."

The waiter nodded.

The violin's song filled the room. Owen marched out of the Winter Garden Room to strains of Vivaldi's Four Seasons. The ring box in his pocket thudded against his hip as he strode to the lift, a constant reminder of his continued failure.

The lift's cast iron grille was shut fast. Cables whirred and rattled as it ascended. He watched the floor indicator rise to the fourth floor. The Grand Central Hotel was a high-class establishment, one of the best in the Commonwealth, and boasted many famous patrons. Even the Prince of Wales had walked its halls, barely two months ago. Most had occupied an apartment on the fourth floor. As did Enid's favourite author, Sir Arthur Conan Doyle.

Owen hissed in a sharp breath. It had to be Mrs Oldham's doing. She, and her cohort, Miss Devin. They were a bad influence. Their reckless adventures would lead Enid into trouble. He needed to warn Enid.

He slapped the grille and bounded up the carpeted stairs to the fourth floor.

chapter eight

Sunlight streamed through the window at the end of the corridor and along the carpet. It glinted off the bronze tubing of the cleaning trolley by a nearby door. Enid glanced along the corridor. It was empty, save for the trolley.

Olive crept up to the door on the other side and motioned for her to follow.

"This is it." She removed her gloves and pointed to the brass number on the door.

"Are you sure he's alone?" Enid glanced over her shoulder.

"Peggy said his family were given another room." Olive clicked open her bag, retrieved her fountain pen, and touched it to the door knob. "*Resera.*"

A small blue spark spat out of the lock. It clicked. The door knob twisted.

Olive pushed the door open.

"Hello?" It was a man's voice, but not Sir Arthur's.

Enid's heart thumped. Olive held her breath.

A middle-aged man with flecks of grey in his hair, and a syringe in his hand turned to face the door. He glanced at the pen in Olive's hand, and scowled.

"Sir Arthur won't be signing autographs today," he said.

"No," said Olive. "We're friends. We're from the..."

"Spiritualists Society," continued Enid. "You've possibly heard about Sir Arthur's lectures last week?"

"Lady Doyle wants an update on his condition," said Olive.

Enid smiled; Olive was an expert in ruses.

"Very well." The doctor stood aside and allowed them to enter.

The fourth floor suites boasted the finest rooms in the Grand Central Hotel. A glass vase, with a red anthurium and thick folded palm leaves, sat on the polished mahogany table a few feet from the door. Their reflections stared back at them from a polished mirror above the fireplace. The hearth had a simple gold surround, with white, funnel-shaped wall sconces on either side. A deep upholstered armchair sat in the far corner.

The wood-framed internal doors, with multiple, square glass panes, opened into a dining room. They followed the doctor past the secondary bedroom.

"How is Sir Arthur?" asked Enid.

The doctor shook his head. "He's stable, at least."

"I told you I should have handled it," Enid whispered in Olive's ear. "You're hopeless at *Memory Magic*."

"Need I remind you," Olive said as they followed the doctor into the main bedroom, "you didn't have your Focus." She frowned.

Enid winced.

The doctor returned the syringe to his bag, and checked its contents.

Enid hovered outside the door. She knew Olive was concerned about Sir Arthur's condition. Perhaps she could distract the doctor for a few minutes?

"Will he be all right, doctor?" Enid followed him into the sitting room.

The doctor shrugged. "I've given him a sedative. It should last until later this afternoon."

"We could sit with him until then," said Enid.

"Well..." he replied. "I do have other patients to attend, and there's nothing else I can do until the tests come back." He snatched his hat off the side table near the door. "Contact me if there's any change. Reception has my number."

"Of course, doctor." Enid smiled and ushered him to the front door.

He opened the door, and stopped.

Owen stood in the open stairwell doorway. Thick-piled carpet lined the corridor. The hallway was empty save a brass cleaning trolley parked outside a nearby room.

A door knob rattled. Owen froze. What was he doing? He trusted Enid.

The door on the opposite side of the trolley opened.

A maid in a black dress and white, fretted cap-band locked the door behind her, and pushed used towels into the sack on one end of the trolley.

Curiosity gripped his chest, smothering his breath. He had to know what trouble Enid's friend was getting her into this time.

"Excuse me." He cleared his throat.

The maid's cheeks paled.

"I'm sorry, Mr Barrington, did I forget something in your rooms?"

He shook his head.

"My friend is staying here while he's in town, but I've forgotten the number." He indicated the door next to the trolley. "I believe that's his room, but I don't want to interrupt another guest."

The colour returned to her cheeks.

"I really shouldn't say, sir, but, since you're a permanent resident it should be all right." She wiped her hands on her crisp, white apron. "That's Sir Arthur's rooms." She grinned, and lowered her voice. "The author."

"Then I haven't missed him." Owen frowned. "I thought he was leaving for Melbourne, today?"

"He's unwell," she whispered. "The doctor arrived just before lunch."

A chill ran through Owen's veins. "It's not the Spanish Flu, is it?" Enid could be in danger.

The maid's eyes widened.

"You don't think?" She twisted her apron in her hands and moved the cleaning trolley between her and Doyle's suite door. "They did move the family to other rooms."

Owen stepped closer to the door. He knew her friends would put her in danger. He clenched his fist; he wanted to burst in and drag her out of harm's way.

"Oh, sir," the maid cried. "Surely the doctor would have said something?" She shoved the cart towards the staff lift. "I must check with the manager."

The lift grille clattered shut. The maid's whimpers faded as it descended. The guest lift rattled behind him, and shuddered to a stop.

Owen stepped back into the stairwell.

Miss Sylvia Devin - the oldest of Enid's friends, with a severe pin-curled blonde hair, and sensible clothes - pushed open the grille with her ornate walking cane. Doyle's room door opened as she stepped out of the lift.

"Sylvia!" It was Enid's voice.

"This had better be an emergency." Miss Devin's footsteps thudded on the carpet as she marched into the room and shut the door behind her.

Owen raised an eyebrow. Why had they called Miss Devin? He leaned against the door frame and waited. He'd have some questions for Enid when she finally emerged.

Sylvia stood in the doorway, cradling a large carpet bag.

"Sylvia?" Enid swallowed. What was she doing here?

Enid avoided her steely gaze, and closed the door.

"Where is the patient?" Sylvia pulled off her linen day gloves.

Enid pointed in the direction of the main bedroom.

Sylvia marched passed the doctor.

"Excuse me," growled the doctor. "Who are you?"

Sylvia paused, eyed the doctor's bag and sniffed.

"I was told Mr Doyle is ill," she replied. "And *who* are you?"

"I'm the hotel doctor." He stared at her bulging carpet bag, and snorted. "I'll not have my patient subjected to quackery. I must ask you to leave immediately."

"I'm not accustomed to being told what to do." Sylvia glared at him.

Olive scuttled out of the bedroom to join Enid.

"Sylvia, you're here." There was a sound of relief in her voice.

Sylvia huffed and strode into the bedroom. The doctor followed.

Enid frowned. "But I thought you didn't--?"

Olive grabbed her arm. "I couldn't be responsible if Sir Arthur..." She bit her lip. "It's obvious it's a reaction to the *Memory Magic*," she whispered.

"You should have let me do it," said Enid.

"I had no choice." Olive eyed the umbrella hooked over Enid's arm.

Enid felt her cheeks burn. At least Sylvia couldn't berate her for forgetting her Focus, this time.

"Sylvia will want to know why you did it," she said.

Olive sucked in a sharp breath. "It's not my fault your friend's sanctuary is riddled with Fae."

"We have to tell her about them."

"All right." Olive took a deep breath. "Just don't mention the quest."

Enid nodded. Sylvia would be livid if she discovered Sir Arthur - a civilian - was responsible for ensnaring the Protectors in a Fae quest.

She abhorred civilians meddling in Otherworld affairs.

"But, you must tell her about the reporter," whispered Enid.

Olive went pale.

"Best get it over and done with." She patted Olive's arm.

They joined Sylvia and the doctor into the bedroom.

Sir Arthur lay on one of the twin beds, his face contorted in pain. Beads of perspiration covered his forehead. His muscles twitched.

Sylvia touched the back of her hand to his forehead, and tsked. She pried open his left eyelid, and shook her head.

"How long has he been like this?" she asked.

The doctor screwed up his face. "I beg your pardon?"

Sylvia ignored him. She stared past him, at Enid and Olive.

"Since Saturday, I believe," replied Enid.

"Why didn't you fetch me then?" she asked.

Enid elbowed Olive in the ribs.

"We weren't aware of any complications until this afternoon," said Olive. "We were told he had food poisoning."

"I should think it's obvious this isn't food poisoning," said Sylvia.

"On that, we agree." The doctor crossed his arms.

"That's why I called you," said Olive.

Sylvia eyed her as she emptied the contents of her carpet bag onto the dresser: a collection of jars, tins, and a rolled up leather satchel.

The doctor raised an eyebrow, picked up one of the jars, and unscrewed the lid.

A foul stench wafted across the room. He wrinkled his nose, screwed the lid back on, and dumped it back on the dresser.

Sylvia removed a silver tube with a funnel-like end from her bag, unbuttoned Sir Arthur's shirt, and placed the flared end of the tube against his chest.

"Madam!" The doctor's face reddened. "I must ask you to leave at once."

Sylvia closed her eyes, listened, then pulled away the stethoscope.

"Do you know what ails him?" She didn't wait for his reply. "No?" The corner of her lip curled. "Then leave me to do my work." She turned to Olive and Enid. "I need two pots of freshly boiled water, and raspberry jam."

"Jam?" The doctor's cheeks puffed out like a fish gasping for air. "I must insist you leave, immediately."

Sylvia's smile dropped. A point of fiery red blazed in her green eyes. She grabbed her walking stick in her left hand.

Enid flinched. She knew Sylvia's anger too well; she stepped back, out of the doorway, dragging Olive with her.

"I'm calling security," he growled.

"Silence!" Sylvia's voice rumbled with power.

"I'll not be spoken to--"

Sylvia raised her walking stick, and pointed it at his head.

Enid resisted the urge to grab Sylvia's Focus. She knew better than to question Sylvia's decisions.

"Who are you?" His gaze darted across the room, to Enid and Olive, then back to Sylvia. He edged towards the doorway, and clawed at the door frame. "The Manager will hear about this." His voice was shaky.

"Sylvia?" Enid whispered.

The doctor froze. He stared at her with wild eyes.

Definitely panic.

Sylvia touched his forehead with the head of her finger. "*Obliviscor.*" Static buzzed along the length of the stick, and crackled around her fingertip.

The doctor's mouth clapped shut. His eyes widened as he reeled back into the wall, with a thud. A thin red light arced through the air and circled the doctor's head. His eyes rolled upward, He froze.

The air sizzled.

The doctor gasped. His eyes flickered. His shoulders relaxed.

The red light faded.

Sylvia leaned on her walking stick.

"Pardon?" The doctor stared past them.

"I'll need two pots of freshly boiled water, four tea cups, a pot of raspberry jam, and a red cloth," Sylvia replied.

"Well, I see Sir Arthur is in good hands." The doctor nodded slowly, eyes still fixed on the wall. "Call me if you need me."

"Lock the door on your way out," said Sylvia.

He nodded and left the suite, locking the door behind him.

"That, ladies, is how *Memory Magic* is done." Sylvia sat in the chair near the window and closed her eyes. Her breathing slowed.

Enid and Olive waited in the sitting room, in silence; Sylvia would need every ounce of concentration to correct the magic.

Owen spied through the narrow crack of the partially open stairwell exit. Sir Arthur's suite door swung open again.

A man wearing a sober, ready-made suit and a confused expression, emerged from the room. He adjusted his black leather doctor's bag, and slipped on his hat. He shook his head and walked towards the lift, tipping his hat in Owen's direction as he entered the lift.

About fifteen minutes later, a room waiter delivered a tea trolley to Doyle's room. It rattled across the carpet. Drips of condensation dribbled down the outside of a silver teapot. Four matching cups chinked against the pot of something sweet-smelling. Its smell reminded him of raspberries.

"Will there be anything else, miss?" asked the room waiter.

"We will require this." It was Enid's voice. She passed him a slip of folded paper.

Owen relaxed his fingers.

"You'll find it in the Chinese Market."

"Very well, miss." He slipped the note into his pocket.

Owen stepped back in to the shadows of the stairwell and started down the steps, to catch the waiter before he exited the lift on the ground floor. He paused. His curiosity was not as important as Enid's safety. He plodded back up to the fourth floor, propped open the door a crack, and waited. He'd always wait for Enid.

The smell of sweet raspberry hovered over the silver food tray. Steam rose from the spouts of two silver teapots on the service trolley. Four china teacups and saucers, and a matching lidded bowl sat on the tray next to it. A long-handled silver spoon lay on a linen napkin, next to the bowl.

The china clinked softly as Enid wheeled the trolley into Sir Arthur's bedroom.

Sylvia opened one eye. "Excellent."

She unscrewed one of the small metal tins on the dresser. A smoky aroma marked it as one of Sylvia's Russian tea blends. She spooned the dried leaves into one of the silver pots, left it to brew, and returned her attention to the array of jars and tins. She measured out various quantities of herbs, added them to a thin paper sachet, filled one of the teacups with the brewed tea, and half-filled the other. She let the sachet steep in the copper-coloured liquid of the full cup.

"Now, tell me." Sylvia settled herself back in the chair and eyed Enid. "Who is responsible for Mr Doyle's condition?"

Enid's frowned. Why did Sylvia always expect it was her? She glanced at Olive. Olive swallowed. Her fingers trembled as she stepped forward.

"I should have realised." Sylvia groaned. "Why didn't you let Enid do it? She's more adept at *Memory Magic*."

Enid's heart thumped. If Sylvia found out she had misplaced her Focus during the picnic, she was in for it.

"The picnic," said Olive. "It was our fault." The words seemed to tumble out of her mouth as if she had no control over them.

"Picnic?" Sylvia raised an eyebrow.

"The Fae Queen--" Olive's mouth slapped shut. She glanced at Enid, her eyes wide with fear.

"Fae?" Sylvia sat bolt upright. A pale veil flashed over Sylvia's face. Her eyes narrowed. "What do they want?"

Enid took a slow, deep breath. She'd promised Olive she wouldn't mention their quest. If Sylvia found out Sir Arthur had made a deal with the Fae, and both she and Olive were entangled in it... Olive had kept her secret about the picnic, now she would return in kind. She stepped forward to join Olive.

"Mr Bellchambers invited us to a picnic,' she said. "He wanted some advice about his bees." *Not a lie.* "They've been out of sorts lately." *Also, not a lie.* "I thought, perhaps, the Howler had returned." *So far, so good.*

"And Mr Doyle?" asked Sylvia, still eyeing her.

Enid heard Olive suck in a quiet breath beside her.

"Apparently, he's enamoured by the local fauna, and asked to visit the sanctuary," replied Enid.

"I see." Sylvia jiggled the tea pot, and sniffed the black liquid in the teacup.

She topped up the unadulterated cup with the hot water from the second pot. Enid's pulse slowed as the sweet, smoky aroma of lapsang souchong, keemun, and oolong filled the room.

"And the Fae?" she asked in a calm voice.

"That wasn't our fault." Olive frowned.

"You should have realised there were Thin Places at the sanctuary," said Sylvia.

"How could we--?" Olive's frown lifted. "The Howler?" She groaned. "Of course."

"But we weren't to know there would be Fae," replied Enid. "How could we? They haven't been spotted in these parts since the colonists arrived."

"They are like lice." Sylvia scowled and shifted in her chair. "Once they infest a place, it's impossible to get rid of them. I'll need to inform the Elders." She shook her head, and gulped a mouthful of tea. "What did they want?"

Olive's fingers twitched.

"Fae always want something," said Sylvia.

"I have no idea," said Enid. That was a lie; best to distract Sylvia as quickly as possible. "They must have left when they saw the bounty hunter."

"Bounty hunter?" echoed Sylvia.

"But it was too late." Olive let out a relieved breath. "The reporter had seen it."

"Reporter?" Sylvia's teacup rattled on its saucer.

"So, you see, we *had* to use *Memory Magic*," continued Olive. "We had no choice."

Sylvia turned her attention to Enid.

Enid's heart sank. Had Sylvia seen through their deception?

"You should have done it," said Sylvia. "You know *Memory Magic* isn't one of Olive's strengths."

Blood pounded in Enid's ears.

"She was searching for the other bounty hunter," said Olive.

Ice pulsed through Enid's veins. Olive was confessing all. Had Sylvia magicked her to wheedle out the truth? Would she be next?

"*Another* troll?" hissed Sylvia. "How many were there?"

"Only the two," replied Olive. "The Shoemaker says--"

Enid winced.

"The Shoemaker?" Sylvia's voice was cold.

Olive didn't reply.

Sylvia's nostrils flared. "And you took Enid?"

Olive nodded slowly.

"Is he still up to his old tricks?" she asked calmly.

"If you mean helping unfortunate creatures escape persecution," said Enid, "then, yes. He was the one who warned us of the second troll."

Sylvia closed her eyes, and took three deep breaths.

"A reporter, you say?" Sylvia picked up her teacup, quaffed the liquid, and placed the empty cup back on the tray. "You erased his memories as well?"

"Yes," Olive replied.

"Then we need to make sure you did a better job with him," continued Sylvia. "Best not having our affairs announced in tomorrow's newspaper headlines." She snatched up her gloves. "Olive, you're coming with me. Enid, the tisane steeps for three more minutes. Mix in two teaspoons of raspberry jam, and repeat the dosage in one hour. I'll return in four hours to check on him." She pulled on the gloves. "Be here when I get back. If the fever breaks, give him this." She handed Enid a small vial of purple liquid. "Seven drops in a fresh cup of tea."

"Can't I stay?" asked Olive.

"No." Sylvia smiled. "He's Enid's favourite author."

Owen's arm ached. He'd spent hours propping open the stairwell door. His foot tingled where it rested hard against the step below him. He stretched his leg, and rubbed his calf.

There were thirty-seven curved diamond shapes repeated in the carpet. Curved arrows at the tips of each one lead from the stairwell along the corridor, towards Doyle's suite; each one beckoning him to fetch Enid. He'd resisted the temptation, remaining out of sight.

The room maid hummed as she moved from room to room. The lift had ascended and descended twice - once for a couple of young women lollygagging and giggling at the lift door. They roused when the maid exited the room at the far end, punched the lift buttons, and returned to ground floor.

Enid's friends had finally left, leaving her alone in Doyle's room.

Alone. With Doyle. He twitched. *His* Enid.

He nudged the door, and hesitated. How would he explain his presence? She'd think he didn't trust her?

The door at the far end of the corridor opened.

Owen pulled the stairwell door closed, leaving only a small crack to peer through.

The cleaning trolley squeaked as the maid pushed it towards him. She paused in front of the stairwell door.

Owen held his breath.

She kicked the wheel with her shoe, and continued towards the service lift.

Guests began to dribble out of their rooms, dressed in fine tuxedos, shimmering dresses and jewellery.

It must be almost dinner time. Owen's stomach grumbled, at the reminder.

A red-headed woman giggled and made her way to the stairwell door. Owen jumped to his feet and let the door close; there was no time to get out of sight. He held his breath as the door knob turned.

A muffled voice came from the other side of the door. "The lift is here."

The door knob spun back home.

"Thank goodness," said the woman. "I didn't fancy walking all the way down."

Owen fell back against the wall, and let his breath escape. What was he thinking? Of course, he trusted Enid. It was her friends he doubted.

He examined his creased trousers and ran his hand through his hair. How ridiculous he must look - hiding in a stairwell, keeping surveillance on his soon-to-be fiancée. He scoffed at himself, dusted off his trousers, picked up his hat and walked down the stairs. He needed a stiff drink.

Owen dashed down the stairs and settled on a stool at the cocktail bar, making sure it had line of sight to the lift, the stairs and the foyer entrance.

"Scotch," he said.

The barman slid a whisky in his direction.

Owen's stomach grumbled again. He glanced longingly in the direction of the Dining Room. He'd have to wait; Enid still hadn't emerged. He tugged at his day jacket; he was under-dressed for dinner.

The lift bell dinged. A woman's laughter filtered through the grate as it opened.

"Ground floor, sir." A white-gloved hand extended through the opening. "The Dining Room is to your right."

The same amorous couple he'd seen enter the lift on the fourth floor, stepped out. The glass beads on her dress clicked gently as she wrapped her slender arm around the gentleman's elbow, then straightened his lapel.

The gentleman's gaze flitted across the foyer, pausing to connect with Owen's inquisitive stare. His pale violet eyes studied Owen, lingering for just a few seconds longer than required. Owen's heart skipped. The man smiled, returned his attention to his companion, and whispered in her ear. His jet-black hair danced on his shoulders as he spoke.

She nodded and smiled, as he ushered her past the cocktail bar, towards the foyer.

Owen's foot fell onto the soft carpet; the familiar arrowed-diamond enticed him to follow. He took a deep breath and drained his glass.

"Another whisky?" asked the barman.

Owen stood, and followed the couple into the foyer. The reception clerk sucked in a breath and eyed the young gentleman as he passed. His companion hugged his arm tighter. The porter nodded as they left.

Owen halted, shook his head, and straightened his jacket. He needed to stay, to be here for Enid. He found a comfortable arm chair with a good view of the lift, and settled into the soft-padded leather.

More guests wandered past, resplendent in their evening finery. Bursts of excited conversation and the faint clink of cutlery escaped into the foyer as the Dining Room door opened for latecomers, both quickly drowned by a lively tune from the resident quartet.

Mouth-watering aromas of roast beef in Burgundy sauce, fresh baked bread and spicy soup wafted along the hall.

Owen closed his eyes, drank in the delicious bouquet, and licked his lips. His stomach growled again.

Ding.

Owen's eyes snapped open, his attention locked on the lift. Another elegant couple stepped out and strolled through the foyer to the front door. A reflection of orange light streamed over its glass panels as the porter held it open.

A shadow flickered across the glass. A tall man ducked into the hotel, and strode to the front desk.

"Ernest Whitington. '*The Register*'." His voice was calm and reassuring. "For Sir Arthur Conan Doyle." He smiled. "I understand he's extended his stay."

Owen's heart raced. If Enid was discovered alone, in the apartment, with Doyle, she'd be ruined. His muscles tensed, ready to sprint up the stairs.

"I'm sorry, sir." The Reception Clerk smiled at him. "He's not available."

Owen slumped back into the armchair. Thank goodness the hotel valued guest's privacy.

The clerk returned her attention to the work on the desk.

"Can you tell me when he'll be available?" Whitington asked. "I have something urgent to discuss."

She shook her head, and returned to her work.

"I see." He rummaged in his jacket pocket, flipped opened a small notebook, and peered at her name badge. "Miss Margaret...?" He poised his pencil above the page.

"Taylor." She patted the neat roll bun above her collar.

"With a 'Y'?" He scribbled in his notebook.

She blushed and nodded.

"I'm doing a story on Sir Arthur's stay in the hotel," he said. "I'm sure you can help me?"

The young woman bit her lip and scanned the foyer.

"He's unwell," she whispered.

"Ah." Whitington raised an eyebrow. "Has the doctor been to see him?"

The reception clerk returned to her work.

Whitington leaned on the desk and smiled. "May I speak to the doctor?"

"I'm sorry, he's not here, sir." She leaned closer. "But he is due back in the morning," she whispered.

"Margaret, you're a peach." Whitington slipped his notebook into a jacket pocket, tipped his hat at the clerk.

"Mr Barrington?"

Owen jumped.

A clean-shaven man in a smart navy suit and brimless hat loomed above him.

"Is there a problem, sir?" asked the porter.

Owen shook his head and slid back in to the armchair, wishing the cushions would swallow him.

"Is there anything I can get you sir?" asked the porter.

Owen recognised his voice. What was his name? Bernie?

"No, thank you, Bernie," he replied. "I'm waiting for someone."

"Shall I organise a table for dinner?"

Owen shook his head. "Not tonight, Bernie."

"Perhaps I could fetch something from the kitchen." Bernie leaned closer. "For two."

"Pardon?" Owen forehead tightened.

The ported smiled.

"For Miss Turner, sir," he whispered.

Owen frowned. "No, thank you, I've decided to eat out."

"Shall I inform the valet Miss Turner will be requiring her motorcar?"

Owen squirmed in the chair. Had he seen Enid going upstairs?

The lift rattled as it descended.

Owen's muscles relaxed. What if Enid stepped out? Would Bernie call her over? He fiddled with the ring box in his pocket. Would she understand he only wanted to protect her?

The lift's bell dinged.

His heart thumped. He'd have to explain fast. He was on his feet, and in the foyer by the time the lift grille opened.

The Reception clerk was busy on the phone. The reporter, Whittington hovered near the desk.

Owen marched to the front door; he couldn't let Enid see him.

The porter smiled and opened the door. "Have a good evening, Mr Barrington."

The comforting aromas of the Grand Central Hotel were replaced by the stink of car exhaust, pipe smoke and a hint of fresh horse dung on the street; glamorous guests and genteel music replaced by a sea of boaters and Homburgs, hurried footsteps, tooting horns and the rattle of horse drawn carriages as they crossed the tram tracks on Pulteney Street.

The late afternoon sun rimmed the roofline, silhouetted the buildings on the opposite side and glared in Owen's eyes. A policeman stood at the corner of the busy intersection, directing pedestrian, carriage, and motorcar.

Owen strode out from the shade of the Hotel's awning. He shoved his hands in his pockets and his fingertips brushed the ring box. His fingers snapped back. His heart sank. He'd failed again.

The reporter stalked past, climbed into a black motorcar by the curb, and drove off southwards. Two women waited at the curb near where the car had been, one with a distinctive carpet bag and silver walking stick.

Owen slid his hat low over his eyes and crossed the street. A bicycle sped past. Its shrill bell rang in his ears as he stepped onto the footpath and into the shade of the buildings.

An acrid stench clawed his nostrils. A metallic rattle clattered near his ear. Something moved in the shadows next to him.

Owen blinked, allowing his eyes to adjust to the lower light.

A figure leaned against the wall. His unkempt beard matched the well-worn khaki uniform jacket and faded trousers. The veteran rattled his tin, and limped forward towards him.

"Please, sir." The veteran spoke in a gravelly voice. "For a poor soldier?" His head remained low, his face shadowed. "And I will tell you a most sad tale." He shook his tin again.

Owen pulled a few coins from his pocket, being careful to avoid the ring box, and dropped them into the tin.

"I was rich, like you, once." The veteran hugged the tin close to his chest. "Before the war. I owned a mansion, only a few blocks away."

He stared past Owen, apparently lost in the memory. The stench rolled over Owen again. He wrinkled his nose.

"Do you have a sweetheart?" asked the veteran.

Owen nodded slowly.

"I had a wife." The veteran lowered his head further. "She betrayed me. Sold my house while I was away, and absconded with every last shilling. I fought for my country, and she turned me out onto the street, she did." He stared across the street. "I blame that old witch." He jerked his head in the direction of the Hotel, and growled. "And her friend. They poisoned her mind, turned her against me."

Owen glanced back over the street. Enid's motorcar was at the curb. A hotel valet held the doors open for Mrs Oldham and Miss Devin.

"Are you sure?" Owen shifted on his feet. He knew Enid's friends were trouble, but hadn't realised he was in danger as well.

"I assure you. Those crones set my wife against me." He spat on the ground.

Owen held his breath, patted the ill-fated soldier on the shoulder, and folded a few notes in his tin.

"You may have saved me, friend." Owen tugged down the brim of his hat, and followed the Lincoln south along Pulteney Street.

chapter nine

nid's red Lincoln Tourer lurched after the reporter's black motorcar. Owen trotted along the footpath after it. They turned west into Grenfell Street. The leading motorcar slowed. Its tyre nudged the curb in front of a sandstone building. Black, Gothic letters on the first floor marked it as the offices of *The Register*.

Whitington alighted from the black vehicle, fumbled with a set of keys, and moved into the shadow of the overhanging balcony.

The red Tourer shuddered to a stop behind his motorcar.

Owen remained in the shadow of the buildings across the street and waited for Miss Devin and Mrs Oldham to exit the vehicle, before he crept across the street. He hovered on the other side of Enid's motorcar and listened.

"Yoo-hoo, Mr Whitington." Mrs Oldham strode to the front door.

Mr Whitington snatched his keys back from the door. His eyes narrowed.

"Olive Oldham." She thrust out her hand. "We met at the picnic at Humbug Scrub."

"You were there when the body was found?" There was a flicker of recognition. "The police interviewed you."

"Yes." Her gaze flicked back, in the direction of her cohort.

Owen's heart pounded; he ducked below the side window of the Tourer.

"This is my friend, Miss Devin," she continued.

"What can I do for you, Mrs Oldham?" Whitington's voice wafted over the motorcar.

There was an awkward silence.

Owen moved to the rear of the car for a better view.

"Olive remembered something from the picnic." It was Miss Devin's voice.

"The police weren't interested," added Mrs Oldham.

"Their loss." Whitington chuckled.

"We thought you might be," said Mrs Oldham.

"Come in." His key rattled in the door lock.

Owen moved out from behind the motorcar as the trio entered the building. He wedged his foot in the doorway as the door closed, waited for their footsteps to recede, and slipped inside.

A light flickered on in a room further along the hallway. The door creaked as it was pulled closed. Owen tiptoed towards the room, and crouched down to peer through the keyhole.

Glimpses of blue silk flashed past the keyhole. He held his breath. His muscles tensed, ready to run.

"You have information about the murder, I presume?" asked Whitington.

Owen placed a palm on the wall to steady himself, and leaned closer. Mrs Oldham paced the room.

Whitington sat behind a plain desk. Behind him was a bookshelf full of scruffy notebooks, reference books, and magazine. He dropped his hat next to a stack of paper and envelopes, and opened a small notebook.

Miss Devin sat on the edge of the desk and flipped through pages near the top of a pile of papers. Whitington slapped his hand on the pile.

"All information is confidential," he said.

"Until it's printed in your newspaper, of course." Sylvia removed her white linen gloves.

"Of course." Whitington grinned.

Mrs Oldham paused in front of the desk, partially obscuring Owen's view.

"What do you remember about the picnic?" asked Miss Devin.

"I should be asking the questions." Whitington leaned back in his chair.

Miss Devin nudged one of the pages Whitington had hurriedly arranged on his desk. A small brown paper packet peeked out.

Whitington lunged for it.

She snatched it away from his reach and jumped off the desk.

"Manners, Mr Whitington." She unfolded the package. "Or I shall have to inform the Police about your little habit."

"You mean he's--?" Mrs Oldham hovered near her shoulder.

"Go ahead." Whitington's chuckled and leaned back into his chair.

She dipped a finger into the packet, licked it, and frowned. "Stone dust?"

Mrs Oldham peered at the packet's contents.

"Yes," replied Whitington, "I have a penchant for collecting rocks."

"Usually one collects entire rock specimens." Miss Devin glared at him.

Mrs Oldham whispered in her companion's ear.

Miss Devin's mouth hardened. She closed the packet and handed it to Mrs Oldham.

"The Police didn't think it important." Whitington's eyes widened. "But it means something to you, doesn't it?" He rested his elbows on the desk. "Why are you so interested?"

"You first." Miss Devin sat on the opposite side of the desk.

Whitington raised an eyebrow. "All right, I'll play."

"This was on the body found at the picnic?" asked Olive.

"No," he replied. "The chauffeur's rooms."

"No surprises there," said Miss Devin.

"How do you know about the second body?" asked Whitington.

"The police were keeping it quiet."

"Second body?" Mrs Oldham joined her fellow conspirator.

The reporter sneered and cursed under his breath.

Miss Devlin chuckled. "Do tell."

"That's not how it works." Whitington crossed his arms and shook his head. "*Quid pro quo.* Your turn."

Miss Devlin leaned closer and whispered something. Whitington's eyes widened.

"The police found a body when they searched the chauffeur's residence." His voice was calm.

Shit! Owen pressed close against the keyhole. *A multiple murderer?*

The women whispered to each other, seemingly unaffected by the revelation.

What had they dragged Enie into?

"Who was it?" Mrs Oldham asked the reporter.

"Unknown," replied Whitington. "His face was bludgeoned. He was unrecognisable."

Miss Devin twisted her walking stick on the floor. A faint red glow wrapped around the stick and snaked up her arm. She leaned closer to the reporter, and whispered.

Owen strained to listen.

Red light oozed from her fingertips and surrounded Whitington's head. His eyes rolled upwards, baring the whites of his eyes.

A shiver trickled down Owen's spine.

Whitington slumped in the chair.

What the--? Owen jumped back, sucked in a breath and flung his hands back to break his fall. His wrist cracked. He cursed under his breath. The veteran was right; she was a witch - he swallowed - and Mrs Oldham was her collaborator. He rubbed his wrist, and peered back through the keyhole.

Mrs Oldham mumbled something.

"No time for that." Miss Devin checked his pulse. "He'll live." She rifled through the pile of papers closest to her. "Check he hasn't written anything down."

The desk drawers scraped open. Mrs Oldham held up several photographs.

Photographs? Owen frowned. What would two middle-aged women want with photographs?

Miss Devin snatched them from her hand, and examined them.

"We're fortunate the police didn't find them." She handed them back to Mrs Oldham. "Any negatives?"

Mrs Oldham peered into the drawer, pulled out a bundle of negatives. She turned on the desk lamp and inspected them under the light.

"Bring them with you." Miss Devin moved towards the door.

Owen scrambled back from the door and stumbled down the hallway, out the front door. He had to protect Enid! Before they bewitched her away from him.

He slipped around the corner of the building into the laneway, and waited.

The two Crones emerged from the building and climbed into Enid's motorcar. Mrs Oldham stashed the photographs under the dash.

Owen flattened himself against the stone wall, as the vehicle jerked away from the curb. Gears crunched as it turned around in the street and headed east, back along Grenfell Street. He hurried after them, keeping to the buildings' shadows, back to the Grand Central Hotel.

Owen waited in the shadows of the buildings across from the Grand Central Hotel.

Miss Devin strode into the hotel.

Mrs Oldham paused for a moment, then marched westward along

Rundle Street; the urgent click of her heels echoed off the buildings. Owen followed, thankful for the soft, leather soles of his custom-made shoes.

She turned down Gawler Place, and ducked into a laneway behind the Pharmacist's building.

Owen paused at the corner and listened; her footsteps were faint. He crept into the lane and hid behind a stack of crates. The acrid stench of decomposing rubbish and chemical compounds engulfed him.

Something thudded in the shadows behind him. His heart raced.

He peered into the darkness. There was nothing. He let out a long, measured breath. He scoffed; he was imagining things. He crept further into the lane.

Mrs Oldham marched up to the rear of the next building and ran her hand over the red bricks, allowing it to linger over one of them. She knocked four times, and pressed her palm against the wall.

The bricks blurred and squirmed in the air.

Owen froze.

The bricks continued to twist, rearranging themselves to form a shadowy archway. Mrs Oldham adjusted the bag on her arm, stepped into the breach, and was swallowed by darkness.

"Impossible." He rubbed his eyes. It'd been a long day; he *had* to be imagining things. But this wasn't the first sorcery he'd seen today. First the older crone, now her apprentice. Blood pounded in his veins. Bloody hell, they were *both* witches!

He stumbled out from behind the crates and staggered towards the doorway. The ground rumbled under his feet. The lane seemed to distort around him. The bricks shuddered and snapped shut. A cloud of brick dust spat over him. Grit scratched his eyes and caught in his throat. He coughed, and waved away the dust as he retreated from the lane.

Blood thumped in his ears. His head whirled. Fingers of pain dug into his temple. He careened back into the street, and towards the hotel.

A whisky. That's what he needed. A very large whisky. Or three.

It was Olive's second visit to the Shoemaker in as many days. Nothing much had changed; the fireplace still crackled, warming the cosy cottage-like room, the door in the corner remained closed. Four chairs now sat under the curtained window. And the voice from the Hall of Portals still whispered in her head.

Orrug sat opposite her. He peered over his metal-half-rimmed spectacles, eyed the cards in Olive's hand, then stared at her as if trying to read her thoughts. Miss Caimanos hovered behind him and glared at her.

Olive smiled back; she found it put people off guard. Orrug shook his head, and pushed another gold coin into the centre of the desk.

Miss Caimanos examined his cards. The corner of her eyelid fluttered. She plonked an earthenware bowl on the desk. The smell of spinach and herbs wafted over the table. Small, triangular pastry-covered morsels jiggled in the bowl.

"What do you call this game, again?" asked Miss Caimanos.

"Poker." Olive slid a gold coin across the desk, leaned back in her chair, and rested her cards against her chest. "It's a bit like *Poque*." She dropped two more coins on the desk. "But with more cards."

"The picture cards are good, right?" Miss Caimanos sniffed.

"Yes." Olive smiled at Orrug. "You're stalling."

Miss Caimanos narrowed her eyelids. "How do you know she's not cheating?" she whispered in Orrug's ear.

"I don't cheat!" Olive straightened in her chair.

Orrug scooped up a miniature pastry and nibbled on the corner. He fanned his cards out on the table in front of him. "Two red threes, a red ten, and two fives."

"Is that good?" asked Miss Caimanos.

"Not bad." Warmth flooded through Olive's chest. Her muscles relaxed. She laid down her cards. Two tens, a Jack, a Queen, and an Ace; all hearts.

"Ah." The Shoemaker shoved the entire pastry in his mouth, and crunched.

"I get..." Olive counted the coins and leaned her elbows on the desk. "Two questions. And you must answer truthfully."

Miss Caimanos snatched up Olive's playing cards and examined them.

"Our guest needs a refreshment," said Orrug.

"Do you have a beer?" asked Olive.

"We have *xiaonero*."

Olive screwed up her nose.

"How about cider?" Orrug chuckled.

Miss Caimanos strode out of the room without waiting for an answer.

Olive leaned forward in her chair. She needed to find out where the trolls had come from, and why one had attacked Enid.

"Is there a fairy door near Albert Bridge?" she asked.

"Yes." Orrug smiled.

That made sense; but how would the troll know Enid would be there? Olive frowned.

"One door? That would imply..." She eyed him. "Is there another one?"

"Still ever the Protector." Orrug ran his hand over his grey beard. His silver jewellery clicked faintly.

Olive's heart sank. Was that all he thought of her now?

He pulled a hand-drawn map out from a desk drawer and unrolled the parchment.

Olive scanned the map. There were several strange markings, on various buildings, that she didn't recognise.

The aroma of warm apple and honey drifted into the room, heralding Miss Caimanos' return with two silver tankards. She glanced at the map and frowned.

"I thought you didn't want them knowing about those?"

"We can trust Olive." Orrug pointed at the map.

"I'll take that." Miss Caimanos rolled up the map and tucked it under her arm. "You shouldn't gamble away our secrets."

"There's rumour of one in the Botanic Gardens," he said, "and a third still active a few blocks south of the Sanctuary."

"So close?" Olive shifted in her seat.

"It's protected," replied Orrug, "on holy ground."

"And you're certain there's no other portals from the Otherworlds?" asked Olive.

"Is that your second question?" asked Miss Caimanos.

Olive shook her head.

"Why would a troll come through a Fae door?" Olive bit her lip.

"Let's just say not all Fae are as..." He returned his attention to the map. "... forgiving."

"There's a war brewing in the Otherworlds, Mrs Oldham." Miss Caimanos leaned over the desk. "And your pact with the Fae has brought it to our door step."

"It wasn't me." Olive's fingernails pressed through her cotton gloves and dug into her palms. "I made no pact." Her hand slipped into her handbag under the table, and wrapped around her fountain pen.

"The Fae are quite adept at twisting fate to their advantage," said Orrug. "It's up to us all to protect this world from Otherworld politics. Don't you agree?"

Olive and Miss Caimanos eyed each other, and nodded. Olive closed her handbag.

"Then that's settled." He grinned.

"I have one question left." Olive relaxed into her chair. And Orrug had promised to answer truthfully. But what to ask? Why would the Fae send a bounty hunter after one of their own? Who was the unnamed criminal the bounty hunter had tracked from the Otherworlds? And when did Orrug acquire an assistant? So many questions. But there was one...

A voice had whispered in her head, ever since the Hall of Portals. A voice she longed to hear. It whispered even now, calling her name. She'd heard rumours about a place. She had to know.

Olive looked Orrug in the eye.

"The grey door, in the Hall of Portals?" she said. "Where does it lead?

The shoemaker's grin faded. The colour drained from Miss Caimanos' face. The map crinkled under her arm. She grasped The Shoemaker's shoulder with her other hand.

"I heard something." Olive stared into the flickering flames in the fireplace. "A voice. It seemed..."

"Familiar?" Orrug snatched up one of the tankards and swigged its contents.

"The Netherworld." Miss Caimanos' voice was shaky. She drew in a sharp breath.

The Shoemaker clutched her hand on his shoulder.

"Then it's true?" asked Olive. "There is a way to reach it?"

Miss Caimanos' knuckles whitened.

"Olive, no..." Orrug shook his head.

Miss Caimanos released her grip on his shoulder, and paced the room.

"It is forbidden," he replied. "Only those who are no longer of this world may pass over that threshold."

Olive's heart twisted in her chest.

"But my Frank..." She struggled to breathe. "There must be a way?"

"The dead must rest." Orrug's hand gently squeezed hers. "That is the way of things."

Olive closed her eyes, trying not to let tears escape down her cheek.

The voice whispered again. Her breath shuddered. It was Frank. It had to be. She picked up the tankard and gulped down the pale yellow liquid. Its tart taste clung to her mouth as the tepid fluid slid down her throat. She squeezed her eyes tighter, and listened for his voice.

The food bowl rattled on the desk.

The whispering voice faded. Olive opened her eyes.

Miss Caimanos stopped circling, cocked her head, and turned slowly to face them.

"Kel?" The Shoemaker stood slowly. "What is it?"

The flames sputtered in the hearth. Miss Caimanos pressed her palm on the wall near the fireplace, and frowned.

"Something's trying to break in," she replied.

Olive placed her hand on the desk. "I can't feel anything."

"She has the Sight," said Orrug.

Olive's eyes widened. She'd heard about the gift. It was rare these days. And didn't require a Focus to channel energy. It wasn't magic; it was something else, something older. Far older.

Miss Caimanos frowned, and moved her hands as if searching for something.

"It's capricious," she whispered.

Olive snatched her fountain pen out of her handbag, and rose from the chair.

"*Revelo.*" A blue glow coalesced around the tip of the pen. She twisted it in the air, and turned slowly to scan the room. The glow flared as she faced the entrance door.

Miss Caimanos froze. "It's coming closer."

The ground vibrated under her feet.

"You need to leave, Olive," said Orrug.

"But I can help."

The entrance door shimmered.

"It's trying to sever our link to your world," hissed Miss Caimanos.

Orrug jumped to his feet. "Go, now!" He was by her side. "Please, Olive, before it's too late."

Flames spluttered and spat. Small plumes of smoke rose where sparks touched the wool hearth rug.

"Go, or you'll be trapped." He nudged her towards the exit.

Olive stumbled forward. The shimmer in the doorway crackled and disintegrated. Its rim of steel-coloured stone blazed as she crossed the threshold. Fine, silvery cracks snaked along the dark stone of the Hall of Portals. Dark patches crept across the silent archways.

A rush of air blasted over her face, yanked at her clothes, and snuffed out the flames behind her.

Enid placed the engraved silver cutlery on the china plate, leaned back in the dining chair and sipped the last of her tea. She glanced into the bedroom where Sir Arthur snored peacefully.

The front door rattled.

She sat bolt upright, her hand already wrapped around her umbrella handle, ready for action.

The door opened.

Sylvia entered, and tapped the door with her walking stick. Its lock gleamed briefly, and clicked.

"All sorted?" asked Enid.

"It shouldn't have been necessary," Sylvia replied. "You let yourself be distracted."

"But there was a murder."

"Protectors must not get involved in the affairs of civilians." Sylvia removed one of her gloves.

"But the victim wasn't human." Enid huffed.

"If you'd both been more vigilant then I wouldn't have had to fix things." She stripped off her other glove. "Why do humans have such a fascination with murder and mystery? I blame those mystery novels of yours. They've infected you, and now you've dragged Olive into your shenanigans." She snorted. "Why can't you take up crochet, like other spinsters?"

"But I'm not a--"

"He had photos." Sylvia slapped her gloves onto the table, next to the plate. "What if the newspaper had published them? They'd come sniffing around to investigate next. We can't allow them to know the Otherworlds exist." She leaned closer to Enid. "That *we* exist."

"But it's the twentieth century," said Enid.

"They still fear the unknown," hissed Sylvia. "Their *Great War* proved that." She eyed the remnants of the dinner plate.

"The hotel sent it up." Enid pushed the plate into the centre of the table. "And Sir Arthur couldn't eat it."

Sylvia's mouth curled. "How is the patient?"

"Sleeping," replied Enid. "The draught worked."

"Of course it did." Sylvia marched into the bedroom.

Enid followed.

Sylvia checked Sir Arthur's pulse.

"He'll be fine by morning." She wiped down her long-handled mixing spoons, slipped them into their pouches in her leather satchel, and rolled it up. "I'll finish up here."

Enid nodded. She pulled on her gloves, picked up her carpet bag, and hooked her umbrella over one arm. A faint shimmer washed over the door as she approached it.

"Same password?" she asked.

Sylvia nodded.

Enid whispered: "*Otkroitsye.*"

The handle buzzed under her hand. She opened the door, and clicked it shut behind her.

Enid stepped out of the lift into the foyer. Music crept along the corridor, serenading late diners. The porter stood to attention by the front door.

"Good evening, Miss Turner." He tipped his hat and smiled. "I'm afraid Mr Barrington hasn't returned from dinner yet."

"Thank you," she read his identification badge on his jacket, "Ernest. Did he say where he was going?"

Ernest shook his head.

Enid smiled sweetly - it was quite effective at distracting men - and sighed. "I was going to surprise him."

"I think he'd like that. He didn't seem himself, if you don't mind me saying. He looked like he could use some cheering up."

"Thank you, Ernest." Enid tipped him a coin and walked outside.

The moon was on the rise. The street light in the centre of the intersection buzzed and flickered. Something stirred in the Aether. The hair on Enid's neck prickled and tugged.

A man strode across the street towards her, his head down. It was Owen.

Her heart raced.

He glared at the top floor of the hotel, frowned, and shoved his hat on his head. He cursed under his breath and stormed into the hotel. Faint music wafted into the street, smothered as the door slammed shut behind him.

Enid hesitated; she'd never seen him so upset, but she didn't have time to console him. Not tonight. Time was short. The Fae Queen would return in less than three days, expecting the Heir to be delivered, unharmed.

Enid slid into the shadows of the lane beside the hotel.

The air shuddered. A faint buzz, like a distant swarm of bees, resonated through the Aether.

Enid raised her umbrella.

Another shudder.

A pulse of unseen energy rolled over her skin. The sharp tang of fresh ozone filled her nostrils. The tip of her umbrella sparked and crackled. Something was wrenching at the Aether, cleaving it apart.

She sucked in a sharp breath, and searched the western sky. Dense clouds cloaked the moon. An eerie, green light flickered across their underside.

A horse and buggy trotted past, seemingly oblivious to the tumult.

Her heart pounded. Her fingers tingled; the buzzing spread through her body. The air shifted, and convulsed, like a tidal wave being sucked toward the green light.

Then silence.

Bollocks! Enid rushed into the intersection and tightened her grip on the handle of her umbrella. Had the Fae returned early?

A loud crack resounded along the buildings. Another wave of energy flung her towards the curb, and slammed her against the post of the hotel's awning. A sharp pain shot down her spine.

A ball of green light belched into the sky from between the buildings, just a few blocks away. It ripped through the cloud cover, and flashed across the intersection. An eerie glow settled over the street.

Enid's heart raced.

The sound of a distant motorcar horn, rattling carriages, and muted music flooded over her. The horse hooves echoed, thudding along the street as if nothing had happened.

The ground rumbled under her feet. She pushed herself off the post, raced to her motorcar in the side lane, and jumped into the seat. A garden gnome, clad in red, with black, pupilless eyes, leaned on the passenger seat.

"Come on, Red. We have work to do."

chapter ten

the steering wheel vibrated under Enid's palms as the red Lincoln sped towards the grumbling green clouds circling the city. A strong wind led her along Rundle Street, drawing with it motor exhaust, horse dung and coal dust.

Raucous laughter erupted ahead of her. An angry shout snapped her attention back to the road. A swaggering knot of uniformed men in the middle of the street gestured at her.

Enid cursed, and punched the horn in the middle of the steering wheel. The revellers scattered. The Lincoln screeched to a halt in front of the shoe shop. A closed sign dangled in the window.

"Wait here," whispered Enid to the garden gnome on the passenger seat. She patted its red cap. "Guard the motorcar."

Enid stumbled out of the vehicle. The ground vibrated under her feet. The shop sign jiggled. She rattled the handle. Locked.

She glanced over her shoulder; the soldiers were preening on the opposite footpath.

Enid wrapped her fingers around the handle.

Bollocks. Her Focus was still in the Lincoln. She groaned. A Protector's magic required a Focus. Without it, she was useless. Sylvia was right; she needed to concentrate on her duties.

Enid rushed back to the motorcar.

She snatched up the umbrella from the passenger seat, and returned to the shop.

Laughter percolated out from the side street. The clicks of high heels heralded a pack of flappers in knee-length dresses and short, bobbed hair. A cloud of cigarette smoke followed them.

The women waved and joined the young men across the street. They drifted back to the footpath and congregated around the Pharmacy next to the shoe shop.

The ground shuddered. Enid staggered forward.

"Had too much to drink, love?" They snickered.

A low rumble spread out from the building, increasing in intensity until Enid's ears rang, drowning out their laughter, the Aether's protestations apparently unnoticed.

Another shudder.

Enid glanced in the wing mirror. Still no reaction. They hadn't flinched.

Cigarette smoke clawed the back of her throat. They wouldn't be leaving any time soon. She leaned against the Lincoln's door and harrumphed. She needed to get inside to access the Sanctuary entrance. But Olive had said they'd used the back entrance of the Sanctuary. Perhaps the front entrance was at the rear of the shop? She pulled her cloche low on her head, strode into the delivery lane behind the buildings.

The service lane was black as charcoaled scones. A remnant of streetlight hovered at its edge. Aether clouds swirled above the buildings. Enid's hair fluttered in the draught. Crates wobbled. She slipped into their quivering shadows.

Another wave of green Aether slammed into the ground, rushed out of the lane, sucked a row of barrels with it, and smashed her into the wall.

The blast reversed direction. Crates creaked. The gale whipped at Enid's skirt, tugging it upwards. A stench of sulphur flowed with it.

Enid crept forward, feeling her way further into the dark lane. A crate rattled. She ducked behind a pile of crates, snapped off her driving gloves, and inched towards the back entrance of the shoe shop.

She raised her umbrella, and whispered: "*Illumino.*"

A faint green thread of light drifted from the umbrella tip, and bathed the brick wall in front of her. Enid ran her hand along the bricks, searching for an entrance. The wall buzzed under her palm.

There!

She touched the wall with the tip of her umbrella. The green glow trickled down the walls of the lane and outlined an entry portal to the left of the shop door.

She whispered again: "*Revelo.*"

The door remained closed.

"Bollocks." Enid thumped the wall. What was she doing wrong? What were Olive's instructions inside the shop? The entrance to the Sanctuary was Otherworld Magic. *Old Magic.*

Enid grinned. Words wouldn't work; she had to *feel* it.

She hooked her umbrella over one arm, placed her palms against the door, and imagined the door opening.

Still nothing.

Her arms dropped by her side. It had worked last time. Perhaps the Shoemaker had re-enforced the portal magic? Or... She sucked in a sharp breath. Or barred her from entry?

The wall vibrated.

The air buzzed. Enid's skin prickled. Her muscles twitched. Something was wrong.

The portal outline shimmered. Bricks twisted and blurred, crumbling as the wall bulged outward. The portal snapped open.

Approaching footsteps slapped on wooden stairs. A familiar face appeared in the darkness.

Enid's heart raced. "What's happening?"

"Don't just stand there." Olive's face contorted. "Run!" She lunged forward, towards the disintegrating portal.

Enid jumped clear, and sheltered behind a crate.

Cobblestones trembled and danced under her feet. The crates shuddered and splintered to the ground. The portal's perimeter pulsed and wavered. Enid's Focus sputtered; the light fizzled.

Aether spiralled downwards, picking up speed. It hissed and shrieked through the lane and towards the portal, dragging her, and the crates, with it.

Enid flung up her arms, squeezed her eyes shut, and braced herself.

A thunderous clap reverberated through her body. Aether swept her up, threw her across the lane, and pinned her against the wall.

Pain wracked her body. Mist engulfed her, crushed her chest.

The very air howled. No, the howl was hers. Her lungs burned. Her head buzzed. She gasped for oxygen.

"No." Enid clawed the brick. "Olive, come back!"

The portal was shut. Olive was trapped inside.

The pressure eased. Enid's fingers twitched. She slid down the wall.

Rough brick scraped her cheek. Enid's stomach twisted. She *had* to tell Sylvia. Her stomach completed the knot.

Enid took a long, deep breath. Her mind raced. What would Sherlock do? Not even his logic could defeat *Old Magic*.

Another slow breath. What would Olive do?

A smile tugged at her lips. She rose to her feet, turned, and knocked on the wall four times.

Nothing happened.

Enid's palms stung. She winced. Small droplets of blood had beaded along fine grazes, tracking along her empty palms to her fingers.

Empty; her Focus was gone. Again. Sylvia would be furious.

Wisps of green mist swirled around her feet. A flurry of eddies rippled across the cobblestones. A barrel rolled into a shamble of broken crates. A sulphurous stench caught in her nostrils.

Enid's muscles tensed. Not from the Pharmacy. Too far away. She searched the shadows. Something glinted red.

Troll. She plunged her hand into the mist again; her Focus *had* to be there. She widened the search arc, keeping one eye on the troll.

Her eyes pricked. Water filled their rims. Her vision blurred. She blinked. Tears rolled down her cheeks. She licked the salty water from her lip, and cursed under her breath. The red glint was gone.

The mist thinned as it flowed over the fallen crates. Soft moonlight bathed the lane, revealing a dark mound amongst the debris.

Something fluttered in the corner of her eye. A scratch sounded on the cobblestones. She glanced in its direction. The umbrella skittered across the cobblestones toward her.

The mound remained motionless.

A faltering light flashed over its surface, and encased it. The mound shivered, and moaned.

Enid's heart pounded. She reached for the umbrella.

The mound convulsed.

"Bollocks." Her fingertips brushed the handle.

Aether crackled. Blue light flared. A wave of warm air rolled over her. Then, silence.

A ghostly figure unfurled from the mound, in a sphere of swirling blue light. Aether mist steamed over its surface, and trickled up the building.

The sphere moved closer, halting a few feet in front of Enid. The figure reached out a hand towards her.

Enid lunged for her Focus. Her fingernails scraped the cobblestones. It was gone.

"Bollocks."

The sphere flickered. Enid held her breath.

The light faded. The figure leaned forward, smiled, and held the umbrella handle towards her.

"I won't tell Sylvia, if you don't." The voice was calm, soothing, and familiar.

"Olive!" Enid embraced her friend.

"I thought you were trapped in an Otherworld." Enid pulled Olive to her feet.

Olive stumbled past Enid, slapped her hands against the wall, and mumbled under her breath.

"The link is severed," whispered Enid. "They're trapped."

"It is I who am trapped." Olive's hands slid down the brick wall.

"But you made it back safely," said Enid.

"But he's... I..." Olive sniffed. Her eyes were red-rimmed.

Enid's heart cracked; the Shoemaker was more than just an old friend. She hugged her friend tight.

Olive winced.

Enid's heart sank into her stomach. "Are you hurt?"

She released her grip, jumped back, and examined her friend.

Dirt covered her peacock blue, silk dress. The hem was ripped, Olive's knees scraped. Bruises had already begun to form on her shoulders. Tousled curls tumbled across her face. Olive flicked them away, smudging the smear of blood on her chin.

Enid grabbed Olive's hands, turned them over, and inspected the palms. Deep cuts and splinters covered them. She gasped.

"I'll fix it." She placed her palm over Olive's.

"It's nothing." Olive snatched away her hands and dusted off her dress. Faint streaks of blood stained the silk. She groaned. "This was Frank's favourite dress."

Enid's heart ached. She raised her umbrella.

Olive shook her head. "If Sylvia found out we'd wasted magic for personal gain..."

"Please, let me do this for you."

Olive's husband had been mortally wounded, the day before Armistice; she'd suffered more than either of them. She deserved this one thing, even if Sylvia would consider it a frivolous use of energy.

"Would you rather Sylvia to find out you've visited the Shoemaker again?" asked Enid.

Olive glared at her.

"Then, I'll do it." Olive reached for her handbag on her arm. "I can't allow you to get into trouble." She froze, and sucked in a sharp breath. "It's gone!"

Olive dropped to her knees and swept her hands through the remnants of mist hugging the ground. She kicked through shards of shattered wood near the walls of the surrounding buildings, and lifted smaller boxes. She leaned against a larger crate, and pushed. It scraped back a few inches, then caught against something. She growled and scrabbled behind it.

"Olive?" Enid tapped her on the shoulder.

Olive pulled away, and shoved another piece of debris out of the way. The grazes on her palms had begun to bleed again.

"Olive, relax."

"I have to find it," hissed Olive.

Tears rimmed Enid's eyes. It wasn't the handbag, but the loss of the contents that tormented Olive; the fountain pen - her Focus - was a gift from her husband the day he left for war. Losing the Shoemaker had disturbed the memory. She had now lost two loves.

"*Revela.*" Enid retreated and arced the tip of her umbrella over the laneway. The handle hummed in her hand. The tip crackled. A pulse of Aether fanned over the area.

She turned slowly, searching every crevice. The handle thrummed. She peered at a glowing smudge on the sandstone wall near the lane entrance, near a collapsed stack of crates.

"I've found it," Enid pointed towards the rubble. Another faint green glow seeped out from behind an upturned crate.

Olive dived in the direction of the pile, pushed aside the crates, and snatched up her handbag. She rummaged through its contents, and pulled out the gold fountain pen. She slowly turned it over, and smiled, then replaced it in her handbag and clipped it shut.

"Everything all right?" asked Enid.

Olive nodded. The blue light of her amulet still pulsed on her chest.

"Your amulet," whispered Enid.

Her Focus tugged towards the sandstone building.

Olive scanned the sandstone surface, and frowned. "There's nothing there."

Enid's heart tightened in her chest. There'd been something there before; she'd assumed it had just been an Aether echo.

"*Revela.*" Enid touched her Focus to the wall, and held her breath.

A second wave of energy spread out over the wall. The stone squirmed. A bulge rippled across its surface.

Enid's Focus sputtered and faded in a sparking pop.

The smell of ozone surged over her, quickly followed by the pungent stench of sulphur. Enid's stomach churned.

"Can you smell that?" asked Olive. "Like rotten eggs?"

Enid screwed up her nose, and stepped back. She'd smelled that stench before.

The wall bulged again. Another wave of stench rolled over them. Olive spluttered and coughed.

Enid sucked in a quick breath, regretting it immediately.

"It's a--" She gagged. Her stomach clenched, pushing acid up her throat.

"Troll!" Olive fumbled to unhook the clasp of her handbag.

"Show yourself, coward." Enid pointed her Focus at the undulating rock; there was little they could do until the creature was exposed.

The stones groaned and ground over each other. A shape formed. Sand trickled to the ground as the creature detached itself from the wall. A rocky limb pulled free of the sandstone. Then another. Its eye glinted red as it turned to face them.

Its leg lurched from the wall. The ground crunched underfoot as it landed. Stone dust spat from the cobblestones.

"You're not getting away this time," hissed Enid.

Olive scowled and raised her fountain pen. "*Sis--*"

It punched the wall. A wave rippled down the building and ripped outward across the lane. The ground trembled and buckled under their feet. Enid's umbrella waggled aimlessly as she struggled to keep her balance.

Olive tumbled backwards and tripped over one of the scattered boxes. She cursed, and flung out her hand to keep her balance. Her fountain pen ricocheted across the lane. Blue light fizzled at its tip.

"Olive!" Enid staggered back to join her.

The stones rumbled back home as the troll pulled clear of the wall. It grinned, and sprinted towards the lane entrance.

"No!" Olive lunged in the direction of her Focus and swung it in the troll's direction. "*Siste.*"

Blue light spewed from the tip, splintered into several filaments, and arced along the lane after the troll, expanding into a glowing net.

The troll roared with laughter. It scraped a gnarled hand along the building as it retreated. Chunks of stone sprayed across the lane, and stung Enid's face.

She growled, flicked her umbrella open as a second shower of stone pellets rained down on her, thrust it up to form a shield, and raced after the creature.

The ground rumbled and shifted under Enid's feet, with each troll-stomp.

It glanced back at her. Its fiery eye flickered. It laughed - a low rumbling chortle, like grating rocks - and lumbered southward, towards Grenfell Street.

"No, you don't." The troll's thuds almost drowned out her voice.

"Enid, wait!"

Enid ignored her plea; she wouldn't let it escape this time. She sprinted after the creature, and skidded on loose gravel at the lane entrance. She caught the corner of the building to steady herself.

Laughter thundered in the distance. The gravel shifted, rolled across the footpath, and spiralled upward, wrapping Enid in its funnel.

Grit scratched her eyes. Dust filled her lungs.

Something grabbed her umbrella and yanked her to one side, free of the whirligig.

"Did you see that?" Enid stumbled forward, gasping for fresh air. A hint of sulphur caught in her throat.

"Yes, very impressive." Olive's high heels crunched the gravel. She glanced at her shoes, and sighed.

Gravel dust had dulled the shine of her black, patent leather *Sunday* shoes - quite impractical for chasing a troll Bounty Hunter. Enid expected she'd dressed up to impress the Shoemaker. She grinned.

Olive's cheeks flushed red. "We're just friends."

"And did you get want you wanted?" asked Enid.

The red of Olive's cheeks deepened. "Where's your motorcar?"

"Round front," replied Enid.

"We haven't got time,' said Olive. "It's getting away."

Enid followed, and sniffed the air. The troll's stench lingered. "Can you smell it?"

Olive nodded. "This way." She sprinted after the creature.

Grenfell Street was deserted. Businesses had closed for the day. A lone light burned in a first floor window of the Grenfell Buildings, to the west. A few stragglers dribbled out of the local eating establishments. A couple paraded along the footpath, taking advantage of the crisp spring evening.

A horn blared. The troll dodged the oncoming motorcar.

No, you don't. Enid stepped into the street, not taking her eyes off her quarry.

"Enid!" Olive grabbed her sleeve and pulled her back onto the footpath.

Horse hooves thudded close by. A whip cracked.

"Watch it!" The carriage clattered. A horse spluttered in her ear. Warm breath blasted her neck.

"Bloody hell, woman." The driver glowered at her. "Watch where you're going."

"It wouldn't risk being seen," whispered Olive. "It must have a *Glamour.*"

"And it's getting away." Enid shrugged her arm free from Olive's grip.

The troll struck a building opposite, and continued onward. Its throaty laugh echoed off the stone buildings and rumbled back along Gawler Place. The buildings trembled as the shock wave approached.

The horse whinnied. Leather creaked.

"What the--" The driver yanked on the reigns. Metal jangled and clattered against wood.

"Easy, easy." The driver clicked his tongue. "Walk on."

The horse pawed the ground and refused to move.

The tip of Olive's fountain pen flashed in the corner of her eye.

"Oh, no. Not *him*." She pulled Enid back behind the fidgeting horse.

"Not who?" asked Enid.

"Whitington," replied Olive. "The reporter from the picnic."

"Where?" Enid shifted to see past the horse.

A tall man, with a camera slung over his shoulder, stood on the opposite footpath. His inquisitive gaze darted along the street. He pulled a black notebook out of his jacket pocket and strode towards the panicking couple. It was the same man who'd taken a keen interest in the dead troll at the picnic.

"What's he doing here?" she asked.

Another rumble. Whitington stumbled towards the couple. The horse shied.

Enid planted her feet on the ground to steady herself.

"Easy," cooed the driver.

"We can't let him see us," said Olive. "Sylvia and I paid him a visit today. It's too soon since Sylvia--" She glanced up at the driver, and wiggled her finger at her head. "If he sees us, it could rouse the memory."

Enid ducked behind the carriage and grabbed the horse's harness.

The Grenfell Buildings groaned. The light on the first-floor balcony flickered. A figure appeared at the corner balcony as the stone balustrade twisted. The promenading couple jumped away from under the balcony. The woman screamed and batted stone fragments from her hat.

The horse reared.

"Woah!" The driver pulled hard on the reins.

Enid grabbed its mane and nudged its shoulder. It huffed, and pawed at the ground.

"Easy, boy." She patted the horse on its neck.

"What's going on?" The driver's head jerked around towards the noise and peered along the building roofs. "Is it the Electricity Works?"

Civilians emerged from the buildings and huddled in the middle of the street, panic in their eyes.

Enid's heart thumped. She had to protect them. It was her duty. But they couldn't know the truth; there had to be a mundane explanation for the destruction. She gripped her umbrella. Green light played across her fingers.

Olive stayed her hand. "We can't let them see--"

"I know."

The building behind them rattled. More stones crumbled to the footpath.

"I have an idea." She sucked in a breath, and yelled: "Earthquake!"

The driver's head snapped in the direction of the crumbling stone. The colour drained from his face.

"Earthquake!" He glanced at Enid and Olive. "Get away from the buildings. Find cover." He wrapped the reigns tight around his hands and slapped the horse's flanks. "Hiya!"

The carriage raced eastward. The civilians scattered. Mr Whitington shoved his notebook into his pocket and unhooked his camera from his shoulder. He dodged some falling debris, and stormed off after them.

Perfect. The way was clear. Enid brandished her umbrella, and dashed across the street. "Come on, Olive. Time to hunt troll."

The troll veered left at the Bank. A trail of fallen stone chunks littered the footpath. Enid and Olive trotted along the footpath, checking alleys between buildings as they went. Enid paused at the next intersection.

Olive halted beside her and adjusted one of her shoes. Stone dust covered the toes.

"Where did it go?" hissed Olive.

Enid inhaled deeply, and screwed up her nose. "Follow the smell."

They tracked the lingering stench eastward along the next cross street. A shadow moved under a street light up ahead.

"There!" Enid yelled louder than intended.

A red glint shifted in the shadows. The troll growled.

The ground reverberated under their feet. Windows rattled in the corner building, beside them. The rumble advanced north, back the way they had come.

"Got you." She sprinted down Gawler Place, after the troll. "Hurry, we can't let it escape."

The troll's thundering footsteps faded around the corner.

Street lamps along the centre of the adjoining road flicked in its wake. The footpaths were deserted of pedestrians.

The wind changed, gusting down from the hills, bringing with it coal dust from the Electric Company, and forcing the lingering trail of sulphur down their throats.

They followed the ground tremors east. A horse-drawn coal cart galloped towards them. A motorcar clattered past, turned north, and sped away from the path of the tremors.

Singing wafted through the open, arched windows beyond the white rectangular columns of The People's Palace. A single, sombre jingle of a tambourine provided musical accompaniment.

The wind shifted again, this time blowing at their backs.

Enid froze. If she could smell the creature, it would likely smell them now.

"Anything in those legends about a troll's sense of smell?" She searched the shadows beyond the pools of street lighting.

Olive shrugged.

A shadow flitted on the opposite side of Pultney Street; it hugged the shadows, avoiding the lights at the intersection, and it was gone.

Enid sprinted across the street; the time for caution and stealth was past. The troll knew they were in pursuit. Olive's faltering footsteps lagged behind.

Enid kept moving. Her heart thumped with each step. Faster. Faster. She had to catch that son of a--

"Enid, wait!"

Enid cursed. She slowed, and grabbed a pale stone quoin of the corner bluestone building. She gulped for air and bent over.

"You're out of shape." Olive hobbled up to her, wincing each time she put her weight on her left foot. "Perhaps you shouldn't drive that fancy car of yours everywhere?" Olive wiggled the shoe on her foot.

Enid drew in a ragged breath. "At least I wear sensible shoes."

"Just so." Olive flicked off both shoes, wiggled her toes, and examined the heels of her shoes. Several chips marred the smooth, black leather. She ran her finger over the leather and frowned. "These were brand new."

"It's gone." Enid scanned the street. There was no sign, or smell, of the creature. Her breaths slowed.

"Perhaps it's melded into the stone?" Olive extricated a silk scarf from her handbag, wrapped up her beloved shoes and exchanged them for her fountain pen.

Enid launched herself off the wall and examined the stone.

Olive poked her on the shoulder. Enid spun on her heel and thrust her Focus forward; Olive caught it in one free hand.

"Ruddy hell, Olive." Her heart sprang into her throat, almost choking her. "I could have--"

"There." Olive nodded towards Wakefield Street.

Enid spun on her heel.

A tram rattled south down the centre of the street towards them. The troll sprinted out of the shadows and veered towards the tram.

Enid frowned. The creature had zig-zagged its way eastward. She'd assumed it was heading for the safety of the hills.

It trailed the tram as it passed them, and ducked behind the wooden carriage.

"No you don't." Enid bolted after it.

Olive footsteps padded behind her.

The clatter of the tram drowned out Enid's footsteps she chased the tram.

The troll grabbed the metal hand rail and swung itself up onto the tram step.

"Oi, you." A smartly-uniformed conductor leaned through a carriage window. "No vagrants allowed."

Enid held her breath. What if the troll's *Glamour* had faded?

"No pay, no ride." yelled the conductor. "Bugger off!"

Enid let out her breath; they saw only a bum trying to cadge a free ride.

The troll pivoted on the rail and raised its arm to strike.

"Enid!" Olive's voice pierced the Aether.

Enid aimed her Focus at the creature. "*Ferio.*"

Electricity sparked on the cable above the tram, snaked down its arm, and enveloped the carriage chassis. The troll jumped free, and sped off towards the fire station.

Enid ran faster.

The creature chortled and stomped the ground. A low rumble rippled outward along the metal tram track. The tram shuddered. Passengers' shrieks pierced the air.

The troll thundered closer to the fire station.

"*Siste.*" Olive hobbled past, her fountain pen fixed on her quarry.

The troll's laugh choked. Its limbs slowed, as if crawling through Enid's prize-winning lemon butter.

It snarled, and slammed its fist into the macadamed road surface. Dust and gravel spewed into the air as the road undulated towards them.

A light flickered in the window at the far end of the fire station's first floor. Enid's heart raced; they needed to finish this before the occupants emptied into the streets to witness the fray.

"I don't think that was a good idea, Olive." The tip of Enid's umbrella scraped against the road. "They'll see us."

"Not through my wards." Olive muttered under her breath and curved the fountain pen in the air above her to inscribe a circle. The Aether glimmered and rippled, creating a translucent blue sphere around them.

The troll jerked forward.

"No, you don't," hissed Enid.

A thread of green light snared the creature. It roared, and pushed its fist deeper into the earth. The ground rumbled.

"*Surge.*" Enid levelled her umbrella in its direction, grasped her Focus with both hands, and concentrated. The thread coiled around the troll's arm and over its torso.

The troll clawed at the ground as the Aether thread thickened, and wrenched its fist from the ground. The rumbling ceased.

The creature howled.

"Be silent." Enid's voice boomed through the Aether.

The trapped troll whipped through the air and smashed into a wrought iron light pole on the footpath. It grabbed the pole and held tight. Enid yanked the umbrella in the opposite direction, trying to pull the creature from its new anchor.

Light flickered in the fire station window nearest the light pole.

"I can't hold the *Concealment Wards* much longer." Olive's voice was close to Enid's ear.

"I'm trying." Enid grit her teeth and pulled the Aether cord tighter.

Tortured metal screeched as the light pole separated from the footpath. The light fizzled. The street went dark. Electric sparks showered the Aether sphere. Dark patches scarred where they touched. Cracks formed in the surface.

The troll dropped to the ground and stumbled to its feet. Enid fell backwards. Gravel ground into her palm, opening fresh grazes.

The troll swung the pole through the Aether cord, and tossed it onto the tram cables. The cables snapped. Sparks snaked along the lines.

Screaming passengers poured out of the carriage. The tram moaned and lurched to one side, the sparks erupting into flames.

Muted bells clanged in the fire station.

"Are you all right?"

Olive stood behind Enid, fountain pen in one hand; the other still supporting the protective sphere. The cracks widened.

"I can't hold it much longer." Olive's arm trembled.

Enid caught her breath and hauled herself to her feet. The occupants of the station were stirring. There was no time.

A siren blared, still partly muffled by the failing *Concealment Ward*s. Lights blazed in the station windows. The front doors clattered open.

"We've got company," she said.

"I can't--" Olive's knees buckled.

Enid searched beyond the *Wards*. A blurred shadow lumbered towards the next street light, in the opposite direction to the burning tram.

Olive muttered under her breath. Blue light engulfed the troll. It howled.

"That won't slow it for long." She probed the fragmented road with her bare toes and lowered her foot gingerly. She sucked a sharp breath through her teeth.

Two fire trucks rolled into the street. Men in heavy uniforms, shiny buttons and hats poured out of the gaping maw on the station's ground level.

"They can handle the fire." Enid tugged Olive out of the crumbling Wards and shoved her towards a dark alleyway next to the neighbouring building.

The bells faded as the trucks raced towards the tram.

"I think I know where it's going." Olive squirmed free of Enid's grip. Her face was pale. "And it's not good." She brushed the soles of her feet and peeked around the corner into the street.

"Well...?" Enid frowned.

"They're gone." Olive returned to the street. "Come on."

"Where's it going?" Enid followed her along the unlit footpath.

"It's heading for a portal." replied Olive.

"There's more than one?" asked Enid.

"There are several hidden around town." Olive caught her breath. "There's one in Botanic Park, and another near St Francis' church."

"How do you know?" Enid asked.

"Orrug had a map."

"The Shoemaker?" Enid shook her head. "He was just trying to impress you, Olive."

Olive glared at her.

"Orrug would never lie to me." She slowed, her breaths shallow. "If a bounty hunter has found one, then the whole portal system could be in danger." She picked her way around a crater of rubble. "We can't let that happen."

The ground crunched under their feet. Olive winced, and propped herself against the closest lamp pole.

"What's wrong?" Enid halted.

Blood oozed from several cuts on Olive's soles. She clenched her teeth as she picked out a piece of glass.

The street light sputtered above her. Glass from the shattered lantern covered the footpath.

Another street light fizzled in the distance.

"Trolls are stronger in the dark." Olive picked another glass shard from her foot. "I'm slowing you down. You go. Catch it."

Enid nodded and sprinted along the footpath towards St Frances

Xavier church. Her heels clicked on the concrete, echoing Olive's words: *Catch it. Catch it.*

Enid raced past the Boy's School. The smell of cooking wafted out of the alley. Her stomach grumbled. She slowed to savour the aroma of bacon and...

There was movement under the trees.

She froze. "Come out. I know you're there."

A motorcar horn blasted behind her. She jumped back, and span on her heel, to relocate the troll.

It was gone.

She sniffed the air for its foul scent. Nothing.

"Bollocks." Enid felt the cool concrete of the footpath. Faint vibrations came from the direction of the church. She crept forward, sniffing the air for the creature's scent. It couldn't have gotten far. She quickened her pace.

The multi-coloured stone walls of St Francis Church cast deep shadows in the moonlight. High peaked roofs, each topped with an iron cross, jutted out at the far end. Tall, Gothic-revival, arched windows - grouped in threes - reminded her of the catechism her father had taught her as a child. A high wood-paling fence braced between square plinths defined the holy ground.

A shadow flickered along the palings. Enid crouched behind the corner of the fence, as the troll hauled itself up a plinth.

"*Ferio.*" A pulse of green Aether shot past its head.

"Is that the best you have, Protector?" Its gravelly laugh reverberated through Enid's chest.

"You know what I am?" asked Enid.

"I was warned there was competition." He swung over the fence.

The ground shook as it landed on the other side.

Enid touched her Focus to the ground. "*Subvolo.*"

She launched into the air, jumped onto the square top of the fence post, and aimed at the troll.

The creature's eye flared red. It waggled a stony finger at her and tsked.

"You can't touch me here." It swung its arms wide. "This is holy ground." Its laugh grated on Enid's nerves. "You know the rules, Protector."

Bollocks. The creature was correct. The *Law of Sanctuary* was clear; all Sacred Places - cemeteries, churches, and shrines - were places of Sanctuary. No being, Otherworldly or not, was to be harmed on such ground.

Enid growled.

The troll backed away, towards the rear of the church. Light shimmered behind it. Colours swirled as the portal grew.

A dull hum filled the air. The fence rippled.

Enid's skin prickled. Her hands trembled. This one-eyed daemon had murdered its kin, destroyed the Shoemaker's Sanctuary, and almost killed her fellow Protector. Most of all, it had attacked her beloved Owen.

Enid's blood boiled. Her fingernails dug into the cuts on her palms.

"Until next time." It turned to face the portal.

She would not let it escape.

"*Clausum.*" She punched her Focus forward.

Green lightning forked from its tip, engulfed the portal in a shifting shell of Aether. The portal shuddered. The lightning contracted, collapsing the edges of the portal with it.

The troll roared, and rushed the opening. The Aether shell buckled.

The wooden fence palings rattled and danced as energy rebounded towards Enid. She reeled backwards.

The troll thrust one arm into the portal. Energy pulsed through its arm. It grinned, and buried its fist further into the Aether.

"No, you don't!" Enid strained to control the flow of energy. Pain flashed up her arm. The umbrella handle of her Focus glowed green, then red. Her skin smouldered. She pulled harder.

"*Dest--*" Her fingers trembled. Beads of sweat trickled down her temples. It felt as if energy was being siphoned from every cell in her body. "*Destruo.*"

Sparks flew from the umbrella's tip. Smoke drifted out between her fingers. Her skin burned.

Enid squeezed her eyes shut and screamed. The umbrella thudded to ground.

Light bled through her eyelids. She was flung backwards. She forced her eyes open.

There was nothing but a blood-curdling scream to fill the void.

chapter eleven

he Maître'D led Owen and Doyle to Owen's regular table in Winter Garden Room. Owen sat under one of the giant palms. Doyle sat in the wicker chair opposite him.

"The usual, Gentlemen?" asked the waiter.

They nodded.

"I regret I couldn't attend the picnic at the Sanctuary," said Owen. "You made quite an impression on my Enie." He shovelled up a mouthful of bacon.

Doyle frowned.

Owen examined Doyle's plate: fried mushrooms, and toast. Was he one of those vegetari-what's-its? He swallowed and washed it down with a swig of coffee.

"I do apologise." He cleared his throat of the offending morsels. "Are you--?"

"I'm mostly vegetarian, except for fish." Doyle unslung his camera and placed it on the table next to his plate. "Don't stop on my account."

Owen picked at the rasher, then slipped his egg on the toast. The yolk broke and seeped into the crisp bread.

"Miss Enid Turner?" Doyle's frown faded. "The lady with the exquisite Red Lincoln Tourer?" He smiled. "Sensible woman. Love those - what do you call them - biscuits?"

"She's quite a fan of yours, you know." Owen dug his fork into his egg. "Unfortunate business about the chauffeur."

Doyle sipped his tea.

"Aren't those at the scene considered likely suspects?" continued Owen. "Perhaps you could assist me in clearing her name?" He crunched on a piece of toast. A drop of egg yolk threatened to escape.

Doyle's frown returned.

Owen couldn't let him lose interest; he needed his insight to prove the Crones' nefarious motives.

"My investigative abilities pale in comparison with your own." He lowered his fork. "Your defence of Sir Roger Casement, for example."

Doyle's teacup clinked on its saucer. "The man was vilified of his predilections."

"The police are investigating, of course." Owen leaned forward.

"Yes," said Doyle.

"There are rumours about fairies." His heart raced. The hotel was abuzz with rumours, yet Enid had still said nothing.

"Fairies? I..." Doyle's voice cracked. He closed his eyes, and rubbed the bridge of this nose. "I'm sorry. Don't remember."

"Give it time." Owen stabbed his toast. "I don't suppose you took any photos?" He tapped the top of the box-shaped camera. "I'd love to see the magnificence of the Sanctuary for myself."

"The Constabulary--" Doyle winced. "I seem to--" He rubbed his temple. "The police confiscated everyone's film."

Owen thrummed his fingers on his knee. "Are you all right, Sir Arthur?"

"Just a headache." Doyle buried his head his hand.

Owen caught the attention of the waiter.

"Aspirin for Sir Arthur," said Owen.

The waiter poked his head past the palm, nodded, and returned with a packet of Bex and a glass of water. The white powder fizzed as it dissolved and sank into the liquid. Doyle quaffed down the drink.

"Perhaps some fresh air?" Owen was determined not to let the author out of his sight. He gulped down the rest of his breakfast. He'd need a full stomach for the day ahead.

Electric lights burned in the wall sconces, casting stark pools of light on the lush hotel carpet; its arrowed diamonds ushered the hotel's patrons to the Dining Room.

Owen Barrington sat in a padded armchair opposite the lift, and waited. He'd woken early and ventured downstairs to resume his post, in hopes of catching Doyle on the way to breakfast.

A bleary-eyed porter snapped to attention as he approached Owen, nodded, and ducked into the kitchen.

The smell of bacon and freshly toasted bread wafted along the corridor and tantalised his taste buds. He drew in a deep breath and licked his lips.

His stomach grumbled. He'd missed dinner last night. He leaned on the arm of the chair and peered at the wall clock above the foyer door. *Half past eight.* He'd been ensconced in the armchair since seven-thirty. He stifled a yawn; he was usually still in bed at this ungodly hour.

He shifted in his seat to relieve the nerve in his leg, and rubbed his sore wrist, still aching from the previous day's surveillance, and lit a cigarette. The smoke burned his lungs, but the nicotine calmed his nerves; its work was done.

He stared at the lift, willing it to open. Enid's 'friends' had already cost one man's life. He wouldn't let them steal hers as well. But he wasn't an investigator; he needed Doyle's help. With Doyle's predilection for the supernatural, and past involvement with the British Constabulary, he may be the only one he could trust to unearth the truth behind the Crones' plans. He just needed to convince the man to help him.

The ding of the lift echoed in the foyer. Owen gripped the arms of the chair. He held his breath and rehearsed his opening gambit as the iron grate rattled open.

"Have a good day, sir." The lift operator's voice was chirpy for such an early hour but, then, he'd only started his shift after Owen had taken up his vigil.

A tall man stepped out of the lift. Hints of grey peppered his impeccable moustache. A camera strap dangled over his shoulder. It slipped as he pressed a coin into the lift attendant's hand. He sauntered towards the Winter Garden Room.

Owen jumped to his feet and cleared his throat.

"Sir Arthur Conan Doyle?" He thrust out his hand. "I'm Owen Barrington, the third. I must congratulate you on your recent lectures at the Town Hall."

The attendant whispered to Doyle.

"Ah yes." Doyle's eyes lit up. Small creases formed in their corners. "The painter in residence." He shook Owen's hand. "Thank you, Mr Barrington."

Another burst of mouth-watering aromas escaped as a couple left the dining area. Owen's stomach complained a second time. He stubbed out his cigarette.

"Will you join me for breakfast, Sir Arthur?" he asked.

"Reg-ist-arr-r." The paperboy's voice rang out over the hubbub of the morning traffic. Owen dropped a coin into the boy's hand, folded the paper in half, and shoved it in his pocket. He was more interested in information he could glean from his newest companion; news the papers wouldn't report.

He guided Doyle south, along Pultney Street.

A tin rattled nearby. A figure in a familiar, worn-out army coat loitered in the shade of a building overhang. The veteran smiled and winked.

Owen tipped his hat.

The Veteran rattled his tin cup a second time.

Doyle paused, patted his coat pockets. He grimaced, and rubbed his temple.

"Are you certain you're all right, Sir Arthur?" Owen dropped a coin in the Veteran's cup and continued towards Grenfell Street.

Doyle groaned. "The nurse said it'd last a few days." He shuffled a few steps and halted at the intersection.

"Sir Arthur?" asked Owen.

"I must have forgotten these." Doyle opened his hand.

Owen's heart leapt. A length of crinkled film tumbled from a cylindrical film canister in his hand.

"I should take them to the Police," continued Doyle.

"No." Owen mind raced. He needed to see those photographs... Perhaps they would shed light on why the Crones stole the reporter's photos, and how much danger Enie was in? He took a deep breath to slow his heart.

Doyle patted his pocket as if checking for another canister.

"Those rumours..." He winced. "Where--?" He shook his head, frowned. "How did you hear about them?" asked Doyle.

"The newspaper," replied Owen. "Rufus wrote an article about your visit to the wildlife sanctuary."

"I don't remember a Rufus." Doyle pressed his forehead and grimaced.

"The reporter, Whitington," replied Owen. "They are one and the same."

Doyle stared past Owen. His eyes darted from one side to the other, as if watching a private picture show. He screwed up his eyes, clearly in pain.

Owen's heart skipped. "Perhaps the film would nudge your memory?"

Doyle's frown lifted. He met Owen's gaze. There was a spark of hope.

Owen continued; he couldn't lose Doyle now: "Your third lecture on photographic images is of particular interest."

Doyle's eyes seemed to sparkle brighter.

"Perhaps you know a photographer, sympathetic to the cause? One who won't pass them onto the Police, or the papers?"

Doyle raised an eyebrow. "I see your meaning." He glanced at the street sign, and smiled. "I believe one has a studio on this very street." He marched east along Grenfell Street, scanning each building as he went.

Owen followed.

"This one." Doyle stopped.

A bell tinkled as he opened the door; another bloody fairy had wings. The irony wasn't lost on Owen.

Metal rings scraped on the curtain rod partitioning the photographer's private office from the darkroom.

"So the rumours in the newspaper were true?" Owen held out his hand.

"Never thought I'd see the like here. Not in my shop." The photographer's hand trembled. "Humbug Scrub, you say?" He held out a brown paper envelope. Several photographs tumbled out.

Owen snatched one as it fluttered to the floor. He examined the image: a paddock of gums and oak. The sky was dark. Mrs Oldham looked directly at the camera. A shiver crawled down his spine. It was as if she was staring into his soul, daring him to catch her.

Specks of light trailed around her. He peered at the largest light smudge, near her shoulder. A dragonfly. His eyes widened; the creature had a face, torso, limbs, and the face of a Botticelli angel.

"Fai--" The word caught in his throat. It couldn't be. He glanced at the photograph again. Was it his imagination, or did it move? He flipped over the photo, and swallowed. If he believed witches existed, why shouldn't he believe in fairies, when the evidence was in front of him?

The photographer collected up the photographs, handed one to Doyle, and slipped the rest back into the envelope. Beads of perspiration formed on Doyle's forehead. He sucked in a sharp breath, and grabbed his head.

The photographer slid a wooden chair behind him, and eased Doyle onto it.

"Migraine?" asked the photographer. "My wife suffers from them. I'll send my boy to fetch a doctor."

"He's under the physician at the Grand Hotel," said Owen.

The photographer nodded and pressed the brown paper envelope into Owen's hand.

"Best not let the cops get hold of these," said the photographer. "They'll hide the truth." He leaned forward, his eyes searching the front shop, and whispered: "I heard they paid a reporter a visit as well. There are some who prefer Sir Arthur hadn't come here. You probably saw them picketing his lectures?"

Owen hadn't; he hadn't attended the lectures. He snatched the folded newspaper from his pocket and flicked it open. The headlines screamed at him:

ADELAIDE CITY EARTHQUAKE
Tram in Flames. Soldier feared dead.

He skimmed the story. The quake had toppled electrical poles and burnt out a tram, with minimal injuries due to quick thinking of the driver. There was concern for an ex-soldier who disappeared, assumed burned in the fire. The Wakefield Street tram line was closed for repairs. Commuters needed to find an alternate route.

What if this wasn't an earthquake? He clutched the envelope of photographs. If Doyle's photographs showed fairies, what was in the ones the Crones had stolen? He had to speak with Whitington.

"Take Sir Arthur back to the Hotel," he said. "Tell them he's had a relapse, and needs bed rest, and no one is to see him."

"And if they ask where you've gone?" asked the photographer. "If they need to contact you?"

"Tell them I won't be long." Owen slapped his Homburg on his head. "Tell them, I'm off to see a man about a paper."

Owen strode towards *The Register*'s office building.

The morning tram rattled to a stop in front of a row of parked motorcars. Two smartly dressed women, with sensible rolled buns at the nape of their necks and notebooks in their hands, stepped off the tram.

"Come on, Sophie, we're late." They rushed across the street. The faint clicks of typewriters escaped as they opened the door to the Stott & Hoare Business School.

An attractive, young red-headed woman with a fashionable bob kissing her cheeks dodged past them. Her piercing green eyes glanced in Owen's direction. There was something familiar about her. He tipped his hat. She smiled, sidestepped him, and continued on.

Owen entered *The Register* Building and made his way to Whitington's office. The reporter leaned on his desk, phone receiver to his ear. He traced lines on a creased map with his finger, and frowned.

Owen stepped away from the door and listened.

"So, you agree? The path of the earthquake was unusual?" Whitington paused, then spoke again: "Yes, it does warrant further investigation." He scribbled notes. "Yes. Three o'clock suits me. Thank you, Professor."

He hung up, and leaned back in his chair.

Owen's heart pounded. The earthquake wasn't natural? No doubt, the work of the Crones. Perhaps he could conscript Whitington, and use his skills to gather information?

A chair scraped in the office.

Owen straightened his jacket and knocked at the door. "Mr Whitington, I presume?"

"And you are?" Whittington slipped his notes under the map.

"Mr Owen Barrington, the Third." Owen extended his hand.

Whitington's shoulders relaxed. "The resident painter at--"

"The Grand Hotel," finished Owen. "Yes."

"I knew your father." He shook Owen's hand. "Shrewd businessman. Hates scotch."

"He was a Temperance man."

"And you?" Whitington sat down.

"I must admit a weakness for a well-aged whisky."

The reporter chuckled. "Which explains why the prodigal son now resides at the Grand. What can I do for you, Mr Barrington?"

Owen removed his Homburg, placed it on the desk, and settled in the chair opposite Whitington.

"I saw your article on Sir Arthur Conan Doyle's visit in *The Register* today. I was hoping to purchase a photograph of his visit."

"You're a fan?" asked Whitington.

Owen shook his head. "My fiancée attended the picnic. She's a big fan of his. I thought I'd surprise her."

"What's her name?"

"Miss Enid Turner," replied Owen.

"Yes." He checked his notebook. "She was there for the murder. Loves biscuits. Accompanied by two friends, I believe." Whitington smiled. "Those photos are popular." He leaned forward. "I'm afraid you're too late. The police have just been here. I'm ordered not to discuss the ongoing investigation."

"You don't have any photos from the picnic?" asked Owen.

Whitington frowned and rubbed his temple.

"No, the Police took everything. I was fortunate they agreed to my request for a few photos of Sir Arthur for my next article."

Whitington propped his elbows on the desk and eyed Owen over his steepled fingers. His eyes narrowed. "You're the second person to ask me about them this morning."

Owen straightened in his chair.

"And I'll tell you the same answer I told her." Whitington rubbed the bridge of this nose. "The Police confiscated my camera on the day of the incident."

"*Her?*"

"A pretty young thing with red hair," replied Whitington. "She was at the picnic too. I think your Miss Turner drove her."

Owen glanced at the camera on the bookshelf behind the desk. If he hadn't seen the Crones at work for himself, he'd suspect Whitington was working with them.

Whitington followed his gaze. "They returned it yesterday."

"And the film?"

"Alas, it remains in evidence."

Owen leaned slowly back into the chair. The Crones already had the photographs. Who else would want them?

His heart leapt into his throat. The woman in the street, with the piercing green eyes; he'd seen her before. He rubbed his chin. The woman in the hotel lift, with the unusually charming man. His heart squirmed back down his throat and slammed into his stomach. Was she following him? Reporting back to the Crones?

Owen was on his feet, making apologies. His mind raced with

theories. None of them good. He needed answers. He had to find the girl.

He snatched up his Homburg and rushed out of the office.

Sunlight glared in his eyes as he emerged onto the footpath. He slapped on his hat and sped along the footpath, dodging pedestrians in search of the young woman.

He crossed the street near the photographer's studio. A tram clanged up behind him. He waited for it to trundle past, scanning the commuters for the red-head with piercing green eyes.

Nothing.

He turned around and examined the way he'd come.

Owen shoved his hands in his pockets and huffed. The girl was gone, and Whitington's photographs were lost to him. At least he had Doyle's photographs, and a warning of the magical threat infiltrating his world.

A flash of sunlight caught his eye, as a motorcar pulled away from the curb. Whitington stood there, watching him.

Another motorcar pulled into the vacant spot, blocking his view.

Owen turned and walked slowly towards the intersection, tracking the reporter in the corner of his eye. Whitington paralleled him, making no effort to conceal himself.

A smile flickered over Owen's lips. Whitington was curious; Owen had something he wanted. He could use that to his advantage... when the time was right.

chapter twelve

the troll glared at Enid. Its eye blazed red. Its grey, stone arm swept aside her fellow Protectors, and snatched up her beloved Owen. It grinned, crushed his lifeless body, and unfurled its hand. Debris trickled from its fingers. It ripped Enid's Focus from her grip and snapped it over its knee, and chortled. The deep rumble reverberated through Enid's body.

Green light engulfed her. She slammed into a jagged rock wall. It exploded. Dagger-like projectiles showered her, slicing into her skin.

A monstrous hand seized her waist, and squeezed. Enid writhed in its grip; her arms pinned, her Focus destroyed. She was defeated.

Flames writhed over the wall, reaching for her. The rocky hand was immune. It pulled her into the wall. She gasped for air as the flames swallowed her.

The smell of smoke burned Enid's throat. She gasped for air, and lunged forward. She clawed at the twisted sheets entangling her, and extracted her legs. Sweat drenched her nightgown.

Light streamed through the bedroom window, burrowing into her brain.

She rolled away from the light. Her muscles burned with every move.

She searched her memories: Olive was there. A burning tram, the church, and... She gasped. Pain shot through her chest. *The Fae portal.*

The troll was going to escape, then...

Pain.

Enid adjusted her breathing: shallower, less pain.

She'd destroyed the portal. The Aether backlash should have killed her.

She rubbed her eyes, dragged herself up onto her elbows, and assessed her surroundings.

Light skittered across her mother's standing mirror, accentuating every spec of grit on its surface. So, not dead then; if this was heaven, someone would have dusted.

Curtains flapped in a warm breeze. A garden gnome-shaped shadow stood motionless on the window sill. Red, her favourite garden gnome and loyal guardian, was never far away. She relaxed, just a little.

Enid glanced across the room. A midnight blue silk bodice, bustle skirt and petticoats hung from the wardrobe. Something she'd retrieved from storage. It brought back memories of tougher times, of family long dead, and of new friends.

She smiled; her Focus would incorporate well with the aesthetic. Sylvia would be relieved she'd kept it in mind when choosing her outfit.

Her heart raced at the thought of dancing with her beloved Owen. He would look resplendent in his frock coat - his Sherlock Holmes to her Irene Adler: the closest thing her fictional hero had to a great love. She sighed.

A hint of smoke tickled her nostrils. A faint smoke haze filled the room.

Enid sat up and swung her feet onto the wooden floor. Pain seared up her calves. She sucked in a sharp breath, and sniffed the air. The smell of smoke was stronger near the door.

She reached for her Focus, by the bedside table. Not there. She hissed; it was likely in the umbrella stand by the front door. Sylvia, no doubt, would scold her, yet again.

She flattened her palm on the door. Not hot; that was a good sign.

Wisps of smoke swirled in the hallway. Enid rushed down the stairs and into the kitchen. The sickly smell of burnt sugar greeted her.

A layer of smoke clung to the ceiling. The lace curtains above the sink were pulled to the side. Smoke slowly siphoned out the open window. Enid's mother's recipe book lay on the table surrounded by flour, empty lemon skins.

Olive fussed near the stove, flapping her apron vigorously at the open door of the main oven. Her hair was tousled. Flour spattered up her arm.

"Olive, what in the blazes is going on?" asked Enid.

Olive's cheeks burned a rhubarb hue. She snatched back her apron, skittered back to the centre of the room, slapped shut the book on the table, and dusted off the stack of cake plates beside it.

"I wanted to cheer you up. I followed the recipe exactly." Olive brushed hair from her eyes. "I just can't get the knack of your new stove."

Enid squashed a laugh.

"Sylvia said you'd need to eat something sweet when you woke up," continued Olive.

"Where's Sylvia?" Another wave of pain through Enid's body. Her muscles tensed.

"In the Sitting Room," replied Olive. "Consulting *The Books*. She's already read mine. Now she's studying yours," said Olive.

The Books was the name given to the Protectors' journals. They each had one, containing notes and information on all Otherworldly incursions since their arrival in Adelaide; more than eighty years of guarding local Thin Places.

Olive wrapped the corners of the apron around her hands, slipped them into the open oven door and rescued a scorched lump. Smoke trailed her to the sink. The metal cake tin clattered on the bench. China clinked on the drying rack.

"Are these new?" asked Olive. "I like the pink roses."

"Owen gave them to me," replied Enid.

"*Another* birthday present?" Olive picked up a teacup and turned it over. "These weren't cheap. But it's usually the kind of present one gets for--" She smiled and raised an eyebrow.

"I know." Enid sighed. "And he didn't."

Olive's smiled faded. She put the teacup back in the drying rack. "He's got good taste."

Enid joined her at the sink.

"Stop trying to distract me, Olive. We're almost out of time." said Enid. "And we have nothing but two destroyed Fae portals for our sins."

"Sylvia thinks someone must be hiding the Heir," said Olive.

"Are you sure it's not the Shoemaker?" asked Enid.

Olive's face paled.

"He would've told me." She lowered herself into a chair by the kitchen table.

"Would he?"

Enid swallowed. She liked the Shoemaker; he'd been kind to her when she'd lost her family. But did she really know him? It seemed their duties now conflicted. Could she still trust him?

Olive avoided her gaze. "Yes, but..." Olive's chin quivered. "He wouldn't."

Enid's heart broke. She'd never seen Olive so flustered.

"I'm sorry." She placed a gentle hand on Olive's shoulder, and smiled; Love, after all, always conquers all. "I'm sure he would tell you," she said, "Returning the Heir is to his benefit as well, after all."

"Have you told Sylvia you went back to visit him?" asked Enid.

"But Orrug said--" Olive cut herself off. Her face reddened. She shook her head.

"She needs to know about the Fae doors, and the Bounty Hunter." Enid leaned over, and sniffed the contents of the thin paper sachet lying in the bottom of one of the new teacups sitting next to Sylvia's rolled, leather satchel. It had a strong, sharp smell. She screwed up her nose.

"Better you, than me." A faint smile touched Olive's lips. She wiped her hands and shook the kettle on the stove top. A drop of water sloshed out of the spout. She replaced it.

Enid glared at her. "There's a parcel in the pantry, next to the opened jar of lemon butter. Get it will you?"

Jars clattered in the pantry. Olive returned with a small package wrapped in brown wax paper. She unwrapped it on the way back to the table. The glorious, rich aroma of sweetened cocoa wafted across the table.

Enid cut two slices and placed them on separate cake plates.

"Devil's Food cake?" Olive's gaze locked onto the parcel.

"I think you need more cheering up than me." Enid slid the larger cake plate in front of Olive.

Olive bit into the cake. "You best cut a slice for Sylvia, or--"

"Have you told her?" Sylvia's voice rang across the room with Enid's green journal wedged under one arm.

Olive spluttered, sending cake crumbs over the table. She shook her head and flicked the flecks off the tablecloth.

"Told me what?" asked Enid.

Olive avoided her gaze and pressed her fingers on the remaining cake crumbs, lifting them from the table one by one. Sylvia huffed and closed her eyes, her lips moving silently as she counted to ten.

"You really mustn't make a habit of this." Sylvia dropped a newspaper on the table as she strode over to the bench. "Recklessly attacking magic portals? What were you thinking? Have I not taught you anything? It's our job to protect this world. I can't do that if you insist on desecrating Sacred Ground." She opened the journal and flipped through the pages. "You should update your *Book* more often. There's only the barest mention of the incident at Albert Bridge. And no mention of any follow up investigation." She slapped the book shut and handed it to

Enid.

The kettle on the stove chirped, and whistled.

A cold sliver pulsed through Enid's veins. Sylvia was preparing to give her a bollocking.

"You told her?" Enid asked Olive.

"She didn't need to." Sylvia slid the kettle off the stove and poured the water into the china cup on the bench, and glared at Enid. "Every Otherworld would've felt the disruption. That's how wars start." She shoved the cup of steaming liquid in front of Enid. "Drink."

A sickly-sweet smell drifted under Enid's nose. She raised an eyebrow.

"This isn't like your last brew?" she asked Sylvia.

"No," replied Sylvia.

Enid narrowed her eyelids. "I don't have time to sleep. The Fae Queen returns tomorrow, and we still haven't found the Heir."

"I promise." Sylvia filled the teapot and cradled the pot in her hands.

Enid's stomach twisted. Sylvia rarely made promises. There was something she wasn't saying. Enid picked up the teacup, leaned back against the bench, and inhaled the vapour: a smoky aroma. And a faint sharp smell, like pine wood. It was Sylvia's special Russian blend... and something else. "Echinacea?"

Sylvia nodded. "I'll make a herbalist of you yet." She sat at the table and commandeered the second slice of cake.

Enid sipped the concoction; it was pleasantly sweet, with a slight bitterness, and a hint of eucalyptus.

"My honey?" she asked.

"The bees seemed quite agitated." replied Sylvia. "Don't worry. I asked them first. I told them it was for you."

"They've been fussing all morning," said Olive.

"They know something is coming." Enid stirred the tea, and let the teaspoon drip tea into her cup. She tapped the china and placed the spoon on the saucer. "They can feel it."

Sylvia's face paled. Her fork clattered on the plate. She returned to the sink and stared through the window.

Behind Sylvia's anger, there was dread every time the Fae were mentioned. Her encounter with the Fae had been decades ago. She never spoke of it. Enid could only guess at the horrors she had endured. Enid sipped her tea slowly, and eyed her fellow Protector over the rim of her cup.

Sylvia was the oldest of the trio, and self-appointed leader. She took control of every situation. No doubt, she was still furious about being dragged into a quest with her nemesis. She stared out the kitchen window, presumably lost in her own visions of hell.

Olive cut another slice of Devil's Food cake and stared at the table.

Enid sipped her tea. A change of topic was needed.

"Was your visit with the reporter productive?" she asked.

Sylvia's gaze flicked back to her. She let out a slow breath.

Olive swallowed a mouthful of cake.

"You were right, Enid," said Olive. "He must have swapped out the film before the police arrived."

"You have it?" asked Enid.

Olive nodded, clicked open her handbag, and frowned.

"Where are they, Olive?" Sylvia growled in a measured voice.

Olive's cheeks flushed. "I'll get them." Her chair scraped on the tiles. She scooted out of the kitchen.

The screen door slapped against the wall. Hurried footsteps crunched on the gravel footpath.

Enid watched through the open window.

Olive ran off the path, through the uncut grass, and dodged the guard of garden gnomes surrounding the Lincoln. Her legs jiggled as she leaned through the passenger door, her skirt wiggling like an orange gelatin dessert. She slid off the door, and waved an envelope in the air.

Papers cascaded onto the driveway. She dove to the ground and scooped them up, like a seagull bombarding holiday-makers.

The thwack of the screen door still echoed in Enid's ears as Olive dropped the envelope onto the table.

"Did he know anything?" asked Enid.

"He was hoping we'd provide him with his next story," replied Olive. "Which of course we didn't."

Sylvia huffed, and flipped open the newspaper on the table. She pointed to an article written under Mr Whitington's pseudonym, Rufus.

Enid scanned the page, and paused at the headline: *ADELAIDE CITY EARTHQUAKE. Tram in flames.*

"It seems you supplied him with an alternative story," she said.

Sylvia rested her elbow on the table and massaged her temple.

The grandmother clock chimed in the hall.

Olive gasped. "Enid, you need to get ready."

"Ready for what?" asked Sylvia.

Enid shifted her weight off the kitchen bench. Her muscles didn't complain as much as expected. She smiled. Sylvia's brews always worked wonders.

"Owen is taking me to the Palais tonight," replied Enid.

"Thursday is Fancy Dress night," cooed Olive.

"You'll have to inform Mr Barrington you cannot attend." Sylvia's clipped voice snapped Olive to attention. "We have a world to save, or have you forgotten? You're bound to a Fae pact. One instigated by your inattention to duty, I might add."

Enid's teacup rattled on its saucer.

"But it's a dance," whispered Olive.

"He'll wonder why I can't go," said Enid.

"And you know how curious mortals can be," continued Olive.

"We're Protectors, sworn to protect this world," Sylvia growled. "We can't get involved with mortals." Sylvia glared at Olive. "It never ends well for us."

"Orrug said--" Olive's lips tightened.

"You've seen that meddling Shoemaker again?" Sylvia stabbed a fork into the cake. "Against my specific instructions? He's as good as Fae." She slammed the fork onto the cake plate. "You can't trust them."

Sylvia lowered her voice: "And did he tell you about the Netherworld Portal?"

Olive bit her lip.

"Olive, you haven't done something reckless?" asked Sylvia.

"Tea?" China cups rattled as Enid removed them from the drying rack. She tapped the back of her hand on the teapot. Still hot. She poured two cups of tea, placed one in front of Sylvia, and the other in front of Olive. "We haven't got time to fight."

"Nothing will bring him back, Olive." Sylvia quaffed a mouthful of tea. "His time is done. You must accept that."

Enid's heart raced.

"We wouldn't know about the Fae portals if Olive hadn--"

Sylvia's death-glare shifted to Enid.

"And the Bounty Hunter is gone," stammered Enid.

"Has it?" asked Sylvia.

Enid's heart froze.

"But I saw... Enid swallowed. "...the explosion."

Sylvia sipped the remains of her tea. She picked up Olive's empty tea cup, turned it twice, and examined the leaves in the bottom. She frowned and replaced the cup on the saucer.

"A dance, you say?" she asked. "At the Palais?"

Enid nodded.

"I was supposed to meet Owen there, at quarter past seven," said Enid.

"Fae can't resist a party. It's like catnip to them." Sylvia retrieved her walking stick, and rose from her chair. "What time do we leave?"

"We're all going?" asked Olive.

"But, Owen--" Enid cut herself off.

"The Fae are devious," said Sylvia. "I know them better than you."

At least Enid wouldn't forget her Focus, this time; it was part of her costume. She opened her hand. Fine red lines marred her palm. She remembered the pain. The handle searing her flesh. She curled her fingers shut.

"Where's my Focus?" she asked.

Olive shifted in her chair.

"There's always a danger when we draw too much energy," she whispered. "You know that."

"Olive, where is it?" The lines on her palm throbbed. "Olive?" Enid's voice cracked. She rushed out of the kitchen, and into the hall. A faint whiff of acrid smoke lingered close to the door, like the smell of burnt hair. Blood pounded in her ears. She staggered forward. The umbrella stand was empty.

She spun on her heel and sniffed the air, following the foul smell. It was stronger near the hall table.

Olive hovered in the kitchen doorway, wringing her hands.

"There was nothing I could do," she whispered.

Enid's hand trembled as she curled her fingers around the drawer handle. She edged it open. The pungent stench reminded her of burning troll. Her stomach wrenched.

Inside was a broken skeleton of twisted metal. The silk canopy had shrunk away from the spokes. She gently clasped the charred wooden handle. Black beads of burnt silk crumbled into a gritty, grey-black powder.

Her amulet hummed once, faintly against her chest, and faltered. She held her breath, waiting for the siphoned energy to seep into her skin. There was no buzz. Nothing.

She struggled to breathe; a Protector needed a Focus - a personal link to the Aether. Without it they were mortal. *She* was mortal.

Enid's knees buckled. Her kneecaps smashed onto the tiled floor. Pain shot up her legs. She wailed, but not from the pain.

chapter thirteen

wen leaned against the dark brick by the entrance of the Palais Royal. Doyle had agreed to meet him at seven, before Enid arrived. Owen lit his pipe. He preferred a cigarette, but Enid had insisted he play the part. He sucked nicotine-laden smoke into his lungs, and scanned the new arrivals.

Many had taken on this week's Fancy Dress Carnival's theme, *Baby Week*, with gusto, rattling silver baby heirlooms as they paraded through the door. A woman wearing a lace christening bonnet sashayed into the hall. Owen held his pipe to his mouth, to hide a grin.

Some of the fancy dress was more a state of fancy 'undress'; no doubt outraged letters would be filling the Ladies' Page of *The Chronicle* in the next few weeks. Fortunately for social decorum, many patrons had decided to digress from the advertised theme: kings and queens strutted past, followed by a score of famous couples, and even a personification of the Eiffel Tower who explained to his partner: "well, Paris is the city of love, and how are babies made?" His young partner blushed and giggled accordingly.

Word had circulated that the author of Sherlock Holmes was attending tonight's dance. Frock coats, corsets and bustles adorned every other attendee. Owen caught a whiff of camphor on more than one occasion, presumably the result of having raided their grandparents' wardrobes. A few ghosts and fairies hovered amongst the crowd, no doubt members of the Spiritual Society.

A clutch of *Petit Garcons* with sleek bobbed hair and colourful, glittering sheath dresses congregated around a cab. A familiar laugh wafted through the group of new arrivals as they paraded through the entrance. The reporter, Whitington, approached them, camera at the ready.

A flash of red hair inside the foyer caught his eye. The woman hugged the arm of her escort, both their backs to Owen. She wore a violet, beaded evening dress with a plunging backline, obviously bound for one of the more private parties attending the dance. She turned to face him. Her smile was familiar - the young woman he saw leaving The Register Building the day before. But there was something else...

His wrist throbbed under his white cotton glove, as if to remind him of recent events. He rubbed the aching tendons, and moved out of Whitington's line of sight.

The woman lifted a long cigarette holder to her lips. It was the same woman exiting the lift at the Hotel, with a handsome young man on her arm.

Her escort whispered in her ear. The beads of her violet dress shimmered as she laughed. The same colour as...

Owen's heart skipped. Her escort turned to face her. Tall. Lean. His fair face framed with ebony hair, highlighted with glints of ultramarine and amethyst.

The gentleman's gaze flickered in Owen's direction. His heart raced.

"Barrington?" Doyle tapped him on the shoulder.

Owen sucked in a breath, and disengaged his attention.

"How was your lecture this afternoon, Sir Arthur?" He shook Doyle's hand. "Unfortunately, it took longer to collect my outfit than I'd expected, and tickets had sold out."

"Very well, thank you, Barrington." Doyle turned to his wife. "This is my wife, Lady Jean Doyle. My darling, this is the Mr Barrington I told you about."

"Pleased to meet you, Mr Barrington." She shook Owen's hand. "Arthur tells me you're a painter of some renown."

"I dabble." Owen nodded his head in quick deference, and kissed her silk glove.

A hint of red flashed over her cheeks.

"Oh, look, Arthur, he has the dearest carved pipe. Are you dressed as Sherlock Holmes?" she asked.

"For tonight, Lady Jean." Owen's cheeks flushed.

Doyle's muscles stiffened, his smile frozen on his face.

Owen tapped the tobacco from his pipe and shoved it in his pocket; he couldn't afford to get Doyle offside. "On the insistence of my Miss Turner, I assure you. She's an avid devotee."

Doyle seemed to relax.

"Ready for battle?" he asked.

"I thought--"

"I'm sure I'm not the only one to have guessed your secret," said Lady Jean.

Was it that obvious? Owen glanced at Doyle. Surely he hadn't told his wife of their plans? Their quest to thwart the Crones had been a secret.

"You have the look of a man in love." Lady Jean tapped his shoulder with her fan. "For what it's worth, I'm sure she will say yes."

"Ah, yes." Owen felt his face flush. He smiled and patted his pocket, the ring box reassuring him all would be well - once Enid agreed to marry him. He leaned closer to Doyle. "I need to talk with you in private, Sir Arthur."

"Of course, young man."

Lady Jean flicked open her fan. "I'll meet you inside later, Arthur."

Owen pulled Doyle to the side, away from the stream of costumed arrivals.

"Mrs Oldham and Miss Devin accosted the reporter," whispered Owen.

"Are you sure?" asked Doyle. "Mrs Oldham seemed a pleasant creature."

Creature? Doyle didn't know the half of it.

"They stole photographs from Whitington at *The Register*'s office," Owen replied. "That's a lot of subterfuge for the sake of a few fairies. I thought the police confiscated all the photos from the picnic?"

Doyle nodded.

"Perhaps he pocketed them, like you did?"

Doyle rubbed his temple.

"We need to find out why." Owen leaned closer to Doyle. "I need someone with an open mind. Someone who's willing to *believe*. Who better to investigate witches than yourself?"

"Witches?" Doyle raised an eyebrow.

Owen took a last suck on his pipe and tapped it against the brick wall behind him.

"They're trying to lure my Enie away from me." It felt like the Crones crushing his heart as he spoke.

"Your Miss Turner seemed too intelligent to be taken in by deception," said Doyle.

Owen took a deep breath and flicked away the spent cigarette. "I plan to ask for her hand tonight."

"Most excellent." Doyle slapped Owen's shoulder. "How can I help?"

"I need to you to distract them," replied Owen. "Keep them away from her."

"Courage, man. The deed will be done before you know it." Doyle pointed into the street.

Enid's shiny, red Lincoln Tourer pulled up to the curb. Owen's heart skipped.

Enid stepped out of the motorcar, straightened her long skirt, and adjusted her bonnet. Owen's gaze skimmed down her figure as she strolled towards him. Her bodice clung to her corseted figure - a very fine figure indeed, and every inch a proper Victorian lady.

He tugged his frock coat.

Doors slammed behind her. Mrs Oldham bounded towards them, in a flurry of green silk and chiffon. Miss Devin followed at a more sedate pace, in a shimmering black evening dress.

Owen's heart sank. Could he not get one moment alone with her? He held out his hand to his love. Hopefully, Doyle would prove as canny as his own creation, in distracting Enid's companions, so he could talk to her alone.

He pulled the pipe back out of his pocket. He needed a cigarette; this would have to do.

Enid parked the Lincoln by the curb. The back of her neck prickled. She gripped the steering wheel and glanced in the rear vision mirror. Sylvia glared back at her.

"What do we do about the stowaway?" Sylvia dumped a garden gnome on the seat beside her.

Olive patted it on the head.

"You'll have to stay here, Red." Enid smiled. "And look after the motorcar."

She gathered up her skirts, pulled them down over her ankles, and straightened her overskirt. It'd been decades since she'd last worn a bustle skirt and corset. She grinned; at least they still fit.

Her bonnet scraped the roof of the motorcar. A sharp pain stabbed her scalp. She adjusted the bonnet, and extracted herself from the vehicle.

Her lower back muscles ached. She hadn't driven in a bustle before. She rubbed her back, and made a mental note never to do so again.

"I still say that's not a costume." Olive slid across the back seat. Sheer green chiffon floated after her and settled onto the satin silk of her gown.

"They don't know that." Enid smiled and tugged tight on her long silk gloves.

Sylvia slammed the door shut behind Olive, and scowled. "I wish you hadn't worn that ridiculous costume."

"I thought it'd make the Heir feel more at ease." Olive grinned. "You know, catch more flies with honey, and all that." She eyed Sylvia's black, beaded gown; a few years out of date, but still chic. "At least I made an effort." Olive preened the wired chiffon wings attached to the back of her bodice. "And it is a party, after all."

Sylvia harrumphed.

"Well, you won't snare a Fae with that attitude," said Olive.

Enid ignored their bickering. Goosebumps tracked up her arms. She glanced over her shoulder, expecting to see the troll lumbering towards her. A black motorcar tapped the curb.

Bollocks. Sylvia's paranoia was infecting her. Surely the troll couldn't have survived the blast?

She scanned the gathering crowd near the entrance. Sir Arthur stood out amongst the princesses, pirates, and djinn, in his well-cut tuxedo. A short, dark-haired woman in an evening gown stood beside him, her hand resting on his arm. He shook the hand of a tall gentleman in a frock coat. The gentleman turned to face her direction and smiled.

Enid's skin tingled. Owen cut a fine figure in his tailored coat, waistcoat and cravat. It suited him. She sighed.

"There's Owen." She nudged Olive. "Stop squabbling. It's a party, remember." She wrapped the cords of her drawstring reticule around her wrist and joined Owen.

"Enie!" Owen threw his arms wide.

Enid laughed and offered him a gloved hand. The warmth of his kiss lingered as he stepped back and regarded her.

"You look ravishing, my darling," he said, "but you seem to have forgotten your parasol."

Enid's heart pounded at the reminder of the loss of her Focus.

"Good evening, Sir Arthur." Olive's fairy wings jiggled as she thrust out her un-gloved hand. "I'm Mrs Olive Oldham. We met at the picnic up the Hill."

Sir Arthur eyed her costume, and hesitated. A frown flickered over his forehead.

Enid's stomach twisted. Would Olive's costume rekindle his erased memories?

He rubbed his temple, and the moment was gone.

"You remember Miss Enid Turner?" Olive continued.

"Of course." He clasped her hand in his, then turned to his female companion. "This is my wife, Lady Jean."

"What a magnificent costume, Mrs Oldham," said Lady Jean. "You know, Arthur dreams of fairies."

Sylvia cleared her throat behind them.

Olive bit her lip. "And this is our good friend, Miss Sylvia Devin."

"Devin," echoed Sir Arthur. "Russian, isn't it?"

"A long time ago," replied Sylvia.

Sir Arthur and Owen exchanged glances. Owen nodded.

Sir Arthur lowered his voice and leaned closer to Olive. "Shall we leave these two love birds alone?" He offered her an elbow. "Ladies, I'd be honoured if you joined us."

Olive grinned and took his arm. He escorted Lady Jean and Olive into the dance hall. Sylvia frowned, and followed.

Enid scanned the crowd one last time. She sniffed the air. Nothing. She was becoming as paranoid as Sylvia.

She relaxed her shoulders, wrapped her arm around Owen's, and trailed her other hand along his coat sleeve.

Owen escorted Enid into the hall behind Doyle and his newly found companions.

Rows of rectangular windows created a wall of glass at the far end of the hall, the top row angled open, creating a breezeway to the entry door. Excitement buzzed through the revellers. Bodies, clothed in a rainbow of costumes, surged across the polished-wood dance floor. A warm current of air picked up their scents: lavender, vanilla, and rose, hints of citrus, and the lingering oaken moss aroma of Aqua Velva.

A lively waltz enticed the dancers to the floor. Shoe heels tapped to the music. Bodies swirled around the hall, in whirls of colour, reminiscent of Van Gogh's *Starry Night*.

Owen fingered the ring box in his pocket. *Still there*. He took a deep breath. Now Doyle had spirited away the Crones, he could woo Enid properly.

A flurry of air, and the ceiling danced.

"Look." Enid pointed at the movement, and sighed. Her breath caressed his ear. "How beautiful."

Balloons wafted overhead, tethered to the metal skeleton arching across the ceiling. Light bulbs strung along the metal ribs winked as the warm spring breeze drifted in the hall entrance.

Owen escorted her across the dance floor.

Enid peered through the gaps between dancers as they wove their way across the packed dance floor.

"Is something wrong?" he asked.

Enid turned, smiled sweetly and met his gaze. "I just wanted to make sure Olive and Sylvia are all right."

Owen's heart sank; it would take longer than he'd hoped to clear her head of thoughts of her so-called friends. He spoke in a calm voice: "They're old enough to look after themselves."

"Yes, they are." A smile flickered over her lips. "And I'm sure Sir Arthur is harmless."

Owen returned her smile. At least Doyle was safe with Lady Jean present.

Enid wrapped her arms around him and swayed to the music.

"Let's dance. You lead." She grinned, closed her eyes, and rested her head on his shoulder. "I trust you."

Her hair smelled of honey. His pulse fluttered. He pulled her close and let the music guide them across the dance floor towards the bandstand at the far end of the hall.

He could feel her heart racing in time with his. He slipped his hand off her shoulder, along her arm, towards his pocket.

The music stopped. Three rapid clangs of the cymbal, and the band's tempo quickened. There was an audible gasp from a huddle near the band. A chorus of giggles rose from their centre.

Enid pushed away from Owen. A breeze cooled his chest. He clasped her hand in his, hoping to cling to the moment.

Enid searched the far end of the hall and drifted towards the laughter, pulling him towards the refreshments table, where Doyle was handing glasses to his charges. Her fingers slipped from his.

Owen cursed under his breath. The moment was gone.

A deep, melodic laugh escaped a large huddle, and resonated in his chest. He glanced in its direction where a mass of gyrating flappers and dappers had congregated. He peered into the pack, for the object of their desire.

"Would you like some punch?" He felt the warmth of Enid's breath on his ear. "I'll meet you at the refreshments table." Her voice faded.

Camera flashes lit up faces like fireworks. A flash of red hair and shimmering violet beads swirled as a couple emerged from their young admirers. The woman glanced back at the group, and smirked; it was the woman from the Hotel. She twirled around her partner, and enticed him to dance.

The tall striking man, with hair the colour of the midnight sky, embraced her. He caught Owen's gaze. Those piercing, amethyst-coloured eyes...

Owen's heart fluttered. There was a certain air about the gentleman; as if he knew a secret; one he would share with no creature but you. The gentleman smiled, like he knew he was better than you, and you didn't care.

"She's attractive, isn't she?" Doyle placed a gentle hand on Owen's shoulder. "The redhead."

Owen nodded, still intrigued by the young man with the amethyst-coloured eyes.

Owen glanced at the girl, and cleared his throat. "I've seen her before."

"She seems familiar to me, also." Doyle clicked his tongue, and grimaced. "That damned lightning strike. It's like something flitting at a window, forbidden to enter." He shook his head. "I think I need a drink. The ladies are at the refreshment table. Best you join us." He patted Owen's shoulder. "You've already won the heart of a good woman. Don't get sidetracked. I'll distract her friends so you can have a clear field, and we'll celebrate with champagnes when the deed is done." Doyle turned on his heel.

Friends was a questionable term for such manipulative creatures. *Crones* suited them better. The Crones hovered around her like vultures ready to feed. Were they already bewitching Enie's mind against him? What had they plotted for him?

The older Crone eyed him. Perhaps they'd bewitched him already? He swallowed. Yes, that would explain his fascination with the red-head and her companion. He straightened his back, resolved in his duty to save his love from their clutches.

Owen and Doyle joined the rest of their party.

"Your new friends are quite entertaining, my dear," said Lady Jean.

Olive drained her glass.

"Shall we have another?" asked Doyle.

"There's Mrs Watson." Lady Jean's face lit up. "You remember, Arthur? She's the wife of Professor Watson. We met her at the dinner with your doctor-friends, last week." She hugged her husband. "Please do excuse me. I must chat to her." She made her way across the hall.

Owen slipped his fingers between Enid's and kissed her hand. Her cheeks flushed the colour of summer roses just after the rain.

"Let's dance," he said.

Enid had been alone for almost four generations. She'd watched Olive fall in love through three of those. She was no longer content to watch. If she was fated to outlive mortals, she'd damned well enjoy herself, and experience all of it.

Owen turned on his heel, taking her with him. She laughed. A real laugh, not some schoolgirl titter, or coquettish giggle designed to ensnare a husband. She leaned back, letting her head fall backwards. She opened her eyes, determined not to miss one moment. The lights whirled above her as they spun.

The music stopped. The crowd whooped. Owen pulled her close.

The room still swirled. Enid blinked, searching for a stationery point to focus her vision. The pirouetting colours steadied.

Sir Arthur was still at the refreshments table, deep in conversation with Olive. Sylvia crossed her arms and tapped her foot. Sir Arthur turned to refill his glass.

Sylvia glared at Enid, tapped her watch, and mouthed an order; Enid understood her intent. A knot of guilt twisted her stomach. Tomorrow the Fae Queen returned, and she was partying with her beau.

Sylvia slipped back into the crowd, leaving Olive alone with Sir Arthur. Olive bit her lip and scampered away, in the opposite direction. Sir Arthur turned, two glasses of punch in hand. They were gone.

Enid straightened her back and set to work. She scanned the undulating mob, searching for any sign of a Fae presence. Groups of dancers had separated from the main crowd. Others had gravitated towards areas set aside for private parties. A six-foot burly pirate with a jaunty eye patch twirled his Queen of Hearts.

Aether buzzed around her.

The troll? Ice filled her veins.

The couple bowed, and walked in her direction.

Enid's fingers swished along her silk overskirt, feeling for her chatelaine where she'd hung her Focus in the decades past.

Bollocks! How could she face her nemesis without it?

She sniffed tentatively as the couple glided past her. Rosewater, vanilla, citrus; pleasantly mundane. She flexed her fingers, stretching out the tense muscles, and scolded herself. There was no need to be paranoid; the troll was dead.

She resumed her search as Owen whirled her across the floor towards the band.

A flourish of drums and the tune was finished. The crowd turned to the band, and applauded. Owen clapped enthusiastically. A chorus of laughter burst out behind them.

Owen turned to face the sound.

Enid checked her Marcasite wristwatch. It was after ten. There wasn't much time. She'd never find the Heir while dancing. She had to leave while Owen was distracted. She let her fingers slip from his embrace.

The band struck up another lively tune. The crowd flung themselves across the floor. Owen swayed, enthralled with the music.

"I need another drink." She wound her way through the crowd, not waiting for his reply. It was a warm night; it was a plausible ruse.

She paused at the refreshments table, collected two glasses of punch, and glanced back in Owen's direction. He drifted towards the bandstand. If she was quick, she'd return before he realised she had gone.

She mingled with the dancers, working her way from group to group, in search of any aura of power to betray the Fae's presence. Each clique nudged the next, making her proximity inconsequential. She continued towards the band, pausing every now and then as she felt a murmur in the Aether or spied an eye patch, resuming only when satisfied there was no foul smell of troll.

Her heart raced as she neared where she'd left Owen. She raised the punch glasses above the jostling crowd, carefully balancing them so not to spill the drinks.

Olive waved in her direction, steered herself around a particularly energetic couple, darted between two groups of dancers, and joined Enid. Her cheeks were flushed. She commandeered one of the glasses Enid was carrying, and gulped down the liquid.

"Nothing." She huffed. "You?"

"No," replied Enid. "But I don't really know what we're looking for. Sylvia didn't leave instructions."

"I've only ever encountered Fae the once, at the picnic," said Olive. "I guess it's supposed to feel the same?"

"I'd have thought if the Heir was in hiding, she'd be using some form of Concealment, or Glamour.

Olive pressed the glass back into Enid's hand and reached for the second. Enid jerked it out of her reach. The liquid jiggled and fizzed, threatening to spill. "This is for Owen. I told him I was fetching a drink."

"And has he...?" Olive grinned and wiggled her eyebrows.

Enid felt her cheeks burn.

"Has he what?" She sipped the punch.

"He's been clutching his coat pocket all night," replied Olive. "And I recognise that look of elated fear. If Sylvia hadn't decided we were going Fae hunting, you'd likely have a ring on your finger by now."

Enid rubbed the fingers on her left hand, with her thumb.

"He'll be wondering what's taking you so long," said Olive.

Enid glanced at her beau. He swayed in time with the music, near the bandstand, where the boisterous gaggle of flappers buzzed like bees to pollen. Their equally-enamoured companions danced and flirted, each manoeuvring to get a better view of the couple at their centre.

"Quick, before Sylvia spies us." Olive nudged her in Owen's direction. "Let him think he's surprised you."

Enid's hands trembled at the thought of Sylvia's anger. But Owen was worth every admonishment Sylvia could ladle out. She joined him.

"Miss me?" She fluttered her lashes - men liked that, didn't they? - and offered him the glass of punch.

"Hmm?" Owen's attention remained focused on the huddle of revellers, and a redhead with long legs and a short, backless dress of shimmering violet. A long string of beads trickled down her back and caressed her skin as she moved.

Enid's heart plummeted. Perhaps Olive was wrong? Owen wasn't going to propose; he wanted one last fling before he discarded her for a young dish. After all, Owen Barrington the Third was the heir to a small fortune. What was she? A middle-aged Protector, doomed to spend eternity alone?

A light breeze, saturated with the rich perfume of roses, wafted over the couple and caught Enid's hair. Warm. Inviting. Her skin buzzed. She shivered.

The redhead draped her arms over a young gentleman at the centre of the seething throng. He was gorgeous; tall and raven-haired. The way Enid fancied her men. His slender hands stroked the woman's hair. He glanced in her direction, and smiled. Her heart fluttered. Thoughts of Owen melted away. It was the gentleman from the arcade Tea Shoppe; she'd never forget his face. He held her gaze. Her skin burned, rising from her chest to her cheeks.

A glass shattered near the refreshments table, distracting Enid's gaze away from the gentleman's charms.

"Intoxicating, isn't it?" She wrapped her arm around Owen's, and offered him the glass.

Owen didn't reply. Enid's heart ached. Perhaps he hadn't heard her over the music? Enid gulped a mouthful of punch. Perhaps Sylvia was right, and there was no such thing as a one true love?

Enid nuzzled closer to him.

The netted balloons shuddered on the ceiling. The breeze caressed her face.

The dark-haired gentleman laughed. Enid's gaze snapped back to him. He buried his cheek into the redhead's locks, her back still facing Enid.

Owen caught his breath. Enid reached for Owen's hand. He clasped her fingers, his attention not wavering from the couple.

"I suppose she's pretty." Enid forced a laugh. "But isn't she a bit young for you?" She squeezed his hand.

Owen flinched.

"No, I--" Fear flashed in his eyes. "I just--" He turned to Enid, and cleared his throat. "I've seen her before," he replied, "with the gentleman."

"Oh?" Enid turned him to face her.

The clarinet swooned. The couple danced, and laughed. Their drones buzzed, eager to oblige. Enid's heart flared with jealousy.

Owen took the glass from Enid's hand.

"They were coming out of the lift at the Hotel." He swigged a mouthful of punch. "And she was outside The Register Building this morning." A second gulp. "If I was paranoid, I'd swear she was following me." His chuckle wasn't convincing.

"Really?" Enid eyed the redhead as the couple swayed. "Perhaps she attends the secretarial school next door?"

She took Owen's other hand and danced closer to the Queen Bee - or, in this case, the King Bee - at the centre of the hive.

The woman giggled, Beads dangling from her embroidered headband jiggled. She raised a long metal cigarette holder, and leaned against the gentleman.

"Butt me," she said in a low voice. The cigarette's tip flared. Smoke spiralled above her head.

"The Tea Shoppe!" said Enid out loud. "They were both at the Tea Shoppe. On my birthday."

The young man looked directly at her. His violet eyes smiled, as if he knew he was the subject of her conversation. The woman followed his gaze. She glared at Enid.

A chair screeched at the end of the hall. The windows slapped shut. The balloons stilled.

Owen's fingers stiffened in hers. He tugged her closer and kissed her. Long. Lingering. His clear blue eyes not leaving hers.

Enid's heart thumped. Perhaps she'd misjudged him? Perhaps he'd been evaluating his potential competition? Perhaps *he* was jealous?

"Is that young Agnes?" Olive's voice was close.

Enid jumped.

Music blared across the hall. The gentleman twirled his partner. The girl's flame red bob skimmed her cheeks. It was indeed Agnes Farrow; but this was not the naive young thing eager to meet Sir Arthur, and reluctant to defy her father.

"Yes," replied Enid.

Olive raised an eyebrow. "I think young Agnes is falling in love." Olive sighed. "It's just like Romeo and Juliet."

The ice burned in Enid's chest now. She spun on her heel and glared at Olive. "Her father definitely won't approve."

"And who can blame her? He is gorgeous."

"You should know better," said Enid. "You're a married woman,"

Olive's smile fell. She hugged her Lapis blue beaded purse close to her heart. She narrowed her eyelids. "You're supposed to be madly in love with Mr Barrington, or have you forgotten?"

Enid's skin burned. A loud hum reverberated through her head. Her fingers flexed. If only she had her Focus. She craved the rush of Aether through her body, to channel it at--

A hand stayed her.

Sylvia stepped in front of her.

"Stop this at once." She pulled Enid and Olive away from the group. "You're Protectors, not school girls." She lowered her voice. "Can't you feel it?"

"Feel what?" Enid shrugged away from Sylvia's hand.

"A Fae enchantment," replied Sylvia. "The air is thick with it. Look at your amulets. Did you not heed their warning?"

A faint green light pulsed though the buttonholes of Enid's bodice. She clasped her hand to her chest. Her fingers tingled. Her amulet throbbed against her skin.

Olive clasped her own amulet. Blue light trickled through her fingers.

"Why--?" She tucked it under the neckline of her gown.

"Did you not see the amulet adorning the young woman's neck?" Sylvia hissed.

Enid looked at Agnes. A pale purple gem glistened around her neck. Enid strained to draw on the little energy her amulet could draw from the Aether for *Sight*. A lavender glow cocooned the girl. A slender cord of Aether tethered her to her companion.

"She's Fae?" asked Enid. "How did we not know?" Her attention wandered back to the young man.

"You were distracted," replied Olive.

"I was not!"

"You both were." Sylvia dropped a hand on Enid's shoulder. "She isn't Fae," Sylvia's walking stick touched Enid's arm. "He is."

The *Charm* was broken. Enid's heart plunged into her stomach.

"Are you sure?" asked Olive.

"I know Fae," hissed Sylvia.

"He seems quite taken by her." Olive's smile returned. "Perhaps the amulet is just a love token?"

"Or a cunning trap," said Sylvia.

Enid's mind raced. Owen had mentioned Agnes earlier. She frowned. Another memory tugged, demanding attention. She bit her lip. Something about the day of the picnic... and the Fae.

Blood pulse screamed in her ears, like steam escaping a boiling kettle.

Enid clasped Olive's arm. "She moved!"

"It's a dance," said Olive. "That's the point."

"No." Enid shook her head. "At the picnic. When the Fae Queen arrived." She took a deep breath. "She moved. The time shift didn't affect her."

"Who, young Agnes?" Olive peered at Agnes.

A thought was growing in Enid's mind. It twisted and turned, pushing its way to the surface. There was no hint she was under the Fae's thrall; there was no whiff of Fae about her at all.

"Perhaps...?" Enid frowned. Sylvia's words echoed in her head. *The Fae love a party.* And dear, sweet, innocent Agnes was accommodating. The Heir was drawn to her, as evidenced by his gift. A gift that could--

"Could the amulet conceal magic?" asked Enid. "Or block the Fae's *Charm*?"

"Never trust a Fae," growled Sylvia. "They manipulate for their own gain. And they don't like to lose. No, the necklace will bind her to him."

Agnes whispered in the Heir's ear. He grinned.

"Or him to her?" Enid watched Agnes. She was not at all like the girl they'd met at the picnic. "Perhaps he didn't give the talisman to her? What if it wasn't a gift? What if the amulet was fashioned to entrap Fae?"

"A honey trap," said Sylvia.

"She's in league with the Bounty Hunter?" asked Olive.

"Or the *Glamoured* bounty hunter itself," said Sylvia.

"The Fae Queen did say the Heir was kidnapped," whispered Olive. "And it could start a war."

"A war? I haven't heard anything about a war," said Sylvia. "We need to get the Heir away from the girl." She lifted her walking stick.

"Not here." Enid stepped in front of her. "Too many mortals."

Agnes led the Heir away from the growing crowd of admirers towards the side door.

Owen staggered forward.

"They're leaving," said Enid.

"Don't let her out of your sight," said Sylvia.

"But Owen?" whispered Enid.

"Your duty comes first. Even Olive knows that," replied Sylvia. "Ditch the mortal,"

Enid hesitated.

"Or shall I do it for you?" Sylvia gripped her walking stick tighter.

Enid shook head.

"Poor Mr Barrington," said Olive. "He will recover, won't he?"

"The *Charm* will wear off, eventually," replied Sylvia, "Though some mortals can't shake it."

Agnes glanced over her shoulder as they slipped out the side door. There was fear there.

Agnes opened the door and glanced in their direction. The Heir spoke to her. She shook her head, shoved him throughout the door, and slipped into the crowd.

"Stop that girl, Enid, and find out whose side she's on." Sylvia and Olive moved towards the side door.

Enid joined Owen and wrapped her arm around his shoulder, her attention still fixed on Agnes. She stroked Owen's hair and whispered in his ear.

"Let's get some fresh air. You fetch the car. I'll make my excuses to Sylvia and Olive, and meet you soon as I can."

She kissed Owen, siphoning off the last of the Fae enchantment; the warmth returned to his lips. He squeezed her tight.

"Don't take long." He trailed his hand along her arm, and kissed her outstretched fingers as they parted. He spun on his heel and strode towards the front door.

The ring box weighed heavy in Owen's pocket. His skin tingled. He walked faster, blocking the memory. He loved Enid.

"Mr Barrington?" It was Doyle's voice.

Owen slowed.

"Is the deed done?" asked Doyle.

"No, I got distracted," replied Owen. "I've been sent to collect the motorcar." He lowered his voice to a whisper: "I don't trust those Crones. Something's going on."

"Cheer up, old chap." Doyle patted his shoulder. "Don't let them stop you. 'The game is afoot', as Holmes would say." A smile flickered over his lips.

As Enie would say. "Yes." Owen smiled.

"Shall we?" Doyle gestured towards the exit.

Owen shook his head.

"I need to do this alone, Sir Arthur," he replied. "Keep watch here.

In case the Crones return."

"Of course," said Doyle.

"And keep an eye out for that reporter. We need to find out what was in those photographs," said Owen.

Owen stepped out of the hall. Music escaped onto the street. The door swung shut, muffling it to a dull thud.

A full moon peeked over the roofs on the building opposite. Enid's motorcar squatted near the curb, its pale leather interior like leather-wrapped corpses lying across the front and rear seats.

A shadow moved across the shrouds.

Owen's muscles tensed. There was a familiar rattle of a coin in a metal cup. A large man, stooped in a drab olive coat stepped closer. His hat pulled low over his face cloaked it in shadow, but the smell was unmistakable. The Veteran shuffled onto the footpath near the rear of the motorcar.

"You startled me." Owen fumbled with the door handle. "What are you doing here?"

"I've been watching *them* for you." A glint of white appeared where his mouth would be. "And these to-dos attract a rich crowd. They can't resist a party. They might take pity on a war veteran who lost all for King and country."

The hall door squeaked. Laughter trickled from the hall. The veteran's head whipped in the direction of the sound. Light flashed across the footpath, and was gone.

"They can't see me with you." He ducked behind the motorcar. His voice rumbled into the distance as he scuttled across the street: "Don't trust them."

Owen didn't.

Footsteps thudded behind him. The dark-haired gentleman emerged from the alley beside the dance hall, ran across the street, and turned north.

More footsteps echoed from the alley.

Owen ducked down behind the Lincoln.

The Crones rushed out of the alley. Mrs Oldham turned full circle on her heel, a fountain pen held out in front of her, like a stiletto ready to attack.

Owen held his breath as her older cohort scanned the curb, and ran past the Lincoln, in the same direction as the young gentleman.

Owen turned to follow them.

Voices drifted out of the side alley; one sounded like Enid. Owen's stomach knotted. He hesitated; the gentleman was gone. Enie was here. Now. Owen had already declared his love to her, and he'd promised to fetch the car. And he was a man of his word.

He opened the driver's door, sat behind the steering wheel, and waited.

chapter fourteen

wen gripped the steering wheel, and frowned. What was taking Enid so long? He thrummed his fingers on the steering wheel.

Something hard knocked his side. He glanced at the ceramic garden gnome on the seat beside him, dressed in red cap, matching coat and trousers. Its pupil-less eyes stared back at him. Its stare followed him like the unblinking gaze of a Masters' painting. He shuddered.

Enid had a penchant for collecting the creepy garden ornaments, and this was her favourite. He'd seen the odd one in gardens, here and there; they were apparently all the rage in Europe. Perhaps it should've stayed there.

He tossed it into the back seat, but it was no use; he could still feel its stare on the back of his neck.

He shifted in his seat. The faint stench of the ex-soldier lingered. Owen wrinkled his nose and sniffed his jacket. Nothing. He reached onto the back of his seat, and hesitated. The garden gnome watched him.

"Stop staring at me." Owen buried its face into the leather upholstery, and searched under the front seat instead.

Still nothing.

He slid his fingers along the shelf under the dash. His nails caught something. He felt along the edge: it was a large paper envelope. His pulse raced. The Crone, Oldham, had stashed the reporter's photographs under the dash after their visit.

He pulled out the envelope and unhooked the string seal. Photographs fell onto his lap. He picked one up, angled towards the street light, and examined it: a group of men stood next to a damaged fence. In the background was a stand of gum trees. He searched their faces. He recognised one as Waite, the Director of the State Museum. Doyle stood next to him. On the other side of the Museum Director was a woman. He peered closer. It was Crone Oldham. Her voice from that night echoed in his head: *We met at the picnic at Humbug Scrub.*

A sharp pain crackled in his left temple. He tried to ignore it, and examined the image. At the foot of the group was a body. Something wasn't right.

His temple throbbed. Pain clawed the back of his eye. His vision blurred. He grit his teeth and waited for the pain to subside.

The photograph crinkled in his hand. His fingers dug into the leather seat. He peered closely at the body. And froze. The photos slipped from his lap and tumbled to his feet. He lunched forward to grab them, and cracked his forehead on the steering wheel.

A wave of nausea washed over him. Visions flooded his memory; images of stone creatures, and the fires of hell burning in a single eye socket. He felt the crack of its attack on the back of his head, the glare of sun on the river, and smelled the stench of brimstone.

He clenched his fist tighter. His knuckles paled. Witches, a stone creature, and fairies? What had the Crones dragged Enid into? And what devilry were they up to now?

He stared at the entrance of the Palais. He had to do something. He couldn't sit here, waiting. He had to stop them. He had to save Enie.

He grabbed the steering wheel, and started the engine. The motorcar's engine rumbled into life.

Owen switched off the headlights, as he drove past the hospital where the Crones had tracked the young gentleman.

He scanned the shadowy footpath under the trees lining the road, for any sign of them.

Nothing.

Owen slowed the motorcar and parked across from the Botanic Park. If they'd entered the Gardens itself, he'd never find them. He cut the engine, and listened for any movement.

The faint sounds of nocturnal animals from the Zoological Garden carried on the North wind. He sniffed the air, as the Crones had done. There was a whiff of exotic manures and the faint but definite smell of rotten eggs.

His temples throbbed a warning.

Owen shook his head, and leaned out of the car to sample the air again. Pain crushed his head like a vice. It wasn't safe to drive in this condition. Besides, Enid would be furious if he scratched the Lincoln. He shoved the photograph in his coat pocket, and stumbled out of the motorcar. He untangled his frock coat.

His head reeled. He leaned on the bonnet to steady himself. The metal buzzed. A sharp tang of ozone and sulphur engulfed him. *Fire and brimstone.*

Owen spun on his heel. The world twisted and whirled. He sucked in a ragged breath. The stench caught in his throat. He spluttered and fell back against the motorcar.

The air crackled around him. Thunder rumbled further north, near the bridge.

Owen staggered towards the Zoological Gardens, under cover of the trees. The crackling grew louder as he neared its iron gates. A hyena cackled in the distance. Cages rattled. An elephant trumpeted. Nervous monkeys chittered.

A shiver snaked down Owen's spine. He froze, eyed the lock on the wrought iron gates, and prayed the Crones hadn't let loose the animals. A zookeeper had died, just six months ago, from a polar bear attack. Owen's stomach churned, forcing bile into his throat. He flattened his body against the trunk of the closest tree, glad he was safe outside the locked gates.

Light flared over the brick wall, illuminating the pale diamond pattern in the brick plinths. Owen flinched. Another burst of light flashed along the road. An unearthly crack followed. Whatever it was, it was coming from the Albert Bridge.

Pain seared behind his eye. He winced. He dug his fingers into the tree bark, burying the image of the stone creature and its flaming eye. He'd kill for a smoke to calm his nerves.

He took a deep breath; the gentleman was in danger and, if the veteran had strayed into the Crones' path, his life was in danger as well. He had to do something. He swallowed and edged closer to the bridge.

The smell of sulphur and ozone grew stronger. Forks of red and blue lightning exploded along the bridge, illuminating three silhouettes: the two Crones moved like cats stalking their prey. The veteran recoiled as they advanced. The taller Crone raised her walking stick. Her voice rumbled in fury.

A jagged red arc erupted from the tip of the stick. Puffs of smoke spat into the air where it smashed the wooden deck of the bridge.

The second Crone moved forward to join her, wand in hand, and forced the veteran to the edge of the bridge. The tall Crone growled and thrust her stick at him again.

His back arched over the guard rail. Another blast enveloped him. He bellowed in pain as his grip faltered. His body twitched, rolled backward, and plunged backward over the edge.

"Bloody h--" Owen dug his nails into his palms to force himself to remain silent. They were witches. *Real* witches.

The hedge rustled between the trees on the opposite side of the road.

Owen spun on his heel to face the new threat.

Amethyst eyes gleamed with the reflected light of the Crone's onslaught. They stared at him, enticing him closer.

The intriguing young gentleman stood up.

Owen caught his breath, shook his head slowly, and glanced towards the bridge. He couldn't help the gentleman if the Crones spotted them. He was no match for a pair of witches.

"Get down," he whispered.

The gleam in the gentleman's eyes faded. Another rustle of leaves, and he was gone.

The taller Crone turned in their direction.

"Get him," she hissed to her cohort.

Her cohort sprinted towards the gentleman's hiding place.

Owen hid behind the tree trunk.

A grinding noise rose from under the bridge; rock scraping rock. A boulder rolled up onto the road at the approach to the bridge. The ground trembled.

A stone creature rose from the ground and lumbered forward. The Crone thrust her walking stick in its direction. The air convulsed.

Red arcs coiled around the Crone's hands and along her walking stick. Light consumed the creature.

The creature yowled and sank into the ground.

Owen's head screamed in pain. His heart pounded. He squeezed his eyes shut, pressed his body hard against the trunk, and ground his fists into the bark, as he slid down the trunk. He buried his head in his lap. The smell of his own blood engulfed him.

This isn't happening. It can't be real. He repeated the words, like a protective mantra. He needed normal. He needed Enie; she was the only person he could trust.

The tree shook against his back.

Pain exploded in his head. His ears rang. He clutched his head, and screamed at the visions in his head.

A flare of magnesium erupted across the hall. A photographer stepped out from behind a clique of dancers. He chatted with those in costume and scribbled in his little black notebook. Enid recognised him as Mr Whitington, the reporter at the picnic; the same one Sylvia had relieved of recent, inopportune memories.

Olive recognised him too. She hesitated near the group of dancers and tugged Sylvia's sleeve.

Mr Whitington tilted his head, frowned, and raised his camera.

"This isn't good," whispered Enid.

Sylvia snarled and pulled Olive out of his path. Another flash caught a young socialite behind them instead. When the light had faded, he was gone.

"Wasn't he that reporter?" Sylvia searched the crowd.

Olive rubbed her eyes.

"Enid, you find that girl," said Sylvia. "And don't let that reporter see you. We'll follow the Heir." She scooted Olive towards the side door.

"That bloody reporter." Enid cursed, and ducked behind a gentleman in a tall stovepipe hat.

The gentleman turned to her, grinned, and invited her to dance. Enid excused herself, and searched the crowd for Agnes. The girl had manoeuvred her way back towards the side exit, where several of the Heir's particularly energetic devotees had fenced her in.

A microphone crackled on the stage at the other end of the hall. A booming voice announced: "Time for the Balloon Chase!"

The Balloon Chase was popular at Thursday night Fancy Dress Carnival nights, with two prizes of ten shillings. Olive had won it several times, though Enid suspected she cheated and used magic.

Realising the King Bee had flown, the dancers abandoned Agnes and swarmed on the falling balloons. Agnes slipped out the door, just as Enid reached the exit.

Low whispers filtered out of the shadows of the alley. Soft giggles hinted there was more than one couple avoiding prying eyes. A sliver of moonlight crept into the entrance, leading the way to North Terrace.

Enid's heels clicked loudly on the pavers. A gasp, then silence. A couple fled back into the dance hall.

The Heir's silhouette moved into the moonlight. He moved like liquid, in graceful movements, and was gone. Sylvia and Olive followed; slower, less gracefully. They paused at the alley entrance, then raced across the street.

Enid glanced up at the sky. The moon was setting. Even Sylvia couldn't track Fae on a moonless night, but a troll could. Enid's heart plummeted into her stomach. Mortals could never hold their own against the creatures of the Otherworlds. They had no choice. She needed to gain Agnes' trust if they were to deliver the Heir to the Fae Queen alive.

Footsteps sounded near the entrance. Enid's skin buzzed.

"Olive?" whispered Enid. "Sylvia?"

Sylvia's voice replied in her head. *Keep the girl out of the way, and find out what she knows.*

Enid nodded, and held her breath and listened at the deepening shadows, as she waited for her eyes to adjust to the light. There were faint, quickened breaths, the smell of cigarette smoke and the sweet aroma of *Tabac Blond*.

Enid's lip curled. Agnes' father would be mortified to discover his daughter had the audacity to wear such an evocative scent.

"Agnes?" Enid whispered in a calm voice.

Footsteps shuffled towards the street.

Enid dashed towards the end of the alley entrance, to cut off Agnes' escape.

"They will never catch him once he reaches the Gardens," said Agnes.

"He's not what you think he is." Enid fashioned a friendly smile on her lips. A Fae Charm had to be broken gently, like a thin-shelled egg, or the whole cake is ruined.

"I won't let you take him," Agnes replied.

The shell was cracking. Enid took a step back.

"Agnes, you can trust me. These feelings... they aren't..." She lowered her hands. "I know this may be hard to believe, but he's affecting your mind."

Agnes shook her head.

Enid bit her lip. She didn't have time to play nursemaid to a lovesick girl. Agnes had to accept the truth; she'd deal with the consequences later. "He's not of this world."

"I know."

Enid raised an eyebrow. Perhaps the girl hadn't heard her correctly? Enid spoke slowly: "He's not human."

"I. Know." Agnes' words were deliberate, as if she were talking to a senile old lady. She feinted to the right.

Enid sidestepped in the opposite direction. She was too old to be fooled by such an obvious manoeuvre.

Agnes glared at Enid's amulet and hissed: "Your magic can't hurt me." She clasped the talisman at her throat.

Enid shrugged her shoulders. "We can dance all night, if need be."

"You can't win," said Agnes.

Enid stepped forward. Agnes' amulet pulsed with a faint purple glow. Enid was forced back. She tried to draw on the residual magic in her amulet. It remained cold at her throat. She narrowed her eyes. So, it was a protective talisman. The question still remained: was the girl a Bounty Hunter, or just a smitten mortal?

"What are *you*?" asked Enid.

"I am in love." Agnes stroked the talisman at her neck, and smiled.

Enid frowned; Agnes' answer had the vague ambiguity of a Fae reply.

"You think you're in love," said Enid. "The necklace is magic. A Fae charm."

Agnes shook her head furiously. "You don't understand. I love him, and he loves me." She cupped the talisman in her hand. It glowed brighter. "Ren gave it to me for protect me from magic. All magic. It proves his love is true. It protected me from the creature, and from--"

"Us?" finished Enid.

Agnes sucked in a sharp breath, and nodded.

"I saw you and Mrs Oldham at the picnic," she replied. "When the Fae magic froze everyone, you weren't affected." She stepped back from Enid. "What are *you*?"

"We're Protectors," said Enid. "Our duty is to protect this world."

Agnes' gaze darted over the alley and lingered on Enid's empty hands. Her shoulders relaxed.

"That's what you say." She stepped forward. "Ren said no one is to be trusted. You're all out to trap him."

The Aether shuddered around them. The hair on Enid's arms prickled. Agnes glanced past Enid, out of the alley.

"You won't catch him," said Agnes touched the talisman at her throat. "Do what you want to me. I'm not afraid of you."

Another wave washed over them. A burst of ozone rolled through the alley. A sharp, acrid taste of sulphur caught in Enid's throat.

"Troll!" She spun on her heel and ran into the street. The smell lingered on the stone wall of the building.

Agnes followed her out of the alley.

"Can't you smell it?" Enid fumbled at her waist for her non-existent

Focus. Bollocks.

Agnes wrinkled her nose.

Enid ran to where she'd parked the motorcar. It was gone. Her heart plunged into her stomach.

"Owen?" She scanned the street. There was no sign of him. She cursed under her breath. She shouldn't have sent Owen to fetch the motorcar alone. She glared at Agnes. "If Owen is hurt..."

Agnes grasped her talisman.

"You silly girl," said Enid. "The Bounty Hunter tracked the Heir, and found a mortal instead." She swallowed.

"It's not my fault," said Agnes.

"It followed you," hissed Enid.

"But, why? Ren's just a nor--"

"Foolish girl. He's the Heir to the most powerful Fae Kingdom in the Otherworlds. If we don't find him, this world will be invaded by the Fae, and they are not the forgiving sort. You will all pay with your lives."

"But it's not our fault." Agnes swallowed. "He just wanted to be with me."

"And doomed this world. The Bounty Hunter will make sure he never returns."

"The Queen won't blame the Earth," said Agnes. "Ren will explain. You'll see."

"Not if he's dead," said Enid.

Agnes froze. A strangled cry caught in her throat. "No, not Ren. We have to save him." Agnes grasped Enid's sleeve. "Please, you have to help me."

Enid glared at the girl's hand. Agnes snapped it away.

"Please, Miss Turner," said Agnes, "If you are a Protector, it's your duty to help me, isn't it?"

Enid grit her teeth. The girl was right; she'd sworn a duty to protect this world and all its inhabitants. She couldn't deny her plea.

A third wave of Aether, much fainter this time, fluttered over her. Agnes' talisman flickered in the gloom.

It seemed to react to each surge of Aether. If she could use it to track the disturbances...? Her heart stirred in her gut, and lifted again.

"He gave you that talisman?" she asked.

Agnes nodded. "It protects me--"

Enid grabbed her hand and dragged her across the street.

"You're hurting me." Agnes struggled against Enid's grip.

"I'm helping you." Enid grinned.

The talisman flickered as they reached the footpath on the other side of the street. It glowed brighter as they strode past the hospital, towards the gardens. Enid searched the dimly lit street. A Lincoln-sized shadow loomed in front of the Botanic Park. Her heart raced.

"There!" Enid let go of Agnes' hand and sprinted along the footpath.

"Owen!" Enid ran up to the vehicle and leaned through the open window. It was empty.

Owen was gone. Her heart pounded.

There was a faint rustle of paper on the floor. A red cap peeked out from under the front seat.

"Red?"

The garden gnome lay on top of a scattered pile of photographs. Enid picked one up. It was one of the reporter's photographs from day of the picnic.

"How did you get these?"

Red stared back at her.

Agnes puffed and wheezed as she caught up.

"You shouldn't smoke," grumbled Enid.

Agnes screwed up her nose.

"There's that smell again," she whispered. "Is that the Bounty Hunter?"

"That's a troll." Enid turned towards Albert Bridge and sniffed the air. The stench of troll was strong. "And it's close."

Agnes spun, and ducked behind the motorcar.

"We have to find them." Enid pressed her hand on bonnet of the motorcar. It was still warm. "They can't be far away." Her hand trembled. She clenched it tight, trying to push visions of a broken Owen out of her mind, and searched the shadows under the trees.

chapter fifteen

the horizon shone with a pale pink hue. Light trickled along the road, highlighting every bump in the macadamed surface. A faint pall of ozone and sulphur still cloaked the area. Enid and Agnes had searched for what seemed like hours. Scorches scarred Albert Bridge, and part-way along the riverbank.

Enid smudged the soot on the bridge and smelled her fingertips. Sylvia had been here, and had obviously intended on taking no prisoners. No doubt, she and Olive were still hunting troll.

Enid leaned over the bridge rail. The River Torrens crawled along the bottom of the small gully. There was no sign of the troll. She shivered. This was the spot it'd first attacked. Poor Owen had taken the full brunt of the assault.

She scanned the river banks. It had survived once before. Her gut told her she hadn't seen the last of her nemesis. Perhaps it had slithered back into the safety of the rock? Without her Focus she had no way to tell.

Enid huffed and returned to the Zoological Gardens where Agnes waited. The gates were locked tight. There was no residual buzz of energy. Sylvia and Olive hadn't gone that way, and Owen wouldn't risk snagging his expensive suit on the iron pickets. He was a city boy; he would've stuck to the streets and avoided the unfamiliarity of the trees.

"There's nothing here," she said to Agnes. "We need to look elsewhere."

They trekked back to the Lincoln as dawn crept over the city. One wheel of the abandoned motorcar sat on the curb, another wedged in the gutter. Enid frowned. She'd taught Owen to drive better than that. Her heart thumped. Horror-filled visions of Owen's fate overwhelmed her, fuelled by the lingering stench of burnt troll. Her hand trembled as she opened the driver's side door. Her nails dug through her gloves into her palm, as her imagination plotted even more terrifying outcomes. She clenched her fingers; she shouldn't drive in this state. She took a slow, deep breath and forced a smile.

"Agnes, time for that driving lesson." Enid stepped aside and held the door open.

Agnes trailed a gloved finger along the chassis, and flashed a grin. She jumped in and gripped the steering wheel, and hesitated.

Her grin faded.

"But Father...?" Her hands dropped from the steering wheel. "He'd never approve."

Enid frowned. No grown woman should be bound to her father's will. The girl was young, and had a lot to learn about how to survive in the world of men. She closed the door. Her frown melted into a genuine smile.

She whispered in Agnes' ear: "I won't tell him, if you don't."

Agnes slid her foot across the chassis floor onto the accelerator. Paper stuck to the sole of her shoe. She picked up an envelope and several photographs, and shuffled through them.

"That's a--" Her eyes widened.

"A dead troll. Best sort, really." Enid liberated the photographs from her and slipped them under the dash. "It's a Bounty Hunter, like the one after your beau, and it won't stop until it has him." She slipped into the passenger seat and pushed the starter. "Now, drive. Put the gear shift lever into neutral." Enid wrapped her other hand around the lever between them. "Open the throttle to..." She pointed to switches and buttons on the dash. "About quarter, and advance the spark lever to about half."

Agnes reached for the lever.

"No." Enid tapped the instrument board. "This one. And then that one. Towards you."

Agnes moved the lever under Enid's watchful eye.

Enid nodded. "Now press the foot start switch, and--"

The engine clicked. Agnes' shoulders slumped.

"Don't fret, dear. It took my Owen several attempts to get the hang of it." Enid's chest tightened at the mention of his name. She snatched her fingers away from the instrument board. Damn it. She was a Protector; she couldn't let a civilian see her fear. "He still has problems on occasion. Try again. Just concentrate on the levers."

Agnes opened the throttle and adjusted the spark lever in her direction. Enid reached across and tapped the start switch with her foot. The vehicle jiggled, and the engine roared to life. The rhythmic rumble calmed Enid's nerves. She'd find Owen. She had to.

"Well done," she said. "I doubt your father could do that."

Agnes giggled.

The Lincoln shuddered as it dismounted the footpath and pulled away from the curb. The post-dawn light flashed in the rear mirror as they turned back towards the city.

Something sharp poked in Owen's back. He shifted his body to get comfortable. His elbow thumped against the bed. It was hard as rock. He groaned. He'd have a word with the manager after breakfast, or possibly brunch. He snuffled, yawned, and rolled over. His hat rolled off his chest.

Something scratched his ear. He'd also have a word to housekeeping about their over-zealous use of starch on the bed linens.

Grit caught in the back of his throat, and ground between his teeth. It tasted bland, with a hint of moss. He sat up slowly, refusing to open his eyes. His head throbbed. He groaned again. The Crones must have spiked his punch. Next time he'd stick to a sensible drink, like whisky.

Owen rocked forward, slowly, and swung his legs off the bed.

Thunk.

Pain reverberated through his heels and up his shins. He moaned. He hadn't made it to the bed. He'd slept on the floor again. He collapsed back onto the ground and let his arms fall back onto his chest. He could still taste the stench of the stone creature. He rested his arm over his eyes and winced. What a nightmare!

He squeezed his eyelids tight, not yet ready to face the morning, and reached out to silence his clock before the alarm trilled at him. Scratchy ribbons tickled his neck. He lowered one hand and brushed the ground. Instead of the plush hotel carpet, his fingers dug into soft earth.

A cockatoo screeched above him.

"Bloody hell." His eyes snapped open.

Spots of sunlight danced across his vision as leaves of a Moreton Bay Fig rustled above him. Water trickled nearby.

Owen wriggled; his bladder cautioned him to move slowly.

A woman's voice carried on the breeze: "Come back, Margaret." The sound of trickling water stopped. A girl giggled. Irregular footsteps receded.

Owen pulled himself out of the concealment of the protective buttressed root walls of the massive fig, leaned against the thick trunk. Rough bark dug into his palm. He scanned the surrounding trees.

The sun had barely risen above the trees. Water dripped from a nearby brass drinking fountain. A young girl, her pigtails flapping, skipped along a path running under an avenue of Moreton Bay Figs. A man in a slick business suit and Fedora strode towards him along the path. He checked his watch, and strode faster.

Owen leaned back into the deep shadows of the fig, and waited for the man to pass, then lifted his leg over the tall roots.

His stomach growled. He snatched up his hat, knocked out the dent, and slapped it on his head. He dusted off his frock coat and checked his hands. The bark had grazed his palms. Dirt caked under his fingernails. His stomach grumbled again. First breakfast, then a change of attire. He would get stares at breakfast, but it couldn't be helped. He couldn't concentrate without a full stomach.

Owen strode along the path south, in the direction the man had taken. He slipped his hands into his pocket for a handkerchief to wipe his hands. A sheet of paper fluttered to the ground. He snatched it up. It was the photo he'd retrieved from Enid's motorcar; the one from the reporter, with the murder scene from the Humbug Scrub picnic. Doyle was there, leaning over a crumpled body of a troll-like creature, like the one that had crawled out from under Albert Bridge. Pain sliced through his temple. He winced. The one the Crones had murdered.

He examined the group gathered around the body. He'd had dinner with Mr Waite from the Museum just last week; they'd discussed a donation for a new exhibit. He flicked a speck of dirt off the face of the woman standing next to him. It was the younger Crone, Mrs Oldham.

Owen froze mid-step. She stared back at him from the photograph. His chest tightened as he met her gaze. He'd seen the same cold, calculating look when her fellow Crone murdered the Veteran on the bridge. Shadows crept over her face. She stared at him as if cursing him. His hand trembled. He crossed himself, folded the photograph into his pocket, and strode towards the Garden's exit.

Leaves churned around him. A sudden gust caught them and dashed them at his feet. His breaths quickened. It wasn't a nightmare. It was real. It had happened. The trees whirled. He gasped for breath.

Owen staggered back a step. He flailed for something to steady himself. His knuckles slammed into the cold metal of a brass water fountain. He turned, slammed the ball of his hand into the faucet, and plunged his face into the stream of cool water. He shook the water from his hat, threw back his head, and flicked his dripping fringe off his face.

Pain cracked through his head. His stomach lurched. If witches roamed the streets of Adelaide, and the troll was real, then perhaps the rumours of fairies in the Hills were real too. He slapped his hat back onto his head. He had to find Doyle. He knew of such things.

Enid tugged her skirts from the door of the motorcar, and rushed towards the door of the Grand Central Hotel. Agnes followed.

"Good morning, Miss Turner." The young porter tipped his cap as she approached. His gaze tracked over her vintage attire. He smiled. "Was the ball to your liking, Miss?"

"Pardon?" Enid halted at the door.

Agnes joined her. "It was a hoot."

The porter glanced at Agnes, in her shimmering beaded evening gown, with its plunging back neckline. The corner of his mouth twitched. He cleared his throat.

"I'm afraid Mr Barrington hasn't returned as yet," he said calmly. "If you would care to wait in the lounge, I shall inform you when he returns."

"He's not here?" Enid's heart pounded. The horrific visions returned, this time more catastrophic.

A flurry of green, pink and black burst through the door. Green, sequined chiffon peeked out from a men's tuxedo jacket, barely covering the V-shaped netting concealing the burn scar on her chest.

"I've been looking for you everywhere." Olive caught her breath.

"Sylvia's livid." She eyed Agnes with red-rimmed eyes.

"Olive, you've been crying," said Enid. "Are you all right?"

Olive nodded, and smiled, unconvincingly.

"Ghosts of the past." She leaned against the door. "That reporter followed us. We split up and lost him, so I went after him to see what he was up to. He went snooping around the chauffeur's rooms."

A few pedestrians stared, and hurried past them.

Olive moved away from the door into the street, and lowered her voice: "The real chauffeur was found yesterday, bludgeoned to death. Been dead for a few weeks. The dead troll from the picnic must've been wearing his likeness since then."

"There was nothing in the papers," said Enid.

"The reporter must've found out," said Olive. "He went straight to the driver's rooms. Seems my Frank knew his father. He died too." Olive handed her a small, metal frame with a photo of a middle-aged man in army uniform.

"The father died in the war?" asked Enid.

"No," replied Olive. "He was found dead, in the Torrens, the day before the picnic."

Agnes stepped closer. "That can't be a coincidence."

Olive pulled Enid closer to the parked Lincoln, and whispered in her ear: "Why did you bring her? We can't trust her."

"I think we can," replied Enid. "She's been trying to hide the Heir."

"His name is Ren," said Agnes. "Mr Ren Fairchild."

"Fairchild?" Enid raised an eyebrow.

Olive glared at the girl. Agnes shrank back.

"Where's Sylvia?" asked Enid.

"She went to the Gardens," replied Olive.

"To look for Owen?" Enid's mind raced with growing nightmares. She needed to know he was safe. "Have you seen him?" Her throat tightened as she spoke the words.

"Didn't you send him home?" asked Olive.

"He took the Lincoln," said Enid. "We found it abandoned near the Zoo."

"We've been looking for the Heir," she said.

Agnes spoke: "His name is--"

Olive glared at her again.

"Please, you have to help him," pleaded Agnes.

Enid patted the girl's hand.

"We are. It's just..." Her mind raced. One vision kept playing, like a looping film; Owen's broken body lying hidden, half consumed by stone. Each thought circled back to the same horrifying conclusion: Owen was dead, and she didn't save him. She wanted to scream, to insist they find him first.

She leaned against the Lincoln's chassis: cool, reassuring. She longed to take a long drive in the Hills, to feel the feel of the wind in her hair. No duty. No promises. To be free.

"Enid?" Olive tapped her on the shoulder.

"Pardon?" asked Enid.

"What do we do now?" asked Agnes.

Enid took a long, slow breath to clear her mind. *What would Holmes do?* All she could think of was: *go back to the scene of the crime.*

"Hop in." She straightened her boned bodice, slid into the driver's seat, and wrapped her hands around the steering wheel.

Agnes jumped in the back seat. Olive hesitated.

"Hurry up, Olive." Enid tapped the wheel. Olive wasn't a keen motorist, but not even Sylvia had mastered *Relocation Magic*. "Or have you got a faster way to get there?"

Olive's jaw tightened. She closed her eyes and sat in the front seat next to Enid, and winced as she closed the door.

Owen's head pounded. He readjusted his dirt-smudged frock coat over his arm. It grew heavier with each step. His foot dragged as it skimmed the curb. He stumbled towards the door the Grand Central Hotel, and cursed under his breath.

The porter's white gloves flashed in the corner of Owen's vision, as he steadied himself. He eyed the young man at the door as he regained his composure.

"Good morning, Mr Barrington." The porter withdrew his hand, and smiled. "Rough night, sir?"

Owen glanced up at the familiar voice. *Bernie*: the youth's name badge confirmed it. Pain clawed at his temple at the reminder of the evening's incidents. He harrumphed in reply, hoping it would dissuade Bernie from enquiring further.

"May I take your coat, sir?" Bernie closed the door behind him.

Owen transferred the ring box to his trouser pocket, and gave his soiled frock coat to him. "Have it cleaned. There's a good chap."

The porter nodded, relieved him of his burden, and folded it neatly.

"What should I tell Miss Turner if she returns, sir?" asked the porter.

"Miss Turner was here?" asked Owen.

The porter nodded. "Her friends were with her. They were asking after you."

A growl caught in Owen's throat. "A brunette, and a severe-looking, older blonde?"

"One was brunette," replied Bernie. "I've seen her before. The other was quite young. A redhead." He grinned. "They were still in their party clothes."

"A redhead?" *The girl from the Palais, the one pawing the raven-haired gentleman.* Owen's head whirled. He blushed at the memory.

"Yes." The young man leaned forward. "She was quite a looker."

"Did Miss Turner say where she was going?" asked Owen.

"They drove off in that trim motorcar of hers. The red one. Mentioned something about seeing the Gardens."

"The Botanic Gardens?" Owen grabbed the porter's arm. "Are you sure?"

"Went off that way." Bernie pointed towards North Terrace, in the direction of that bridge.

Owen's stomach knotted. The brunette would have been one of the Crones, Mrs Oldham. But where was the blonde one? He frowned. What was she up to? He had to find Doyle. He knew about fairies and such things. He'd know what to do.

"You don't look so hot, Mr Barrington." The porter clasped Owen's elbow and steadied him.

Owen straightened his shoulders, trying to ignore the pain ricocheting between his ears.

"Anything else, sir?" asked Bernie.

"Yes." Owen shuffled into the foyer. "Have you seen Sir Arthur?"

"I believe he's at breakfast, sir."

Owen's stomach rumbled, reminding him he hadn't eaten since luncheon yesterday. He started towards the Winter Garden Room.

"Mr Barrington...?" Bernie cleared his throat.

Owen halted.

The young man pointed in the direction of the mirror in the foyer. Owen glanced at his reflection: no tie, his unbuttoned collar caught in his hair, and his waistcoat was askew. His dress shirt was crumpled, smudged with grass and clay, and had escaped his trousers. Dark patches marred the elbows of his sleeves. His cuff flapped as he lifted his hat, and ran his fingers through his dishevelled fringe.

A stray leaf - emerald green with a dollop of chrome yellow worthy of Van Gogh's palette - clung to his hand. He flicked it onto the carpet, and tucked in his errant shirt as hotel guests dribbled out of the Dining Room and waited for the lift.

"Are you all right, Barrington?" Doyle escorted his wife and two sons from breakfast. His camera dangled around his neck. Their two sons poked each other, and circled their parents using them as mock shields. He frowned at them. Lady Jean ushered them to one side.

"Only just getting in?" Doyle winked, and beamed at him. "Are congratulations in order?"

Owen wrangled the loose sleeve cuff, and fastened his collar button. "I need to talk to you, Sir Arthur."

"A formal salutation?" Doyle whispered. "This must be serious."

The lift dinged behind them.

"I'll catch you up later." Doyle waved his wife on.

"Don't forget we're on the train to Melbourne this afternoon," she said.

"I won't, my dear." Doyle kissed her and tussled the boys' hair.

Owen tipped his hat as she corralled the boys into the lift. The metal cage jostled as the boys re-commenced their mock duel.

He glanced beyond the lift, and spied Whitington in the foyer. The reporter strode up to the front desk and smiled at the Receptionist. She pointed in their direction.

Owen stepped in front of Doyle to shield him from the reporter's view, and lowered his voice. "You're an expert on the supernatural and otherworldly creatures." He retrieved the unfolded photograph he'd commandeered from Enid's Lincoln, and handed it into Doyle. "What do you know about this creature?" He stood back and caught his breath. He had to know he wasn't imagining things.

Doyle rummaged in his pocket, perched a pair of spectacles on his nose, and studied the photograph. He frowned.

"A troll?" He peered closer at the image. "Is that Mr Waite? And me?" His eyes widened. "The murdered chauffeur was a troll? But where...?"

Owen's eye throbbed. The pain was returning. He grit his teeth and pressed his fingers against his temples.

"I saw another one, under the bridge near the Zoological Gardens," he whispered. "The Crones attacked it."

Doyle's eyes widened. "Show me."

Owen shook his head. "First, can you help me, please? Enie is in danger."

"Of course." Doyle pocketed his spectacles.

"Thank you."

Owen led Doyle along the edge of the foyer, keeping between him and Whitington.

"Into the breach, go the valiant." Doyle grinned.

chapter sixteen

nid's heart raced as her Lincoln motorcar sped along the street towards Albert Bridge, partly due to her growing fear for Owen's life, and partly from the exhilaration of wind tugging her hair, and a short taste of freedom.

"What is that thing?" Agnes shrank away from the ceramic garden gnome on the seat between her and Olive.

"Red?" Enid's attention didn't waver from the road. "He's a garden gnome."

"They're all the rage in Europe," said Olive.

"It keeps staring at me." Agnes squirmed, and tossed it in the front seat.

Enid nestled him into the seat next to her and patted Red's head.

"Hands on the wheel, Enid!" Olive gripped the back of the passenger seat, and squeezed her eyes shut tight. "And please, slow down."

Buzzing voices filled Enid's head.

"Did you hear that?" asked Olive.

"Over there." Agnes lunged across the front seat and pointed along the side road up ahead.

An undulating shadow streamed out of the road. An insect splattered the side window. Pale amber ichor streaked the glass. The Aether trembled at the edge of Enid's vision.

Enid turned the motorcar into the Carriageway between the Zoological Gardens and Botanic Park.

A surge of bees swarmed out of the trees, towards them. The buzzing intensified. The swarm swooped closer, and engulfed the vehicle.

"Bees!" Agnes batted her hands near Enid's face.

Enid wrenched the wheel. Horns blared as oncoming traffic swerved to avoid them. Agnes braced herself. Olive cursed - a word that would've made a soldier blush.

Enid slammed on the brakes. The Lincoln mounted the curb, shuddered, and slid on the grass.

Several bees shot into the motorcar's cabin. They hummed around Enid's head. Agnes swiped at the air again.

"Listen." Enid grasped the girl's wrist to stay her hand. "They're trying to warn us."

A bee settled on Agnes' nose.

"It won't sting, will it?" She stared, cross-eyed, at it, cocked her head, sucked in a sharp breath. She nodded.

"Hush!" said Enid. "I can't hear." She held out a finger. A bee landed on the tip. It wiggled and twirled. "But where?"

The bee hummed.

"That's not good," She murmured under her breath.

"What's not good?" asked Agnes.

"The Aether is thinning," replied Enid.

"The what?" asked Agnes.

"The Earth's protective Shell is cracking."

The bees hovered in front of Enid's nose, as if listening, then sped away.

"She is coming," said Enid.

"But it's too early," said Olive. "It's not even time for morning tea yet."

"Since when do Fae play fair?" Enid removed her driving gloves, flung them over the steering wheel, and slipped out of the vehicle. "Botanic Park is riddled with Thin Places." She scanned the trees in around them. "We'll never find a portal in time."

"This way." Olive grinned. "Follow the bees." She led the way into the wilderness garden.

The flight of bees led the way.

The landscaped Plane trees lining the Carriageway gave way to native species, and bushes. The trees were wild here, less curated than in the Gardens itself. Gravel crunched under Enid's feet as she ran along the gravel path behind Olive.

"This way." Olive chased the bees. "In the clearing, up ahead." Olive's pace slowed.

The bushland thinned. The bees slowed and circled a grassy clearing, keeping out of the shadows of the trees. Half a dozen trickled back to the clearing and buzzed around Enid's head.

"Here?" Enid raised her hand and tested the Aether. Her amulet remained cold on her chest. "Are you sure? I can't feel anything."

"There's a Fae door near here." Olive's face was pale. She leaned against a gum tree and took several ragged breaths. "I saw it on Orrug's map."

"I thought I was the one out of shape," said Enid.

"Don't--" Olive glared at Enid and caught another breath. "Don't tell Sylvia. She'll have me doing calisthenics." She pressed her hands on her thighs and bent over. "Not my fault. Fought that troll last night. Nasty bugger. No rest since." She gulped down more air.

The bees buzzed louder.

"They're worried," said Enid. "They keep repeating: *She's coming. The portal must be close.*"

Olive leaned back against the trunk. "We still haven't found the Heir, in case you've forgotten." Colour slowly returned to her cheeks.

"Then we need to prepare to fight." Enid scanned the clearing. "Where is Sylvia?"

"Still looking for the Heir. We're on our own." Olive peeled off her linen gloves and dropped them onto the grass. "But I don't have the strength to confront a Fae foot soldier, let alone the Queen herself. And you have no Focus" She pushed herself off the trunk. "We need Sylvia."

Three bees sped off in different directions; the others stayed close to Enid.

Enid glanced along the path behind them and frowned. "Where's Agnes? She was right behind me."

Olive groaned.

"That little minx," hissed Enid.

"I knew we couldn't trust her," said Olive.

"She said she loved him." Enid rolled her eyes. "And I believed her. I--"

One of the remaining bees hummed in her ear.

She waved the messenger away. It returned, hovered in front of her nose, and buzzed furiously in unison with the other two stragglers.

"Enid, I think you should listen," said Olive.

The bee buzzed again - a high, nervous pitch - then sped away, followed by its companions.

"They know where she is." Olive marched after the bees, towards a thick stand of trees. She paused, ducked behind a large tree trunk, and motioned for Enid to join her.

A creek wound between the gum trees and trickled over a small waterfall behind them. Enid shook water droplets off her ankle, and peered through the low hanging branches.

A young couple embraced in the shade of an oak. The man was tall, dark-haired, and impossibly handsome. Enid caught her breath; it was the exquisite young man from the dance.

He leaned back against the trunk, the woman's body against his. Her beaded, backless gown shimmered in the morning sunlight as he ran his pale hand along her exposed spine. Enid's cheeks flushed.

He caressed the woman's hair. Red hair. *Agnes' hair*. His laugh resonated through the Aether.

"Isn't it romantic." Olive's breath warmed Enid's ear. "Just like Romeo and Juliet."

"Mortal and Fae?" Enid harrumphed. "Fated to end just as tragically, I'd say."

Olive clicked her tongue. "Jealous?"

"Of Agnes Farrow?" Enid ran her gaze over his perfect skin. He was Fae; her feelings were a Fae trick - an illusion to entice and compel. "But don't you wish..." She took a deep breath and tore her gaze from his smile.

Olive chuckled quietly. "Protectors aren't immune, you know."

"You seem to be." Enid dug her nails into her palm.

"I have the memories of my Frank. I need no other."

"And you have your Focus," said Enid.

"That, too," replied Olive.

A northerly wind shook the gums. Their shadows darkened.

"We haven't got time for this." Enid stepped into the clearing. "Banks closed." Enid turned to Olive. "Is that what they say?"

Olive nodded.

Mr Fairchild - The Heir - opened his eyes. His gaze settled on Enid. Her heart skipped. Piercing violet eyes that could melt any--

She dug her nails deeper into her palm.

His smile slipped.

"You brought *them* here?" He pushed Agnes away. "You betrayed me?" His eyes darkened, their pupils elongated into slits.

Enid swallowed. Olive grabbed her sleeve and dragged her back, behind the gum.

"No, my love." Agnes cooed in a soothing voice and stroked his hair. "Never."

Enid peeked around the trunk.

"No, Enid," Olive whispered.

"I can resist a Fae *Charm*." Enid straightened her shoulders and dug her nails deeper into her palm.

"If you had your Focus, perhaps." Olive retrieved her fountain pen from her handbag. "But as you don't..."

She clasped Enid's wrist. A blue glow crept from Olive's hand and seeped into Enid's skin. Enid's chest tightened.

Olive whispered in her ear. A foreign word. A familiar word. A word that buried deep into her soul, excising the desire the Fae Heir had interred there. Enid's head cleared as the last of the *Charm* lifted.

The Heir's eyes narrowed. An inhuman presence flitted through her mind. There was no amour. Nothing. No remorse, no emotion at all. It attempted to wriggle back into the vacated space in her heart.

She shivered, suddenly cold. Suddenly alone. How could she have longed for such a creature? Sylvia's warning rang in her ears: *They can't be trusted.*

Get out! Enid pushed back the presence.

Thief. His voice reverberated in the Aether. "You steal your power," he hissed out loud.

"We don't steal," replied Olive. "We borrow."

A growl rumbled in his throat. "You mean to take me."

"No," said Enid. "We are Protectors. It's our duty to protect this world from--"

"Creatures like me?" His perfectly-formed brow arched. His smile distorted.

"Sometimes." Olive slipped her fountain pen behind her back. "If we must."

The Aether rippled. The sky rumbled. A few drops of rain dribbled from the leaves and plopped onto the ground.

Enid flicked a droplet from her hand and eyed the darkening, cloudless sky. The wind caught her skirts. Enid swallowed. The Aether shell would crack at any moment. What should she do without her Focus? She took a deep breath. What would Sylvia do?

Protect the civilian.

She turned to Agnes. "Come away, child."

"No." Agnes clung to the Heir's arm.

"If the Fae Queen discovers you..."

"But we love each other," she replied.

Chilled air rushed over Enid's skin. Another drop of water splashed on her bare hand.

Fae are fickle. Fae are dangerous. They are like cats: unpredictable and easily offended.

"We don't have a choice." Vapour streamed from Enid's mouth as she spoke. "The Heir must return to the Fae."

Another rumble rolled across the sky. Closer this time. Lightning crackled above. A cockatoo screeched and fussed in one of the gum trees at the edge of the clearing.

The sky was streaked with purple, the sun fading.

They didn't have much time. "*She's* coming."

"I won't go back." The Heir stared into the clearing. A ripple in his jaw muscles betrayed him. A chink in his armour. The Fae Queen was getting closer, and he was afraid. "I shall never leave you, *a ghràidh*." He kissed Agnes' fingers.

"I know." Agnes wrapped her arms around him.

Enid frowned.

The trees creaked and swayed along the edge of the creek, as the ground rippled towards them.

Olive lost her balance. "That wasn't the Fae. It's under the ground."

The disturbance darted to one side. Enid flicked another water drop off her leg. She cursed under her breath and glanced in Olive's direction.

"Troll!" they yelled in unison.

Enid launched into the clearing.

The Heir pushed Agnes behind him.

Enid searched for any sign of the creature. Rain drizzled in the half-light, blurring the edges of the clearing. There was nothing.

"You fools," hissed the Heir. "You let it follow you."

"It's been tracking you, like a bloodhound," said Enid.

"I would have known if it was following me." The Heir dusted off his trousers.

"It could scent the smell of a Fae," said Olive.

"I do not smell, Thief." He glared at her.

"Quiet." Enid bent down, brushed aside the grass, and flattened her palm against the soil. The ground vibrated faintly under her hand. "It's close. It hasn't finished with you yet."

"It can't have him," said Agnes.

"Nothing will separate us, *a ghràidh*." He slipped his hand in hers.

Enid spread her fingers wider. There was something. Under her thumb. The ground rumbled again. Closer. Stronger. Her heart raced.

"Get back." She frowned, rose slowly, and examined the ground to her left. The stream gurgled innocently.

"What is it?" Olive joined her.

"Last time, I had to destroy a Fae Portal to stop the troll," Enid whispered. Her voice shook more than she expected.

"I know." Olive patted Enid's shoulder. "We've got this. We just have to keep the Heir alive until the Queen arrives."

"Oh, that's all." Enid took a deep breath. "I wish Sylvia was here."

Energy cracked in the black sky above them. Thunder rumbled in reply.

"*She's* coming." The Heir pulled Agnes close.

"She's taking her time," growled Enid.

"Toying with us," said Olive.

Enid huffed. Sylvia was right: *like a cat with its prey.*

Olive wedged her handbag on her arm, raised her fountain pen. A faint blue glow fanned out over the clearing.

"I can't find the doorway," she said.

The Heir waved his free hand across the clearing. The Aether buzzed fitfully. He frowned.

"What's wrong, Ren?" Agnes clutched him tighter.

He shook his hand. "Something's not ri--" His foot sank into the soil.

Agnes grabbed for him.

The ground collapsed beneath him. He tumbled backwards, into the creek with a splash. Leaves on the overhanging trees shuddered, drenching him with droplets. The water shivered in their shadows. Enid's muscles tensed.

The creek bed rose.

"Get out," she yelled.

A stone fist burst from the water, showering them with water and mud.

Agnes screamed. The Heir cursed; his voice cut through the air with its venom, twisting the words. A faint cord of Aether whipped out from his hand, floundered at a nearby tree trunk, and fizzled.

The troll roared with laughter, grabbed the Heir, and shoved him under the water.

A flickering light enveloped the troll. It snarled, twisted out of the water and pushed the Heir's face into the stones of the creek bed.

The Heir lashed out. Another rumbling laugh. The troll pushed harder.

"Ren!" Agnes' scream gurgled in her throat.

Enid snatched her away. "Let us do our job."

Olive stepped in front of them, and thrust her fountain pen in the direction of the troll. Blue lightning blasted from its nib.

A crackling beam of blue light shot past, forking as it blasted the troll. The creature roared and recoiled from the light.

It shook its head, then pushed the Heir's face further into the stones. The Heir's light wavered.

"Save him!" Agnes struggled to escape Enid's grasp.

Olive stabbed her hand into the air a second time. Another pulse burst over the troll. It yowled in pain.

The troll raised a hand and gestured in their direction. Several large rocks rose from the creek bed and flew at the trio.

Enid cursed, shielded Agnes behind her, and squeezed her eyes shut.

Rain crawled down Enid's face. Flaming light blazed through Enid's eyelids.

Agnes screamed.

Enid's eyes snapped open. A faint red glow bathed the dark clearing.

Rocks hung in the air around them - for a heartbeat - then plummeted to the ground.

Another blast of red light rushed past them.

"Sylvia?" Enid spun on her heel, keeping Agnes behind her.

"Your bees are in a tizzy." Wet hair clung to Sylvia's cheeks. "I thought I'd taught you better than that."

She scowled and blasted the troll again. Stone dust exploded off its shoulder.

The troll released its grip on the Heir. Its eye blazed at the newcomer.

Sylvia attacked again. A jagged line of light pierced the troll's chest. Splintered rock showered them. The creature roared and rammed its fist into the creek bed. The water churned. The trees trembled. The strong scent of fresh eucalyptus caught in the wind and burst through the clearing.

The Heir vaulted out of the water, spluttered and scrambled up the embankment. Agnes dragged him out of the troll's reach, and smothered him with kisses. Enid rushed to help them.

"Leave him alone." Agnes pushed her away. "I'd make a better Protector than you."

The Heir brushed them both aside and rose to his feet.

"Whom do you serve?" The words growled in his throat, slamming the Aether into the ground and flattening the grass in the direction of the troll.

Enid covered her ears. His words sliced through her veins. Sylvia flinched. Fear flashed in her eyes.

"Your..." The troll grit its teeth. "Enemy. Closer than you think."

Compulsion Magic; Enid had heard of such power. She licked her lips. If she could borrow its power...

"Why did you kill the other Bounty Hunter?" Her words tinkled in the Aether, riding the Fae's harmonics.

"Competit--" The troll dug its fist deeper into the earth.

The Heir wobbled and fell against the nearby oak. Beads of perspiration rolled down his forehead.

Sylvia raised her walking stick.

The creature roared and slid back into the earth. The ground rumbled under them. The trees shivered tracking the troll's retreat.

Sylvia eyed the Heir. There was no fear in her eyes this time. Only hate. She smiled. A crooked smile. A triumphant smile - like a cat cornering a mouse and preparing to spring on its prey.

"Remember me?" She circled him with feline stealth. "Typical Fae, flirting with mortality amuses you." Sylvia's voice rose like a knife ready to flay its victim. She turned to Agnes. "You did know his power fades the longer he remains separated from the Fae Kingdom?" Her stick hovered close to the Heir's face, its red glow reflecting in his pupils.

"Your power is fading, isn't it, Fae?"

He sneered and embedded his fingers into the bark of the oak. "Not anymore."

A dark veil flickered over his eyes. He caught his breath.

"Ren?" Agnes stepped closer.

"Stay back." He glared at her through slitted eyes.

"What have you done?" she whispered.

"You've lost control, Fae." The corner of Sylvia's mouth curled higher.

"You won't have me, Thief." His voice scraped the Aether.

A shiver ran down Enid's spine.

Dark, smoky tendrils squirmed out of the ground, slithered up Sylvia's walking stick, and burrowed into her skin. They clawed along her arm and infested her eyes.

"Sylvia!" Olive tried to pull her free.

Tendrils coiled around Olive's arm.

The tree shuddered. The Dark Magic pulsed stronger, channelling through the Heir. The tendrils thickened, growing more opaque, tightening around her fellow Protectors.

"This is all your fault." Olive turned to Sylvia. "You cost me my Orrug." She edged closer to Sylvia, her eyes now tinged with Darkness.

Enid's heart pounded: this was *Old Magic*.

"I thought you were Protectors." Agnes shrank away from them.

"Olive?" Enid swallowed. "What's happening, Sylvia?"

Neither of them responded.

The ground rumbled with laughter.

Enid wrapped her hand around her amulet and concentrated, praying she could access enough energy to combat the Fae's *Dark Magic*. The gem warmed in her palm.

"Ren?" Agnes stepped in front of him.

The Darkness flickered in the Heir's eyes. He gasped. His body shuddered and doubled over. Agnes hugged him, kissed him on the forehead. His violet eyes stared back at her.

The tendrils snaked away from him, and latched onto Sylvia's walking stick.

The rain sizzled in the air behind Enid. Hairs stood up on her neck, and prickled down her arms.

Enid glanced over the silent clearing. The bees had long departed. There was no trickling water from the creek. No birds. Only the constant crackling drone of reshaping Aether.

Sylvia turned to face Olive.

"Stop it!" Enid rushed forward and kicked away Sylvia's walking stick, severing the link with the *Dark Magic*. "The portal is opening."

The ground yowled beneath them. The tendrils recoiled and snapped back into the earth.

Sylvia lost her balance and growled. Olive shook her head, her curls stretched with weight of the rain.

The Darkness faded; their link to the *Dark Magic* was broken.

"See, girl?" growled Sylvia. "This is the true nature of the Fae. How long do you think it will be before it turns on you?"

"I would never harm you, *a ghràidh*." The Heir leaned on her.

Enid wiped a raindrop from end of her nose and sniffed. The sharp, sweet smell of manipulated Aether caught in her nostrils. A light shimmered at eye-level, in the corner of her vision. It elongated downwards, hissing when it touched the wet grass. It extended horizontally at the top, for a few feet, then angled down to the ground, parallel to the other side. The Heir's violet eyes paled in wide-eyed panic. Agnes tugged him closer.

Light flared along the fractures in the Aether. Enid stared at it, the hypnotic whisper of the evaporating raindrops sizzling in her ears. The strips of light widened.

"Don't look." Sylvia turned Enid to face her.

The Heir snatched Agnes' hand, and bolted towards the gravel path, keeping to the safety of the trees.

A pale violet beam of light shot upward and tore a fissure in the twilight Aether. In place of the faded mid-morning sun, shone a full moon in a starless night sky.

A harrowing howl pierced the darkness. The ground shuddered. Enid braced herself.

The Heir muttered. His voice resounded through the Aether, both lyrical and dreadful at the same time. A faint purple glow bathed his hands illuminating the shadows under the trees.

Shadows...? What had Sylvia said about trolls and sunlight? *An old wives' tale,* she'd said. Yet, this one was avoiding it. Perhaps it weakened them? If so, perhaps shadows could strengthen them?

She lunged in the lovers' direction.

"Get out of the shadows," yelled Enid.

Cracks formed in the earth under the trees, near the couple.

Agnes and the Heir lurched forward.

The troll erupted from the ground. It latched onto the Heir with one arm and yanked him further into the shadows; the other burrowed into the earth. Clods of soil thudded to the ground around them.

"Help us!" Agnes grabbed the Heir's coat. Her feet ground into the gravel.

"I'm cursed with children and love-sick women." Sylvia moaned. "Why did you have to like detective stories? Why couldn't you have a passion for crochet, instead?" She grasped her stick in both hands, and muttered a stream of archaic words. Red Aether crackled around its tip.

"Stay." Sylvia glared at them over her shoulder. "Both of you."

They froze.

"We must complete your bargain," she continued, "or this world won't survive. I'll stop the creature. You distract the Fae. Two Protectors should be able to hold a Fae prince."

Olive nodded, and raised her Focus.

"No!" Agnes wriggled to get free.

The Heir's magic sputtered and fizzled.

The troll laughed, grabbed the Heir with both hands, and reeled him closer as it slipped into the earth. The Heir writhed as his feet sank into the ground; his screams raked Enid's nerves.

Sylvia punched her stick into the air. Shockwaves of Aether rippled towards the troll. Fiery-red light flared around it. It howled, and relinquished its prey.

The Heir collapsed to the ground, scrambled backwards, and ran. Agnes wrenched herself free of Enid's hold, and rushed after him.

The troll followed.

Sylvia pointed her stick in the direction of the fleeing couple. The Aether cover split above them, catching them in a shaft of moonlight.

Iridescent dragonfly-creatures slipped through the rectangular crack of the invisible door. One flitted around Enid's head and raced back towards the opening portal. The rest of the Guard flanked the area.

The troll halted, and edged away from the moon's Fae light.

Sylvia grinned and continued the onslaught, striding closer to it with every step. The troll slid back towards the moonlit shaft. It snarled and grabbed a tree trunk, halting its momentum.

Sylvia gripped her stick in both hands. It crackled. Its red light flickered and fizzled.

Olive rushed forward.

"No!" hissed Sylvia. "Make sure he returns to his own kind, where he belongs." Her teeth clenched. "Promise me!"

Olive nodded, joined Enid. They moved to join the couple in the moonlight circle. The Fae Guard blocked them.

"Don't move." Enid grabbed Olive's arm and shook her head.

Sylvia rammed her walking stick into the damp earth. It slipped in easily, like a skewer into a perfect sponge.

"Sylvia, no!" Olive's handbag dropped onto the grass with a soft thud. "It's too unpredictable."

Sylvia tapped the ground beside her, three times.

Wind howled in the trees.

She struck the ground again. Three times.

The increasing wind yanked at her skirt.

Grey tendrils of Aether curled along the silver walking stick. It surged along its etched decoration, mixed with her own red Aether, and gushed out of her hand, smothering the troll.

Her hand trembled.

She tugged her walking stick. It remained wedged in the earth, the *Old Magic* holding fast; it wasn't about to give her up that easily. Sickly orange sparks spewed from the tip of her stick.

Sylvia's body stiffened. The flesh on her palm hissed. Wisps of smoke rose from between her fingers.

Olive rushed forward as pale violet light bathed the group.

The wind stilled. The trees stopped moving. The cockatoo squawked and took flight. Its wings blurred, glitched, and froze. The rain halted; the suspended drops glistened in the air.

Agnes clung to the Heir.

The troll fled along the edge of the Guard wall, its movements slowed as if it was wading through molasses. Time was slipping.

Enid's heart raced. The Fae Queen was coming. She glared at the troll.

"Who sent you?"

The troll pushed forward in fractured, jerky movements, laughing like a jumping gramophone.

The Aether portal cracked open and dissolved into the air. Light rushed out of the portal and swirled around the troll. It slowed, and froze.

The drone of flapping wings flooded the clearing. Hundreds of Fae illuminated the area. The aroma of pine washed over them. What was once a clearing surrounded by gum trees was now a thick forest of firs and oak.

The tendrils withered. Dark Aether trickled from the etchings on Sylvia's walking stick, and seeped back into the earth.

A soft breeze caressed Enid's ears - warm and enticing. It smelled of roses, and honey, and fresh earth after a spring rain. She turned slowly.

"You should listen to your comrade, Protector. I thought you'd learned your lesson. *Old Magic* is not yours to command."

chapter seventeen

wen stepped aside as a well-dressed couple paraded, arm-in-arm, past him in the laneway, guided by a feisty Terrier. It yanked and strained its tether in the man's hand. Its paws clicked urgently as it tugged them towards Rundle Street.

"Hurry up, Sir Arthur." Owen glanced back to his companion, and paused. Doyle wasn't there. "Sir Arthur?"

He peered past the couple. Doyle crouched near the footings of the nearby hotel.

He waved for Owen to join him. Owen sighed, threw up his hands, and hurried back to retrieve him.

"What are these?" asked Doyle. "I've never noticed them before."

"Noticed what?" asked Owen.

"These doors. There's one around the corner at the furniture store, as well."

Owen examined the concrete footing. There was something. An arched outline. Pain clawed his eyes and seared through his head. His vision blurred. Bloody headaches! He massaged his eyelids with his thumb and forefinger.

His vision cleared slowly: moulded into the concrete was a small, brown door edged with dark stone quoins and a fanlight above.

"Huh." Owen frowned. "Never noticed that before." And he was a regular at the Exeter.

Light pulsed behind the fanlight. A burst of heat rolled over them.

Owen braced himself. Doyle wobbled. Owen steadied him.

A man stood nearby, holding his coat over one shoulder by its lapel, and watched Doyle from the corner of his eye. He caught Owen's eye. He was likely a Nitpicker, watching for the constabulary to warn the publican. Owen shook his head.

"He's with me." He chuckled. "He's a tourist." He pulled Doyle to his feet.

The gentleman's shoulders relaxed, but he didn't move. He kept an eye on them as they strode towards North Terrace.

The thumping behind his eyes eased. He grimaced. This was all the Crones' doing; they'd likely cursed him. He tugged Doyle's sleeve.

"We need to go," he said. "We've no time for gawping. I need to save Enie." He halted mid-step, and let go of Doyle's jacket.

But how? Where? What would Enid do? Scratch that; what would Holmes do? That's what she would do. All he could think of was: the bridge.

"Where are we going?" asked Doyle.

"Albert Bridge," replied Owen. "The crones murdered the old soldier, and attacked that creature there, last night." He strode along the lane, towards North Terrace. "Return to the scene of the crime. Isn't that what your detective does?"

"Yes, observe the scene of the crime for ourselves." Doyle grinned. "Excellent thinking."

Owen glared at him. "If you call me Watson, I'll thump you, knighthood or no."

Sun glinted off the River Torrens below. Owen searched the banks for any hint of the previous night's slaughter. The bridge looked less foreboding in the daylight. Perhaps it had all been a bad nightmare? He rubbed his temple. Perhaps someone *had* spiked the punch.

"Look at this, Barrington." Doyle beckoned for Owen to join him on the bridge.

Owen's stomach churned.

Scorched smudges pock-marked the wood planks. He peered over the bridge where the Veteran had fallen. He felt sick.

"No, no, no." He spun on his heel, searching for any sign that could lead him to Enid. His heart pounded. He had to find her.

"There's patches of stone dust near the burns," said Doyle. "They went this way."

Owen hurried after him.

The stone dust led past the Zoological Gardens, along the Carriageway into the Botanic Park. Lines of rubber marred the road. Owen tracked them to the Park. A hint of red peeked through the trees, just off the carriageway, and along a gravel path.

"The Lincoln!" He rushed up to Enid's motorcar, grabbed the door, and leaned in. "Thank God, you're--"

Enid's gloves draped over the steering wheel, but there was no Enid.

Thunder rumbled beyond the trees ahead. The crones? Owen caught his breath. "I'm coming, Enid."

Owen jumped into the driver's seat. One of Enid's garden gnomes sat in the front passenger seat. Its creepy black eyes stared at him. Enid loved the diabolical-looking things. They just gave him the willies. He tossed it into the back seat and wiped his hand on his trouser leg.

Owen snatched up Enid's glove and stared down the gravel path. Somehow the vehicle's metal chassis made him feel safer. Like armour. Eighty horse-powered armour.

Doyle caught up and leaned on the door next to him.

"Crank it up," said Owen.

"You can't drive this in there," said Doyle. "The path is too narrow."

"You catch up, then."

Doyle's camera clunked against the radiator as he cranked the vehicle.

Owen stomped the accelerator all the way to the floor. The engine roared. The wheels spun, spitting up stones from the path.

Doyle jumped clear of the motorcar.

Owen pulled the lever into low gear. The engine stalled. He thumped the steering wheel and cursed, acutely aware of the ring box weighing down his trouser pocket. He'd failed. Yet again. His hands trembled. He caught his breath and slipped his hand into his pocket. His hand nudged the ring box. His stomach knotted. He'd planned to spend the rest of his life with Enid. He had it all planned: they'd travel the world, have a brood of children. And he'd paint it all.

He turned the box over in his fingers. A two carat Asscher-cut diamond in platinum - the biggest, most fashionable one available in Adelaide - with perfect symmetry, to match his Enid. She loved him; he was certain of that. So, why couldn't he find the courage to ask her the simple question?

The pain returned, slicing through his temples and skewering his skull. Tears stung his cheeks as his head fell onto the steering wheel.

"The bounty hunter will not bother us now." A tall, lithe creature with pale skin, hair of midnight, and captivating violet eyes stood in the portal's threshold. A sleek, grey hound tugged at its silver chain in her right hand.

"It seems you have kept your part of the bargain." The Fae Queen smiled at them.

Enid smiled back. A wave of calm washed over her. Her fingers relaxed.

Olive lowered her Focus and turned to face the Queen.

The Aether shuddered. Pale light flashed over the Heir's hands. He wiggled his fingers and frowned.

"Ren?" Agnes gripped his hand.

"It's nothing, *a ghràidh*." He squared his shoulders, wrapped his arm around Agnes, and returned her gaze.

The Queen's eyes flared.

Agnes flinched and lowered her eyes.

The girl wasn't affected by the Queen's *Temporal Magic*; the talisman was still protecting her. The Fae Princeling had given her a valuable keepsake. His mother would not be pleased.

Sylvia turned, smoke still rising from her scorched palm. Her Focus crackled and whined.

"I didn't ask for your help." She glowered and leaned on her walking stick.

The Fae Queen's gaze fixed on her son, and the mortal in his arms. She stepped out of the portal, onto the grass. Another division of Fae Guard swarmed out behind her and circled the group, separating them from Sylvia and the frozen troll near the moonlit barrier.

A gentle wind swirled through the clearing, warming the chill air. The tips of Olive's chiffon fairy wings thrummed in the breeze, above the borrowed jacket.

Pale violet light rolled over the clearing. What was once gum trees and native vegetation, was now a thick forest of firs and oak. In place of grass, a field of bluebells swayed silently in the breeze, filling the clearing with their sweet scent.

The Fae door shimmered. Shapes writhed and glinted inside its shifting surface. Three more hounds snapped at the gateway, held back by tall, lithe Fae brandishing swords in their other hand. Behind them, hovered ranks of Fae soldiers.

The gate shimmered again, and the spectacle was gone.

Enid's heart plunged into her stomach. It seemed the Fae Queen was indeed prepared for war if she didn't get her way.

Olive tried to push past the Guard. The sound of rapid-beating wings pounded the Aether.

The Fae Queen nodded to the Guard. "Let the Protector pass."

Olive manoeuvred through their ranks and rushed to Sylvia.

Sylvia waved her away, shifted her weight off her walking stick, and stood tall, the immobile troll behind her.

"I didn't expect we'd ever meet again, Protector." The Queen's eyes darkened to the colour of ripe mulberries.

The Fae guards' wings fluttered faster.

"Did you not learn your lesson last time, Sil'viya?"

Sylvia flinched.

Enid swallowed. To know someone's true name gave you power over them.

The Queen eyed Sylvia, her gaze lingering on the silver walking stick in her hand. Her lips quivered in anger.

"Just try it," hissed Sylvia.

The Queen's caught Sylvia's direct gaze. This time Sylvia didn't flinch. She gripped her walking stick tighter. The Fae Queen turned to her son.

"Time to come home, child." The Queen's voice was calm, her words soothing, like honey. "Playtime is over. You must return to your rightful place where you belong."

Agnes gasped. "But, Ren--"

He pulled her close and kissed her forehead. "Don't fret, my love. I promised. I won't leave you." He glared at the Queen.

"If you stay, you will be in danger." Only a sliver of mulberry rimmed the Queen's enlarged pupil. The Aether shuddered. The troll twitched forward - and froze again.

"Listen to your mother, boy," growled Sylvia. "You endanger us all by remaining."

The corner of the Queen's lip curled.

"I love your son." Agnes wrapped his fingers in hers.

"She is but a child, not even adult in the human world," said the Queen to her son. "What does she know of love?"

She curled a finger under Agnes' chin and lifted it up to face her. She leaned close, and drew in a slow breath. To the girl's credit, she didn't flinch. She stared back. Water rimmed her eyelids.

The Queen sniffed again, longer this time, and caught her breath. She chuckled softly. Her gaze flashed over the Protectors.

"I love Agnes." The Heir clasped her hand, and stepped between them.

"Careful, Little One," said the Queen. "Time was, you would shudder at the mention of a human." She sniffed in her son's direction. "The stench of human mongrel has already infested you." She sneered. "Or perhaps, it is lust?"

"I love this mortal, and you cannot change my mind. I am resolved to stay," he replied. "I shall stay."

"Love?" Sylvia scoffed and thumped her stick onto the ground. "Fiddlesticks! It's not in your nature." She stepped forward.

The Fae guard buzzed angrily and blocked her path.

"Where are my manners?" The Queen waved her hand at them, as if shooing flies.

The Guard parted. "It's an honour to receive a Protector into my domain." She swooped low, in an exaggerated bow.

Sylvia eyed the Guard, and motioned to Olive.

A frown wrinkled the queen's smooth, alabaster skin.

Olive hesitated, then stepped inside the Queen's circle. Two of the guard flitted back to partially close the gap.

A slight movement caught the corner of Enid's eye. She scanned the area. Sylvia hadn't moved.

The Queen smiled sweetly and placed a slender hand on the Heir's shoulder. A faint purple light glowed between her fingers. His shoulders relaxed.

"She is but a child, my son." Her melodic voice commanded everyone's attention. She trailed a finger along his cheek, tracing a faint, momentary glow on his skin. "Your mind is clouded. How can I expect you to make such a decision without all the facts?"

"I will not change my mind, mother."

"If you stay with her," the Queen's voice flowed like syrup, like over-sugared coffee, "This world will suffer." And there was the bitter aftertaste.

Muffled stirs came from the other side of the shimmering portal.

The colour drained from Agnes' face. Her gaze darted from the Heir to Enid. Hope was fading from her eyes; they pleaded for her help. Enid's heart sank. The poor girl. He would break her heart. Olive was right; their love was like Romeo and Juliet's. The best she could do is ensure the girl survived.

A tear rolled down Agnes' cheek. "I'll go with you."

The Heir's eyes widened. "Are you sure?" he whispered.

"There's nothing to keep me here," she replied.

"What about your father?" asked Sylvia.

"I'm old enough to make my own decision." She wiped tears from her chin. "I am determined."

He ran his hand down her back. She closed her eyes and smiled.

Enid's heart clawed back into her chest. It was done, out of her hands. It looked like Olive would get her happy ending after all.

"Then it's settled," he said. "Agnes will return with me, and be my bride."

The Queen twisted the hound's chain around her fingers, and glared at him with eyes black as coal.

"You can't love a mortal. It is forbidden!" The air shook with her venom.

The troll's body lurched forward. A white light flared behind it. Its arm jerked.

Olive cried out and stepped forward, almost tripping over her handbag. She reached down and picked it up.

Another flash of white light from behind the troll.

"Sylvia, behind--" Glass crunched. Purple glinted in the grass at her feet.

Agnes clutched at her throat. The Fae talisman was gone. It must have been smashed in the fight with the troll. If it was broken, then...

Olive gasped. "How are you not--?"

"Only a Protector can--" Sylvia glared at the Fae Queen.

The Fae Queen smirked.

"Impossible!" hissed Sylvia.

Enid examined the bluebells at Olive's feet. Purple glinted between the leaves. She ran her fingers over the ground and picked up a gold chain, its links snapped near the, now empty, setting.

"It must've broken when the troll grabbed me," said Agnes.

"You gave her your talisman?" The air shivered. The Fae Queen glared at her.

The troll's limbs grated. Stone dust trickled to the ground.

Bollocks! Enid held her breath.

It froze again.

Enid breathed, edged closed to Olive, and tugged her borrowed jacket.

If it broke before the Fae Portal opened...? Enid hefted the shards of shattered gem in her hand. "Did you have this at the picnic?" She pocketed the broken remains of the talisman.

"No," replied Agnes.

The Heir ran his hand though Agnes' hair. A faint glow shone at his fingertips.

"Impossible." Sylvia frowned.

Olive grasped her handbag to her chest. Everyone turned to face Agnes.

Agnes frowned. "What's wrong?"

"You." Sylvia moaned. "No mortal can ward off *Temporal Magic*."

"You're one of us, dear." Olive grinned, and reached out to embrace her.

"No." Agnes shook her head and stepped away. "I can't be."

"But this is excellent news, my beloved." He hugged her.

The Queen stepped closer and glared at him. Colours shifted and darkened on the portal's surface. Silhouettes twisted and loomed larger on the other side.

"The Fae world will not tolerate you, Protector," said the Queen.

"I don't want..." Agnes pulled the Heir closer. "I shall renounce it. I'll--"

Sylvia shifted her weight off her walking stick.

"That's not an option, dear." Tears rimmed Olive's eyes.

A crack of thunder shook the air. Owen jumped. The ring box thudded to the floor. His hand snapped back to the steering wheel. The chassis rocked gently. The engine idled.

Damn. He'd fallen asleep. He rubbed his eyes and examined the darkened path curving through the trees ahead. Doyle was gone.

The ground rumbled. The motorcar steering wheel vibrated under his palms. Owen's fingers tensed. Another earthquake?

Light flashed in the shadows ahead. Owen's heart lurched into his throat. His headache returned - dull, throbbing, and growing more persistent, playing havoc with his vision.

He stomped on the accelerator. The transmission crunched as he forced the Lincoln into gear. The wheels spun in the gravel. The motorcar lurched forward, fishtailed, and skidded along the path. The garden gnome tumbled along the back seat and righted itself.

A blurred red light bled through the trees caught in a mist. Shadows moved.

Owen glanced in the rear vision mirror. Crisp-edged gums waved at him in the morning sunshine. The garden gnome stared at him, its creepy eyes daring him to action.

"Enie!" He pressed the accelerator to the floor.

The smell of eucalyptus faded. The Lincoln slowed. The air dragged at his skin. An eerie twilight engulfed him. He swerved to avoid a stand of fir trees in the middle of the path, then a large oak.

Another crack. A rumble.

Owen flicked on the headlights and sped towards the pulsing lights. Enid needed him.

They stood in silence: Enid and Olive flanked the love-struck couple corralled within a line of Fae Guard; Sylvia was separated on the other side, sandwiched between them and the moonlit barrier. The troll, still frozen in time, was silhouetted by a bright, white light. The Fae Queen cast a flickering shadow across the glade, as she studied them.

The Queen's hounds' ears twitched to one side. A twig snapped in the shadows of the trees.

"What the--?" Enid tensed. Fae magic played tricks on the mind; the Aether wall should've distracted any curious mortals, persuading them to avoid the clearing.

Another crack. Leaves rustled in a nearby stand of black Alder.

Enid clenched her fingers and cursed the loss of her Focus.

The hound strained on the leash. The Queen tugged it back.

Sylvia raised her walking stick.

The underbrush shook. A man burst out of a clump of wormwood at the base of the Alders. He tugged free of the trees' sticky branches and stumbled into the clearing.

"Sir Arthur?" Enid stepped forward to shield him from the Queen.

"Miss Turner?" He smiled with relief.

"Shouldn't you be boarding the train to Melbourne?" Olive lowered her Focus.

"I'd heard the--" He turned to face the rest of group. His eyes widened. "You're--" He snatched up the camera around his neck. "How exciting." He fumbled with his camera. "Do you mind if I...?"

Enid shook her head. He lowered his camera.

"You have come to honour your promise?" The Queen's voice was calm. "Or did you send your Protectors to defy me?"

Sir Arthur's moustache twitched.

"You know this man?" asked Sylvia.

"He is your Ambassador, is he not?" asked the Queen.

Sir Arthur nodded and bowed to the Queen.

"But you were supposed to forget," whispered Olive.

"You let a mortal make a pact with the Fae?" hissed Sylvia.

Olive's hand trembled.

The Queen tightened the hound's chain and turned to the Heir.

"You would betray your own kind?" The Queen narrowed her eyes.

"Love is everything, mother."

"*Love is smoke, made with the fume of sighs*, as the bard said." The Queen scoffed. "Who do you think was his muse, Little One?"

"Have you forgotten what it is to love, mother?" he asked.

"Stay. Become mortal," she hissed. "It's your choice. But, what kind of mother would I be if I didn't remind you: the longer you remain in this world, the weaker your magic will become. Your tether will diminish, and you will become mortal." She paused, as if to let it sink in. "The bounty hunters will continue to hunt you, and you will not be able to fight them. It will destroy you both. And, if the Protectors do help you survive, you will age, and watch your mortal die." She leaned closer and whispered in his ear. "You will die."

He shied from her touch and wiggled the fingers of his free hand. Fear flashed in his eyes. He closed his fist, and held Agnes tight.

"You lie." He unfurled his fingers. Energy hummed between them. He held his hand up to her. "It has returned. I have enough to protect us both."

The Queen's laugh sliced through Enid's heart. "What you have is borrowed from me, a reminder of what you will lose. You will be cut off. Forever. You cannot save her. You cannot save yourself. You cannot save this world."

His hand trembled. Fear flooded his eyes. He shuddered. He knew the truth.

"What's happening?" Sir Arthur whispered to Enid.

"The end of the world, if we're not careful." Enid pressed a finger to her lips. "Be silent and don't move."

The Heir relaxed his embrace on Agnes and pulled away.

The Queen held out her hand to greet him.

"Ren, no!" cried Agnes.

"Be quiet, girl. You embarrass your kind," said the Queen.

The swarming warriors on the other side of the portal stood to attention.

The Heir took her hand. "I shall return before you know it."

Agnes' shoulders slumped.

Olive's face paled. "You can't," she whispered.

"I--" His hands fell to his sides.

"He has no choice." Sylvia's voice rang in the silent glade. "Unless you want war."

Enid's heart twisted in her chest. She wanted to scoop the girl up and tell her all would end well. She understood what it was to love a mortal. They all needed a happy ending.

He took the Queen's hand. His eyes glistened in the light of the portal. He stepped onto the threshold.

The portal surface cleared. The Fae guard stepped away to allow the Heir entry.

Olive knelt beside Agnes and cradled her in her arms.

"I shall never love another," whispered Agnes, her eyes red with tears.

"Love is nothing but a trick of the mind, girl." said Sylvia. "A whim. Nothing more. It will pass. Best you learn that while you are young. The Fae's magic will return, and he will forget." She leaned on her walking stick. "You will recover, Miss Farrow."

"They're leaving? Our quest is complete?" asked Doyle.

"Silence, human," said the Queen. "I keep my word."

"Are we safe?" he whispered to Enid.

"Enough!" hissed the Queen.

The portal solidified. A dull thumping echoed from on the other side of the closed portal. A shadow squirmed against the surface.

Stone ground behind them. The troll jerked closer to the path.

"Sylvia!" yelled Olive.

Sylvia spun on her heel, and raised her walking stick.

The troll froze.

The forest groaned. Trees shuddered. Rain thudded to the soil around them.

The motionless cockatoo twitched in the air. Its wings flapped, completing their beat. It squawked, swooped, and darted out of the clearing through the flickering barrier of moonlit Aether.

The white light beyond flashed and dipped. The silhouetted troll glitched, and threw up its arms to shield itself from the shuddering light.

Enid shoved Sir Arthur behind the nearest tree.

Olive jumped to her feet.

Sylvia rushed the creature, her stick raised bayonet-style. A single red pulse shot from its tip. The troll rolled its shoulder, and glanced off into the trees.

Sylvia stumbled. The stick sputtered.

"Traitor!" The troll roared and slammed its fist into the earth.

A ripple of energy surged across the glade, slamming Olive into a tree trunk. Enid struggled to keep her balance.

The Fae Queen hissed.

"Get back." Sylvia plunged her walking stick into the soil. She lowered her head and mumbled. Tendrils of energy erupted from the soil and coiled up the stick, taking hold, quicker this time. Shafts of light pierced the troll.

"Sylvia, no!" Olive blasted the troll. Blue energy fizzled along her fountain pen.

Sylvia's body shuddered. The tendrils flickered.

"What does she think she's doing?" Enid pulled Agnes to her feet. "She can't control Earth Magic."

"Do something," Olive screamed at the Queen.

"This is your world." The Queen's face remained emotionless. "Protect it."

Swirling light filled the portal's surface. Two of the Guard flanked her. Yet, she remained, as if waiting for something.

The white light flashed out of the trees, across the clearing. The familiar sound of the Lincoln's engine filled the clearing.

Enid grinned.

The light jumped up into the trees, and flicked back into the bushes.

The engine revved. Gravel crunched and grated.

"That'll be Barrington," Sir Arthur grinned. "The cavalry has arrived."

The motorcar rumbled closer. Branches cracked. The light bounced over the glade.

"I can't--" Olive's breaths were ragged.

Enid clasped Olive's hand. Green light sparked across her fingers. She pointed the Focus in the direction of the troll, and funnelled the Aether through the metal nib.

"*Scutum.*" The words echoed and twisted in her head.

Olive gasped.

Aether belched across the glade in a ball of searing light.

Enid released her grip, thrust her arms over her face, leaving nothing to muffle the sound of cracking wood, crunching bones, and the scream piercing her eardrums.

chapter eighteen

the energy flash blinded Enid. Agnes no longer leaned on her. Enid reached out, probing for the tree behind her, to get her bearings. Her fingers brushed rough bark.

The cockatoo screeched in the distance, to her left. The creek gurgled to her right. A slow hiss - to her front - grew louder.

Stone dust caught in her throat, and the smell of petrol fumes and smoke drowned out the scent of freshly cracked oak, alder and pine. Enid longed for the aroma of fresh baked scones and a wood fire, and a strong cup of coffee. To be anywhere but here.

She turned to her left, and edged northwards - or what she thought was north - towards the hiss of escaping steam, keeping the trickling of the creek to her right.

Something scrabbled behind her. There was a beat of wings.

She hesitated, squeezed her eyes shut, and waited for the spots to fade.

Shadows formed and separated from the light, first between the trees, then the above. The Fae moon was still in the sky. Agnes was curled up against a tree, knees to her chest, weeping softly.

A sputter of steam drew Enid's attention back to the glade. Half way up a clump of broken alder and oak, her precious Lincoln Tourer was wrapped around a trunk, a long scar rent along one side. Steam gushed from the radiator. Branches poked out from under the twisted axle. The crumpled bumper hung from one side, and skimmed the ground. Beneath it, the body of the troll lay in a shroud of stone dust, its limbs shattered.

Olive knelt a few feet away. Sir Arthur stood next to her.

Enid's heart faltered.

"Owen?" She took a step forward, and hesitated. He had to be alive.

Sir Arthur leaned into the motorcar. He shook his head and frowned.

"But, where?" Enid swallowed.

Sir Arthur shrugged.

Agnes stopped sobbing. She cocked her head in their direction, and rose slowly.

"He can't be--" Enid held her breath and approached slowly.

"I'll check the bushes," said Sir Arthur. "I'm sure he'll be all right."

Black circles rimmed Olive's eyes. Her hands were soaked in blood. Another body lay at their feet in a patch of crushed heather and bluebells, its limbs at awkward angles. Olive pushed pale pin curls back in place. Blood trickled from her nose. Sylvia's nose.

Enid stumbled towards them, and fell to her knees. "Not Sylvia." Her voice was shaky. "She can't die."

She mopped blood trickling from Sylvia's lip.

Sylvia's eyelids trembled and opened. The lower half of the whites were stained with blood. One eye looked up at them, the other restricted.

A faint smile flickered over her lips. "Why couldn't you just learn to crochet, like I asked?"

Her fingers twitched in the direction of her stick. Enid retrieved it and placed it into Sylvia's hand.

"Keep it." Sylvia's voice was weak. "It's yours."

Olive fell back onto her haunches. "But I thought--"

Enid shook her head. She didn't want it. Olive was the natural successor, she'd trained to take Sylvia's place.

Enid lay the stick on her lap. "But, Olive is--"

"Don't argue," whispered Sylvia. "It doesn't make you leader. Your focus was destroyed. You need a new one, that's all."

The stick thrummed in Enid's hand. Its etchings twisted. Energy pulsed into her hand. Warm, comforting, familiar. And strong. The energy surged into her chest.

"Good." Sylvia's smile faded. She shivered. "It's cold." Her breaths slowed.

Enid stood to face the Fae Queen. "She's dying. You have to save her."

"I can't help you." The Queen's voice was emotionless.

"You mean, you won't help us." The stick throbbed in Enid's hand. She jumped to her feet, emboldened by the rush of power. She tightened her grip.

"No." The Queen stepped away from the portal. The surface dimmed. "Death is the way of this world. I have no dominion over it. She made her decision, did her duty. Let her go with dignity."

Olive held Sylvia's hand.

Enid's fingers relaxed. The Fae Queen spoke the truth; no one had power over life and death. She slid her hand down the stick and crouched next to Sylvia.

"We're here," she whispered. "You're not alone."

Sylvia's hand slipped to the ground. Olive cried. Enid struggled to breathe. Sylvia was gone, and they were left behind. A tear slid down her cheek.

"You'll want this." Agnes was beside them. She bent down and parted the bluebells. There was a glimmer of red light and the sound of metal running along a chain as she raised her hand. She flinched, shook her hand, and cursed. Silver flashed as the object fell to the ground.

"What the--?" She kicked the offending item away.

Sylvia's garnet amulet lay in the grass, its silver chain snapped. Enid reached to pick it up. Burning Ice coursed through Enid's veins. She snatched back her hand.

Olive raised an eyebrow. "Pick it up, Agnes."

Agnes hesitated.

"I think it belongs to you, now," said Enid.

"You're one of us," continued Olive.

"No, I'm not." Agnes shook her head and backed away. "I can't be." She rubbed her hand. "I don't want to be. I refuse."

"I'm afraid you are, dear," said Enid. "The amulet had chosen its next keeper. It called. You accepted."

"There's no backsies, I'm afraid," said Olive. "Part of you must have wished to be a Protector."

"No. I wanted to be with Ren. I--" Agnes wobbled. Enid steadied her. "I wondered what it would be like to have magic. To be Fae."

"In your heart, you accepted," said Enid.

Agnes gasped. "No, no, no."

"You made your decision." The Queen's eyes glinted in the Fae twilight. "You must accept your duty."

"Well played." Enid glared at the Queen. No wonder she'd waited; she'd seen Agnes' fate. She wanted to ensure Agnes would remain in this world, and not reclaim her son. The girl could never join her sweetheart now; a Protector would never be permitted to enter the Fae Kingdom.

Agnes wailed.

The Queen smiled.

"You must pick it up. We can't touch it." Olive cupped Agnes' hand in hers and guided it to the ground where the amulet had fallen.

It hummed as Agnes' hand drew nearer. She stretched out her fingers. The red stone glowed, its light reflecting in her eyes. She picked it up.

Olive patted her on the back.

Muffled whistles broke the silence.

Olive gasped. "The police!"

The Queen's hound pulled on its leash, and growled. She pulled it to heel, scanned the trees at the edge of the glade. What more was she waiting for? Why was she not leaving? She'd risk being exposed to mortals.

"You've won. Now let us be." Enid gripped her new Focus.

"The troll," said Olive. "We can't let them see it." Her shoulders slumped. "I can't. I'm exhausted. You'll have to do it."

Enid concentrated on the fallen troll surrounded by shattered stone and wood debris, and drew the Aether's energy towards her, channelling it through her amulet and new Focus. It coursed through her body. New, yet familiar. She drew a deep breath, savoured the power, and braced herself as it neared the handle. Her fingers buzzed. Her palms tickled. The energy flowed with no resistance, tracing the spiral vinework etched along the length of the stick.

The police whistles grew louder.

"Enid?" Olive's voice was muffled.

Enid lifted the tip and touched the troll's leg. The energy slid into the creature before she had time to utter the invocation, transforming stone to flesh as it pulsed through the troll's body. The creature's face shifted, slipping between a weathered and lined visage of a middle-aged man, and the bronzed face of a man in his thirties, both with an eye patch. The mask flickered, and settled on the younger man. The green glow pumped along its torso and limbs, shrouding them in a tattered chauffeur's uniform.

Leaves rustled in the bushes. Branches cracked. Someone cursed; a familiar man's voice. Owen stumbled into the glade.

"Owen, you're alive!" Enid rushed to him.

Owen clasped his side. His crumpled dress shirt was torn and soaked in blood. A braces strap dangled from his shoulder, and his trousers ripped open down one side.

He limped forward and leaned on the motorcar, and wheezed as he caught his breath. His dark fringe fell over one eye as he lifted his head.

"Enid, thank God you're safe." He froze. His gaze darted across the glade, from the love-sick Agnes weeping under a tree to the Fae Queen in front of her shimmering portal, then settled on Enid standing over the dead, *Glamoured*, body of the troll bounty hunter. He reeled backwards, catching himself on a mess of twisted brambles caught under the front wheel arch of the Lincoln, and slumped back against the chassis.

"What's going on?"

The hound growled. The Queen raised an eyebrow.

The green glow around the troll's *Glamoured* body faded. Sylvia's stick hummed in Enid's hand.

"Enid?" Owen stared at the corpse at her feet, and sucked in a ragged breath. He edged back along the body of the car, dragging his injured leg. There was fear in his eyes.

Enid's heart raced. "Owen, it's not what you think."

"Not you, Enid," he whispered.

Enid stepped towards him.

"No!" His hands jerked in front of him, forming a defensive shield. "Don't come near me. You're one of *them*." He lowered his hands. "But, I--"

Her stomach twisted in knots, ramming its contents up her throat. She'd planned to explain everything, after the ball.

"You can't be..." He shook his head slowly.

"I'm still the same person," she said. "Nothing's changed. I love you, Owen."

Owen took a long, slow breath, and raised his unbloodied hand.

The knots in Enid's stomach loosened.

"Come with me, Enie," he whispered as if trying to coax a soufflé to rise. "We can go away. Just you and me. Away from these..." He eyed Olive and the Fae.

"But they are my friends." Her stomach knotted again.

"They are... unnatural." He motioned for her to join him. "Please, come with me." His eyes pleaded with her. "I can save you."

Enid swallowed. "But I don't need saving, Owen."

"They've poisoned your mind."

"It's what I am, Owen. What I've always been." Her stomach reached up, ripped out her heart and forced it into her throat. She wanted to scream, to slap his face, to shake him until he saw sense.

The stick thrummed in her palm, willing to do it for her. She flexed her fingers.

"I am one of them, Owen," she said.

"You don't have to be," he replied. "Forget this nonsense. You can change."

Enid's heart plummeted into her gut. Sylvia had been right. Enid felt ill.

"I still love you, Enie."

Enie: she was beginning to loathe the pet name; it made her sound like a helpless child.

They stood in silence, each holding their ground. Owen's eyelids narrowed. Hard creases formed at their edges. Full of hate.

"I..." Enid looked away, unable to bear the torture of his glare. "I have my duty, Mr Barrington."

He frowned. "I can't lose you, Enie. Once we're--" He swallowed.

"We're what?" she asked.

The Fae Queen sighed loudly. "Enough of this."

Agnes caught her breath and sobbed louder.

"It's all your fault," Owen hissed at the Fae Queen.

"Silence, insolent mortal!" Aether waves shuddered over the glade.

Owen clasped his hands over his ears, and winced.

Agnes' sobs were silenced in her throat.

The Queen's eyes flashed obsidian. A guttural growl gurgled deep in her throat. She pointed at Owen. His feet lifted off the ground. She flicked her hand to one side. An unseen force flung him to the opposite side of the glade.

"No!" screamed Enid.

Olive jumped to her feet and joined Enid.

"Observe, girl," said the Queen, "the true nature of Man."

Owen raised his head slowly, and lifted himself off the ground. "You bit--"

The Fae Queen raised her hand again, and twisted her wrist. Owen's body jerked upwards, swivelled in the air and flew back towards her, and fell at her feet. Blood pooled at his side. His face paled.

Enid moved to join him. Olive grasped her arm and shook her head.

The Queen grasped his chin, turned his face to her and examined his eyes. Her own eyes blazed violent purple.

He flinched, and squeezed his eyes shut.

"Get out of my head." His voice was slurred.

"Leave him alone." Enid wrenched her arm from Olive's grip.

The hound growled. She hesitated.

"You bound yourself to this... mortal?" The Queen screwed up her nose. "He smells of troll." The Queen let him go, and wound the hound's leash tighter around her hand, shortening its tether. "You may proceed."

Enid stepped forward, one eye on the Queen and her hound. She tore a strip from the bottom of her skirt, dropped to her knees, and pushed it into his side to slow the flow of blood. So much blood. It oozed through her fingers.

"Perhaps you should acquaint yourself with his true nature," said the Queen.

"No." Owen whimpered at her feet.

"I trust him," whispered Enid.

"He made a deal with the bounty hunter." The Queen ran her fingers along her hound's back.

A shiver slivered down Enid's spine. Sylvia had warned them. *Never trust a Fae.*

"And endangered us and all this world by doing so." The Queen circled them. "He betrayed you."

"No, you're lying." Enid pressed the cloth harder into Owen's wound. "You can't let him die."

"*Can't?*" The Queen stood up straight; she seemed taller, darker. Her voice rumbled through the glade, shaking the leaves of the alder and oak.

"You have your Heir." Olive shielded Agnes and Sir Arthur behind her. "The contract is fulfilled."

"Your point being?" said the Queen.

"Sylvia died." Olive's chin trembled. "You owe us a life debt."

Agnes sniffed and wiped her nose on the back of her hand.

"There is nothing I can do," said the Fae Queen.

Enid cradled Owen in her lap. He was a bigot. And a fool. He deserved punishment for his betrayal, but not death.

"Please." She held him close.

"He has betrayed you, Protector." The Queen raised an eyebrow. "You care for him, even now?"

Enid nodded slowly. "Mortals can change."

The Queen bent down and whispered in Owen's ear. His eyelids flickered, and closed.

"He is of your world," she said. "Save him if you can. But be warned," the Queen cooed in Enid's ear. "This one's face may be fair, but his heart is duplicitous."

Enid placed her bloodied hand on Owen's chest and tucked her fingers under his torn shirt to touch his skin. She felt his breaths - shallow, almost non-existent - and concentrated on collecting life-giving Aether.

"*Sano.*"

Its warmth spread through her torso, into her open hand, and crawled over the wound.

Owen gasped. His eyes snapped open.

Enid touched his cheek with the back of her hand.

His muscles tensed.

"I'm too late," he whispered. He brushed her away and scrambled clear, not stopping until he backed into a tree.

"Owen?" Enid's legs trembled. "Please?"

He slid down the tree and turned away from her.

"See, Protector?" said the Queen. "You cannot trust him. He is the enemy. He led the foul creature to us."

"Now, see here," Doyle stepped forward. "That's not what happened."

"She's lying." Owen's voice trembled.

"Silence, mortal." The Queen turned on him.

Owen pulled himself back up the trunk.

A shrill whistle pierced the forest.

Owen launched himself off the trunk at the Queen.

The Queen snarled. Aether erupted from her finger and enveloped him.

Enid shielded her eyes. When the light faded, Owen was gone. Only a pile of torn clothes remained.

Agnes screamed.

The police whistles shrieked in earnest.

"You've destroyed him!" said Enid.

Enid was at the pile of clothes before she realised she'd moved. She prodded them with her foot, knocking something hard in the pocket of the trousers. She rummaged in the pocket, found a folded photograph and a small, velvet box. She opened the box. A platinum ring with a square-cut diamond. Her hands shook as she snapped the box shut.

"Such betrayal deserved punishment," said the Queen. "I've saved you from heartache. My gift to you, Protector. For returning my son."

The shirt shivered, and jerked away from the rest of the clothes. It sped off towards the trees, in the direction of the police whistle.

"The life debt has been paid." The Queen smiled.

A lump rippled along the sleeve and emerged at the cuff. A cat, with ruffled charcoal fur, skittered to a halt near the motorcar. It glanced back at them, with Owen's piercing blue eyes, and hissed.

It yowled as it levitated off the ground, squirmed mid-air, and was deposited in the back seat of the vehicle.

"What have you done?" asked Enid.

"It will spend the rest of its days serving the Protector he betrayed." She patted her hound.

"And how long is that?" she asked.

"Let me guess," said Olive. "Nine lives?"

"Eight," replied the Queen.

"But he's a cat!" sniffed Agnes.

Olive tugged Agnes back behind her.

"The first is forfeit," said the Queen.

The cat yowled.

"Quiet, Mr B," replied Enid.

"And, as for you." The Queen turned to Sir Arthur. "I can't have him telling your authorities about the Otherworlds"

"Me?" asked Sir Arthur.

"You can't!" Enid's heart raced at the thought of him being transformed. "They'd be too many questions."

"What do you propose, *Protector*?"

"*Memory Magic?*" asked Olive.

Enid bit her lip. It hadn't proved successful in the past.

The police whistles circled them. A bicycle bell dinged along the path.

"Your Majesty?" Enid grit her teeth; there was no time for pride now.

The Queen's lip curled. Her eyes gleamed. She leaned forward and kissed Sir Arthur on the forehead. As she pulled away, a faint strand of pearlescent Aether trickled out of his skin, into her parted lips. She drank it in. It faded as she moved away.

Sir Arthur gasped for breath and collapsed to the ground.

Crashing sounds moved closer. A dog barked. Running footsteps crunched on the gravel path.

"Make sure your story is believable." The Queen wiped the corner of her mouth with her finger. "He's an intelligent being. It would be a pity if I had to return, and drink him dry." She turned, and glided towards the portal. Her gown rippled over the carpet of bluebells, sweeping them away behind her.

The Fae Forest faded as she stepped over the portal threshold. The portal snapped shut.

The creek trickled behind them. A warm breeze rolled over them, bringing with it the smell of fresh eucalyptus.

"Wait up, Whitington" yelled an authoritative voice.

The reporter rushed into the clearing, brandishing his camera.

He stopped, pressed a camera against his body, scanned the area, and studied the viewfinder. He snapped a few shots before the constables arrived.

"I said: 'wait'." Detective Leonard strode into the clearing after them, pistol in hand. He noted the position of the bodies, rolled his gaze over the dented Lincoln, and sucked a quick breath in through his teeth.

"Miss Turner? Mrs Oldham? Are you all right?" He directed a constable to the deceased 'chauffeur's' corpse, and another to Sir Arthur's limp body lying at Olive's feet.

"Detective Leonard." Enid gasped, in the best damsel-in-distress tone she could muster. "Thank goodness you're here." She slipped the photograph and ring box into Olive's handbag as they huddled together.

"Sir Arthur?" Detective Leonard shook his shoulder gently.

Sir Arthur moaned and sat up groggily, with the detective's assistance.

Enid thrummed her fingers on her new stick handle, and continued to speak, before the detective had time to ask Sir Arthur any questions.

"Sir Arthur saved us." As his memories of the Fae and their dealings were lost, she would replace them, as instructed, with heroic ones befitting the creator of the great Sherlock Holmes. "Isn't that correct, Olive?"

Olive nodded, clutched Agnes close, and whispered in the girl's ear. Agnes' face contorted. She wailed and buried her head into Olive's shoulder.

"That--" Enid waggled her finger at the troll's *Glamoured* corpse. "That man attacked us, and stole my car." She faked a loud sniffle. "Then he tried to run us over."

"Is that how the vehicle came to be damaged?" Detective Leonard flipped open his notebook.

As did Mr Whitington.

"Yes," replied Olive. "Sir Arthur must have been taking a stroll before he caught his train. Isn't that so, Sir Arthur?"

Sir Arthur nodded and cradled his head. "I think so."

"Where is Mr Barrington, and the foreign chap?" asked Mr Whitington.

Agnes wailed louder, on cue.

"There, there." Olive patted her back and glared at the reporter.

"Whitington," growled the detective. "You were warned."

"The man said he'd finished with them and we were next," continued Enid. She had to make it believable, for Sir Arthur's sake.

"What do you think he meant by that, Miss Turner?" asked Whitington.

"Oh, no!" Enid caught her breath. "Do you think he--?"

Leonard cleared his throat. The reporter kept scribbling.

"I--" She bit her lip. "I-- Oh!" She buried her face in her hands.

"Can't you see how distraught they are?" Olive scowled. "They've both lost someone they love."

Enid smiled, unseen, behind her hands. Olive was good.

Detective Leonard lowered his notebook and waved over a constable.

"See these ladies are looked after, Jenkins. We'll get a statement from them in the morning. And get a doctor to check out Sir Arthur."

The constable nodded.

"And get that dog searching for more bodies. Could be two of them," ordered the detective.

They followed Detective Leonard and the constable towards the path leading back to the Carriageway.

"What about your lovely motorcar?" Agnes asked Enid.

"It will be returned after the scientific investigators have examined it," replied Detective Leonard.

Enid eyed the vehicle. Blood smeared the radiator grill. The Lincoln had been her pride and joy, her symbol of freedom. All she saw now was death and betrayal. Her shoulders slumped.

"My driving days are over," she said.

"But, Enid, you can't possibly mean that?" Olive frowned. "It's just grief talking. You'll feel better after lunch at the Hotel."

"There's nothing here, in the city, for me anymore," said Enid. "And my bees need tending. Sylvia reminded me I was neglecting them." She took a deep breath. "I'd like you to have it, Agnes."

She patted Agnes' hand and smiled.

Agnes' eyes widened. "You mean it?"

Enid nodded.

Agnes' smile fell. "But Father won't allow it."

"Fiddlesticks!" Enid glanced along the gravel path. Detective Leonard was no longer visible, and his footsteps were faint. She leaned closer - just in case - and whispered: "You're a Protector now. No man can make you do anything you don't want to."

epilogue

the smell of freshly brewed coffee filled the Sitting Room. Enid slathered a scone with lemon butter and took a bite. The tangy lemon curd was smooth as silk - an award-winning batch, even by Sylvia's standards.

Enid caught her breath. *Sylvia.* The memory still hurt. The coroner's inquest had ruled her death a murder. The troll's *Glamour* had lasted long enough to go with it to the grave, and allow their secret to survive. With four witnesses, the 'chauffeur' had been declared guilty posthumously, and Sir Arthur had left for Melbourne - almost to schedule - to complete his tour of Australia and New Zealand unhindered.

Mr Owen Barrington had not been seen after breakfast on that day and was assumed to be another victim. His body was never found, nor was that of the mysterious Mr Ren Fairchild.

Enid had worn black, for an appropriate period, and donated Mr Barrington's vast art collection to the South Australian Museum - to Mr Waite's delight.

Enid licked her fingers, and returned to her crocheting. It was her way to honour Sylvia, a sort of last request.

She gathered up her ball of yarn, and checked her pattern: *Cortedelli Sports Hat No. 938*. The crown was done, now onto the brim. She cut the stiffening cord, inserted her hook into the next stitch, twisted the yarn around her finger, and finished the row. Duck egg blue would accent Agnes' fiery red curls, and possibly prove a calming influence. The girl had taken on the life of a flapper a little too exuberantly.

She sighed and continued along the row. She'd just enough silk yarn left from Agnes' sport coat to make a matching cap to shade the girl's pale, freckled skin while driving. Agnes had been a quick study, and was proving to be an excellent driver.

Enid smiled. Her Lincoln was in good hands.

A soft tap on the window caught her attention. She peered through the window and shielded her eyes against the afternoon sun.

The front door screen slapped against its frame. Agnes marched into the room, pulled off her driving gloves, and sank into the armchair opposite Enid.

"Why do I always have to be chauffeur?" She harrumphed. "Olive's fingernails are wearing a hole in the seat leather."

Enid chuckled.

The screen door slapped again.

"Yoo-hoo! You've got mail." Olive dropped a brown paper parcel in Enid's lap. "From England."

"From Sir Arthur," cooed Agnes. "With love?"

"Agnes!" Olive slapped her gently on the knee.

Enid grinned. She had been corresponding with Sir Arthur since the Coroner's inquest.

"Friends, that's all," she said. "He keeps bees."

Agnes rolled her eyes.

Enid tucked her fingers under the string, slipped it off the parcel, and removed the brown paper wrappings.

"A book?" She turned over the navy, cloth bound book to read the title: *The Coming of the Fairies.*

"He remembered." Agnes leaned closer.

Olive raised an eyebrow. "Surely, not with the Fae Queen's magic?"

Enid swallowed. If the Fae Queen found out...

"Perhaps she took pity on him?" asked Agnes.

"Fiddlesticks," replied Olive.

"You can't trust the Fae." Sylvia's words spilled out of Enid's mouth before she realised what she'd said. "Perhaps She had some other mischief in mind."

Enid flicked through the pages, and paused at a photograph: two girls with what appeared to be fairies.

Olive peered at the image, and scoffed.

"I don't think we need to concern ourselves." She leaned back in her chair and shook her head.

Enid flicked through a few more pages. A folded note fell onto her lap. Agnes snatched it up, and grinned.

"It's from Sir Arthur." She sat next to Enid.

"What does it say?" asked Olive.

Agnes cleared her throat.

My dear Miss Turner,

I hope this letter finds you, and your bees, well. Thank you, again, for your support during the events of last year. Without your assistance with the local constabulary, we would not have been able to honour our scheduled tour commitments. For this, we are both very grateful.

I thought you, and your friends, may be interested in an advance copy of my latest book.

These photographs haunt me still. Something about them reminds me of my visit to Adelaide.

Do give my regards to your friend, Mr Bellchambers. I do hope my letters have helped find patrons for his excellent wildlife sanctuary.

Yours sincerely,

Arthur Conan Doyle.

Agnes sighed and flopped back into the chair.

"I could use a drink." she said.

Olive grunted disapproval. "It's only just gone lunch."

"There's fresh coffee in the siphon pot on the stove."

"No, thank you." Olive screwed up her nose. "I'll pass." She turned to Agnes. "Tea?"

"If I must," replied Agnes.

A sad mewing drifted in from the hallway. Agnes sucked in a breath.

"He's still hanging around?" She tucked the letter back into the book, and slipped it back into its brown paper wrapping.

Olive glanced at Enid. Enid nodded.

"Agnes, help me in the kitchen, will you?" asked Olive. "The scones need buttering."

Agnes jumped to her feet and followed Olive out of the room. China rattled in the kitchen.

A sleek, charcoal feline inched into the room, and hugged the walls. He glanced in Enid's direction and hesitated.

"Good afternoon, Mr B." Enid picked up her crochet work, and twisted the yarn around her finger.

Mr B's tail twitched as he slowly patrolled the room's circumference as he'd done every day for the past eighteen months.

Enid slipped the crochet hook into the next stitch. How long were 'eight lives' anyway? *Generations?* She'd never defined her term.

Mr B finished his second round, and halted at her feet. His tail twitched again. He looked at her, with his pale blue eyes, and meowed.

She'd forgiven him, of course. Sylvia's death had been an accident. And everyone deserved a second chance, didn't they? Besides, if they were to be stuck with each other for eight generations, they had to make the best of it. They were partners whether they liked it or not.

She finished the stitch.

She'd thought he'd revert to human state once she'd forgiven him. Yet the feline form persisted. To own the truth of it, she was glad he couldn't talk. She was still angry, and couldn't guarantee her words would be civil. And words made in anger were often regretted later.

He nudged her foot. His tail brushed over her skin. He circled her legs curling his tail around her calf. The fur was soft.

This time she didn't flinch, didn't push him away. He'd become her guardian - not in the way he'd planned, yet he stayed. If she couldn't love him anymore, at least she could pity him.

Enid smiled, and patted her lap. Mr B leapt onto her knees. She raised her hand above him, and hesitated.

"This doesn't mean I'm not still very angry at you," she whispered.

He purred.

Olive's voice drifted in from the kitchen. "One scone, or two?"

"Just one, thank you."

"Are you all right in there?"

"I'm fine." Enid patted Mr B's warm fur.

"Now, Mr B," she whispered. "There are some rules we need to discuss."

THE END

Acknowledgements

As an indie author, it's down to me to ensure I produce a story worthy of my readers. But, contrary to popular belief, authors are not all solitary creatures. Not only does it take a village to raise a child, but it takes one to produce a book. I couldn't have completed this book without the assistance of amazing and generous people.

Firstly, I'd like to acknowledge my alpha reader, David, my beta readers, and my editor Sharon Kemmett (*The Word Tailor* - https:// smkemmettwordtailor.wordpress.com) who helped me wrangle belligerent words into their final form.

I love creating alternate histories (this time 1920 Adelaide), making research a key element.

I'd like to thank the South Australian Museum, and Francesca Zilio in particular, for supplying information and photographs on Sir Arthur Conan Doyle's visit to Adelaide in September, 1920. Fortunately, Sir Arthur also provided key insights to his visit in 'The Wanderings of a Spiritualist', published in 1921 by Hodder & Stoughton.

Many years ago, I saw a small moulded fairy door at the base of a shop in Rundle Street. I've been fascinated with them ever since. No one really seems to know when the 'fairy doors' first appeared in the Adelaide CBD, or who created them. It was originally thought they appeared sometime in the late 1900s, but it seems some were more recent. I'd like to thank Deb Williams, of Save South Australia's History from Demolition group, for information on, and photographs of, the fairy doors in Adelaide CBD.

I'd also like to thank John Cooke and Matthew Lombard, from the Birdwood Motor Museum, who supplied information on their 1919

Lincoln Tourer (on which Enid Turner's beloved motorcar is based). They tracked down the handbook supplied with the vehicle, answered detailed questions, and even took photographs for me during the Covid-19 lockdowns in 2020. Image my surprise when I discovered the motorcar was donated by a family named 'Turner'!

Thank you to Tim Scammell and the volunteer researchers from the South Australian Police Historical Society Inc. for their help.

A final thank you, also to those who helped with various translations required for this story. Racheal Hay, Ronald McCoy, Miriam Staples, and David Greagg assisted me with Scots Gaelic translations. David Greagg assisted with multiple Latin translations, and Susan Rehorek and Nicolas Cowall helped with Russian translation. A special mention to David Greagg for attempting to explain both Latin and Gaelic grammar.

Thank you, all. Without your help I'd still be on page one.

If you enjoyed this book, please take a moment to leave a book review where you purchased it, or on Goodreads.

-Karen J

About the Author

Karen Carlisle lives in Adelaide with her family and the ghost of her ancient Devon Rex cat. She loves fantasy fiction, gardening, historical re-creation, and steampunk and can often be found plotting fantastical, piratic or airship adventures.
Karen has always loved chocolate and rarely refuses a cup of tea. She is not keen on South Australian summers.

www.karenjcarlisle.com
www.instagram.com/karenjcarlisle
twitter.com/kjcarlisle
www.goodreads.com/kjcarlisle

You can support me on Patreon
www.patreon.com/KarenJCarlisle
or buy me a cup of tea at
ko-fi.com/karenjcarlisle

Other Works by Karen J Carlisle

Available in paperback:
The Aunt Enid Mysteries
Aunt Enid: Protector Extraordinaire

The Adventures of Viola Stewart series
Doctor Jack & Other Tales
Eye of the Beholder & Other Tales
The Illusioneer & Other Tales

The Department of Curiosities
The Department of Curiosities: For the Good of the Empire

Also available separately as eBooks:
The Adventures of Viola Stewart series
Three Short Stories
Doctor Jack
Three More Short Stories
Eye of the Beholder
From the Depths
Tomorrow, When I Die
The Illusioneer

The Aunt Enid Mysteries
Aunt Enid: Protector Extraordinaire

The Department of Curiosities
The Department of Curiosities: For the Good of the Empire

Short story collections
With a Twist of Nib: For When Time is Short
Another Twist of the Nib: Shorter Tales with a Darker Twist
Quarantine Reads: Escape to Adventure

bonus extra

devils food cake recipe

The first recipe for Devil's Food Cake was published in *Mrs Rorer's New Cook Book* in 1902 (page 619), though it is thought to have been in use in the Southern US before that.

This recipe uses chocolate (assuming modern equivalent of unsweetened or dark baking chocolate) instead of cocoa, and decorated with white icing (or frosting).

devils food cake recipe

(Sarah Tyson Rorer.)

Ingredients:

1/2 cup of milk

4 ounces of chocolate (unsweetened/dark baking chocolate)

1/2 cup of butter

3 cups of pastry flour

1 1/2 cups of sugar

4 eggs

2 teaspoonfuls of baking powder

Method:

Put in a double boiler four ounces of chocolate and a half pint of milk; cook until smooth and thick, and stand aside to cool. Beat a half cup of butter to a cream; add gradually one and a half cups of sugar and the yolks of four eggs; beat until light and smooth. Then add the cool chocolate mixture and three cups of pastry flour, with which you have sifted two teaspoonfuls of baking powder. Beat thoroughly for at least five minutes; then stir in the well beaten whites of the eggs. Bake in three or four layers. Put the layers together with soft icing, to which you have added a cup of chopped nuts. The success of this cake depends upon the flour used.